THERESA NATALIE

A Tale of No Face

Reaper
Press

First published by Reaper Press 2026

This novel is entirely a work of fiction. The names, characters and incidents portrayed in it are the work of the author's imagination. Any resemblance to actual persons, living or dead, events or localities is entirely coincidental.

Theresa Natalie asserts the moral right to be identified as the author of this work.

Theresa Natalie has no responsibility for the persistence or accuracy of URLs for external or third-party Internet Websites referred to in this publication and does not guarantee that any content on such Websites is, or will remain, accurate or appropriate.

Designations used by companies to distinguish their products are often claimed as trademarks. All brand names and product names used in this book and on its cover are trade names, service marks, trademarks and registered trademarks of their respective owners. The publishers and the book are not associated with any product or vendor mentioned in this book. None of the companies referenced within the book have endorsed the book.

First edition

ISBN: 979-8-9941562-0-9

Cover art by Theresa Natalie

This book was professionally typeset on Reedsy.
Find out more at reedsy.com

For anyone surviving on hope and a dream

Acknowledgments

I would like to thank the team at Reaper Press for all your hard work and dedication on this project. Thank you for taking a chance on me. Big thanks to my editor Halley Sutton, your insights have been priceless and you truly helped make this a better book.

Rocky Richard, I couldn't have done this without your support. Thank you for putting up with me (I know it isn't always easy) and encouraging me every step of the way. Your friendship means the world to me. Brian Doré and Brandy Prince, thank you for reading and rereading and rereading all the different drafts of this book. You've believed in me since day one and I will forever be grateful. To the PJ's crew, I couldn't be more thankful for an amazing group of friends to be my chosen family. Our years of friendship have made me a better person and I wouldn't be who I am today without all of you.

To my parents: Dad, thank you for teaching me the value of hard work and how to persist in the face of obstacles. You've always been there for me and you have given me a solid foundation to stand on. Lana, thank you for passing down the gift of storytelling. You've taught me that sometimes it's okay to throw all the rules out the window, and if it wasn't for you I wouldn't have anything interesting to write about. I love you both.

Content Warning: Reader, beware; this book contains graphic descriptions of body horror, sexual assault, and domestic violence. Read at your own risk.

I

Ville Morte, LA May 1945

Chapter 1

Suzy Quibodeaux wasn't sure she would like being fingered, but to her pleasant surprise, she found it quite delightful.

It was a moonless spring night out on Lover's Lane. The young couple parked under a cluster of cypress trees. Spanish moss dangled from branches and swayed against a warm breeze.

The serenade of the bayou, with its symphony of bullfrogs and cicadas, went unnoticed. Even the jazz music that drifted from the car radio was drowned out by Suzy's cries of pleasure. Her complete abandonment of all propriety resonated through the night. She expressed herself freely because she thought they were alone.

But hidden in the thick foliage just beyond the clearing was a monstrous man stroking himself vigorously. He was well over six feet tall with broad shoulders and an extra-large frame, his face horribly disfigured. He had made a habit of coming to this spot during the new moon to spy on backseat lovers. He could shroud himself more easily in the darkness of those nights.

Tonight, however, something was different. Just looking wasn't enough. Hatred gripped his heart. He hated himself for the disgusting being he had become. He hated the girl because she reminded him of his past and all that was lost to him. He hated the boy and his beautiful face; he, too, had a beautiful face once. Why should that little bastard get all the goods while he was left with less than scraps? His mind began to cloud with a thick rage as he silently crept from his hiding place.

Suzy Quibodeaux and Bobby Fontenot were in love, practically engaged in her mind. It's not like they were going all the way, she thought, they were only sixteen, after all. She'd still be a virgin, so what was the harm?

They officially met in band class the school year before the summer of '45. She played the clarinet, and he sat behind her with his French horn. They smiled and made eyes at each other daily; it was love at first sight. When homecoming came around in early October, he finally mustered up the nerve to ask her out and the two had been inseparable ever since.

They spent many late afternoons sitting on her parents' front porch swing, watching the sun go down and making plans for their future.

Suzy's face was flushed and dewy from her very first orgasm. Bobby lifted her chin and gave her a gentle kiss on the lips. "Did you enjoy it?"

"Yes," she replied with a shy smile.

Tucking her hair behind her ear, he asked, "Can I have a turn?" Suzy looked down at her hands nervously. "I don't know how." "I can show you," he whispered sweetly.

Suzy looked up at him with willing eyes and a wide smile. "Ok," she answered.

Bobby enthusiastically unbuckled his pants; he was thrilled to finally have a hand other than his own to touch him. But

4

before he could get his pants down past his hips, the car door flew open. Suzy let out a bloodcurdling scream as a pair of powerful hands yanked Bobby out of the car.

Confused, Bobby found himself thrown to the ground, looking up at a ghoul. His first instinct was to fight back, but before he even had a chance to comprehend what was happening, the figure raised a .32 caliber pistol and shot Bobby in both kneecaps. Everything went white as searing pain pulsed through his entire body, leaving him breathless and gasping for air. He began to panic as Suzy's hysterical screams rang out from the shadows of his torment.

The maniac loomed over him as he raised the gun once more, bringing the butt end down on Bobby's temple. One. Two. Three times. Now that he had ensured the boy was out cold, he could turn his attention to the shrieking girl and shut her up.

Suzy's screams suddenly came to a stop as the stranger climbed into the back seat of the car. She was paralyzed with fear as she laid eyes on the monster. He grabbed her by the ankle and dragged her body across the backseat. He crawled on top of her and pinned her down with his massive body weight. Suzy's stomach turned as his pungent, musky stench engulfed the air around her.

Her body began to shake involuntarily as she looked upon his face of melted flesh. The skin around his sunken eyes was so thin she could see the bone right through it. Infected scabs freckled his face. She watched in horror as a maggot came out of the hole where his nose should be, and crawled across his face down to his mouth, of which only half of the top lip remained. The rest was nothing but rotten teeth and gray gums. Her stomach turned again as he breathed heavily in her face; the smell of his sour hot breath was so repulsive she could feel the bile rise in the back of her throat.

He took his grimy hand and slipped it inside her panties. As he pushed his filthy body harder against hers, he pressed his mouth to her ear and grunted. The vibrations invaded her ear canal and sent chills all through her. She tried to squirm away, but he grabbed her firmly between the legs, and in a deep guttural voice, he whispered, "I'm gonna *boucher*[1] your meat, bitch."

---

[1] *boucher: butcher*

II

New Orleans, LA July 1945

Chapter 2

Frank could feel the eyes of Mr. Butcher's young secretary on him as he waited anxiously outside of the office. He wished she'd stop glancing over at him; he was already nervous enough about this interview.

Being a bit shy, he had never quite gotten used to the effect he had on women. Frank was handsome, tall with broad shoulders and an athletic body. A chiseled jawline framed his face, giving him a classic masculine beauty, and his big blue eyes made him simply dreamy.

The smell of old wood on a humid Louisiana day and freshly lit cigarettes wafted through the air. The clicking of a dozen typewriters pulsed around the bullpen of *The New Orleans Post*, and everything felt alive with a sense of purpose.

Frank had always wanted to work for a newspaper, and he couldn't believe his good fortune when he saw the ad for this job. He hadn't had much luck in the way of work since he had returned home from the war. He often wondered if it was because of his slight limp. But on warm days like today, his bad leg didn't bother him much, so the limp was hardly noticeable.

"Mr. Martin?" Mary Ann, the secretary, called to him in a

squeaky voice.

"Yes?"

"Mr. Butcher will see you now." She stood and escorted him to the office. As she opened the door for him, she whispered, "Good luck."

Frank gave her a charming little smile that made her swoon, and she floated all the way back to her desk.

Mr. Butcher was overlooking Frank's résumé as he sat behind an oversized wooden desk in the center of the room, which faced a large picture window overlooking the bullpen. The shades were pulled up halfway and fully open. He liked to keep an eye on things while maintaining a sense of privacy.

"Frank Martin, I presume."

"Yes sir."

"Alan Butcher," he introduced himself as he stood to greet Frank. Alan was a big man with salt and pepper hair. He had a round belly, plump jowls, and a commanding presence. "Have a seat." He gestured to a chair facing his desk.

"So, Frank," Alan began as he sat down in his chair and grabbed himself a cigarette from a silver box on his desk, "I see until recently you were serving our country in the war. Army Air Corps?"

"Yes sir," Frank answered proudly.

"Ah, I was a navy man myself during the Great War. I take it you saw some action?"

"A little too much action," Frank replied with a half-smile. "I was injured in the line of duty and subsequently discharged."

"I see. I have a similar story myself. We'll have to exchange war tales over whiskies." Alan took a deep drag of his cigarette. "But for now, why don't you tell me why you want to work for *The New Orleans Post*."

"Well, sir, I've always been interested in a career as a reporter. I studied journalism in college for a couple of semesters before joining the military."

"Now I'm gonna stop you right there, Frank. I want to be clear, this job is for an assistant, not a reporter."

"Oh yes, sir. Your ad said the position is working for one of your top reporters. In my opinion, there's no better way to learn the ropes than working under the best. I'm a hard worker. I'm disciplined, a fast learner, and I'm not above grunt work."

Alan chuckled as he took another drag of his cigarette. "I like your attitude."

Frank was feeling quite pleased. The interview was going swell, and he just knew he was going to get the job. But he watched as the smile on Alan's face slowly faded. He was looking past him out the picture window.

"Shit," Alan mumbled under his breath as he stamped out his cigarette.

Frank could hear a commotion going on behind him and turned around to see what could possibly have caused such a formidable man to shrink down a size. To his surprise, he saw a beautiful young woman arguing with Mary Ann. She had the looks of a movie star; tall, blonde, and sharply dressed in a navy-blue victory suit. But even from across the room, Frank could see the anger burning in her eyes, and he watched in shock as she shoved Mary Ann away from the door and stormed into the office.

"What the hell, Alan?!" she yelled and threw the newspaper onto his desk; the ad for the job was circled in red.

"Now, Betty," Alan said, keeping a cool head as he stood up to face her, "just calm down."

11

"Don't you dare tell me to calm down." She pointed her finger directly in his face. "An assistant, Alan, really? You might as well have just taken an ad out for a babysitter." Even though Alan towered over her, Betty didn't back down an inch.

Alan sighed and hung his head; he had really hoped to avoid all this. Clearly, he made a mistake by not telling her, although he was never going to admit it. He turned to Frank. "I'm sorry about all this. Would you mind giving us a moment?"

"Not at all," Frank replied politely as he prepared to leave. Even though the situation was making him uncomfortable, he was amused and disappointed he wouldn't get to watch the rest of this showdown.

"Here," Betty said, tossing a quarter in his lap, "there's a diner down the street. Why don't you scram."

Frank, who always prided himself on being a gentleman, found it very difficult to mind his manners. He stood up and shook Alan's hand. "Mr. Butcher, it was a pleasure." Then he turned to Betty. "I wish I could say the same about you, miss," and with a smirk, he flipped the coin back at her and walked out the door. The coin danced on the floor before falling flat.

"The nerve," Betty huffed.

"Yes, Betty, I'd say you've got some nerve barging into my office and causing a scene like that. Take a seat," Alan said in a commanding voice.

The last thing Betty wanted to do was take orders from Alan, but she knew she had pushed him just far enough. If she was going to get anywhere in this situation, now was the time to behave. So, she grabbed a cigarette from the silver box on his desk, and with all the grace of a Southern beauty queen, she sat down.

Alan took his place behind his desk and lit himself another cigarette. "Now, Betty, what's this all about?" he said, switching to his soothing fatherly tone.

Betty took a deep drag of her cigarette and let her temper cool before answering. "You didn't consult me, Alan. Didn't ask if I needed or even wanted an assistant. You just decided for me, as if I were a child in need of a babysitter. You think I'm just some silly little woman who needs looking after."

"Betty, I may think you're a lot of things, but a silly little woman is not one of them." It amused him that she thought anyone could possibly think of Betty Boudreaux as a silly little woman. "Look, you're my best reporter, your articles are the reason people buy our paper, but you tend to get yourself into some pretty hot water doing it." He looked at her, and a stream of cigarette smoke drifted from his nostrils, making him look like a bull. "How many times have you been arrested this year, Betty?"

Betty stared at her fingernails. "Twice," she answered with a bit of reluctance.

"Three. And it's only July. Listen, your father and I were good friends, and I promised him I'd look after you, but you can't keep calling me at all hours of the night to bail you out of trouble. I'm old, and it upsets my wife. Would it really be so bad to have another person around to help level things out a bit?"

"So, a babysitter."

Alan sighed with frustration. He really didn't want to go around this circle again. "If that's what you want to call it, Betty, but you're in charge; he's your assistant. Besides, you can get him to do all the grunt work, like typing."

"I like typing."

"You hate typing."

Alan was right; she did hate typing.

"Now, you're going to go down the street to the diner and apologize to that young man. I like him, I have a good feeling about him."

Chapter 3

Betty stepped outside the office of *The New Orleans Post* and onto the bustling city sidewalk. It was only nine o'clock in the morning, but the heat had already eclipsed the day, and she felt smothered by the dense humidity. While she strutted down the street toward the diner, she pulled a handkerchief from her handbag and blotted her face where the sweat was beginning to collect.

The weather was doing nothing to improve her mood; she was still feeling vexed about this morning. It didn't matter what Alan said, she knew she was being treated differently because she was a woman. If she were a man and had an outburst like that in a meeting, she wouldn't be forced to hunt down this character, apologize, and offer him a job. No. If she were a man, she would have been consulted about all of this, there never would have been a secret job interview in the first place. But there wasn't a damn thing she could do about it, Alan made that quite clear.

Betty reached the diner and walked inside, hoping he wouldn't be there. But immediately she spotted him sitting alone at the counter, reading a newspaper and drinking a steamy cup of coffee, despite the oppressive summer elements.

She took a deep breath to compose herself before walking over to Frank.

"May I have a seat?" she asked in her polite voice.

"That depends," Frank answered without looking at her, continuing to sip his coffee and skim over his paper, "are you going to throw more loose change at me?"

She knew she should feel bad about their earlier encounter, but truthfully, the thought of it tickled her pink. She looked down at her hands to hide the faint smile forming on her lips. If she was going to get ahead of this situation, she was going to have put on her charm and feign sincerity.

With her natural smoothness, Betty sat down on the stool next to him. "Well, you see, Mr. ummm..." She stopped, realizing that she didn't know his name.

Frank put down his paper and smiled as he turned to her. Betty had been so worked up earlier that she hadn't noticed how handsome he was; it was almost enough to make her lose her focus.

"Martin. Frank Martin." He held his hand out to her.

"Miss Betty Boudreaux," she replied, shaking his hand. "Well Mr.

Martin, I came..."

"It's a pleasure to meet you, Miss Boudreaux," he said, cutting her off mid-sentence, which was very out of character for him. He wasn't sure why he had done it; Frank was usually much more quiet and polite. Maybe it was the heat or maybe he was sore about Betty ruining his interview. Either way, a spark was lit in him that day.

Betty fumed as she smiled through a clenched jaw. Nothing pissed her off more than being interrupted, especially by men, especially in a professional setting.

"Now, Mr. Martin, I came here to apologize for my outburst this morning. It was very unprofessional of me and I'm sorry if I offended you."

Frank said nothing and only smiled at her.

Betty had to clutch her hands in her lap to keep from slapping that smug look right off his face. "The job is yours, if you still want it."

"Well, that's wonderful, Miss Boudreaux. When do I start?"

"Monday morning. Eight o'clock sharp."

"Alright then, I'll see you Monday morning."

Betty gave him a tight smile as she stood up. She pulled the quarter they had tossed at each other out of her dress pocket and slapped it on the counter.

"Coffee's on me," she said, and walked out the door.

* * *

Jasmine was in full bloom in uptown New Orleans. Its deep green vines grew freely, crawling up lamp posts and creeping along fences. The sweet fragrance of the tiny white flowers floated through the streets, all lined with classic shotgun houses.

Frank strolled down Magazine Street with a pep in his step as he mindlessly thumbed Betty's coin in his pocket. Nothing could get him down today, not even the beginnings of a painful throb in his bad leg. He had just come from the corner store and was making his way home with a brown paper bag tucked under his arm. He turned onto Eleonore Street and realized that for the first time in years his heart didn't feel heavy to come home.

17

He arrived at his house, 624 Eleonore Street. Frank always felt lucky that he found a single shotgun instead of a double; the thought of sharing a thin wall and front porch with a perfect stranger made him feel a little uneasy. He opened the gate of the wrought iron fence that bordered the small lot and stepped onto the front porch of his light blue house with white trim. Frank had painted the house himself, a project he undertook to avoid his feelings. He walked into the house and hung his hat and suit jacket on the coat rack by the front door.

"Daddy!" Avril called out as she ran into the living room. The toddler looked like a perfect little doll wearing a soft pink dress with a lace Peter Pan collar and matching Mary Jane shoes. Her golden curls bounced as she ran to her father.

Frank scooped up his tiny daughter with one strong arm and held her tight. Avril threw her chubby arms around his neck and hugged him.

"Well, hello there, Sunshine," Frank said as he gave her a big kiss on the cheek. It was their usual routine and always the brightest moment in Frank's day. He often thought that she was truly the only good thing in his life. Even when he felt lower than dirt, Avril had the power to make his life endurable.

Still holding the brown bag under his left arm, Frank carried her to the kitchen in the back of the house. There, standing over the stove, looking like a frail little bird was Frank's wife, Ava. Her dull mousy brown hair was tucked into a bun at the nape of her neck, and she wore a faded blue house dress that hung loosely over her body. She was much too thin and bordered on scrawny.

Ava had been a plain girl who had grown into a plain woman. She was the type of person who easily faded into the background and there seemed to be nothing extraordinary about her. She had always been a little insecure but since coming to America, it had gotten worse. People always assumed that when Frank said his wife was from France, she would be glamorous and cultured. Even though over time Ava had come to expect the bafflement in their eyes when she was presented as Frank's wife, it always made her feel second rate, as if she were unworthy of his love because she was not beautiful and outgoing. It didn't help matters that behind his smile, Frank wore a slight look of embarrassment when introducing her. It stung every time, so she had become resistant to social events.

"Something smells good." Frank said from the doorway.

"*Bonjour, mon chéri*[2]," Ava greeted him in her native tongue. "It's coq au vin, your best."

Frank chuckled as he put Avril down and turned his face away from Ava. He didn't have the heart to tell her that the thought of her coq au vin made his stomach turn. "Favorite," he corrected her. "Coq au vin is my favorite." He leaned down and gave her a gentle kiss on the lips.

"Ah, *favorite*," she repeated, her heart racing just a little. Ava was deeply in love with her husband, but he rarely showed her affection. His melancholy had become so cumbersome these days. She tried her best to comfort him, but the only thing that seemed to help was to leave him to himself.

"I have a little something for you." Frank handed Ava the paper bag. "Champagne!" she exclaimed as she pulled out the bottle. "Does this mean you have the work?"

Frank laughed to himself again. "Yes, darling, I have the

---

[2] Bonjour, mon chéri: Hello, my darling

job."

"Tell me, tell me." Ava fluttered around the kitchen setting the table up for them to dine.

"Let me get this bottle open and I'll tell you everything over dinner." Frank turned to Avril, who was clinging to his pants leg. "Now, Sunshine, this is champagne. It's something grownups drink to celebrate. But when you open the bottle, it makes a loud pop. I want you to cover your ears, so you don't get frightened."

Avril's face lit up with excitement as she put her tiny hands over her ears. Frank shook the bottle a little for showmanship. Then he aimed the cork down the hall and popped the champagne open. Avril squealed with delight, watching the foam spill over the top of the bottle.

"Again, Daddy, again!"

"I'm afraid I can't. Once the cork is out, you can't put it back in." Avril frowned at him.

"Oh, come now, don't pout," Frank said cheerfully as he put the bottle down on the table and picked her up, tossing and catching her in the air a couple of times. It was her favorite game and never failed to make her giggle.

Ava loved watching them play; the two of them had such a special bond. She always knew Frank would be a wonderful father. He never had a harsh word or a raised voice for his daughter. He was always gentle and patient with her, taking the time to explain the ways of the world in a manner that a young child could understand.

They all sat down at the table to eat, and Frank went about retelling the story of his day. Too occupied with her own thoughts, Ava only half-listened. She was thrilled that after everything they had been through, Frank was finally opening up to her. As he went on, Ava drifted away on hopes of a fresh start. Maybe this job would usher in a happier chapter for their little family. The closeness that she longed for with her husband could be just around the bend. But suddenly, Ava was snapped right back into the moment at the mention of Betty.

"I mean, there's no doubt about it, the woman is crass. But I have to admit that I admire her gumption. And the courage it takes to apologize, well, that's to be respected. Not to mention Betty's a fantastic writer. I was reading her latest article today when she came in to offer me the job."

There was something about the way Frank said her name that made Ava's skin burn, the way the corners of his mouth turned up in a secret smile that could not be suppressed. It disturbed Ava to her core. But she swallowed those feelings down with one big gulp of champagne and self-deception.

Chapter 4

Frank stared at the empty desk across from him. It was pushed up against his, the pair facing each other. His patience was wearing thin as he looked at his watch, again. Betty had instructed him to be at the office by eight o'clock, he'd gotten there at 7:45, and it was now nine o'clock and still no sign of Betty.

Today was his first day on the job and there was little for him to do without her there, so he had to just sit around, waiting. Bored and anxious, he must have reorganized his desk about a hundred times. He had spent a good twenty minutes trying to find the perfect place for his pencil cup.

Finally, he settled on a spot at the top right-hand corner.

"Now that's the ticket," he thought as he leaned back in his chair to admire his work. Everything was neat and tidy, positioned for maximum efficiency and productivity, exactly how he liked it.

Just as Frank took a deep breath of satisfaction, Betty strolled into the bullpen, carrying about a dozen newspapers under her arm. She was impeccably dressed, her blonde hair curled and pinned to perfection with not a hair out of place. Her brilliant red peplum dress matched her lipstick and hugged her waist just right, while a pair of heels showed off her shapely legs. As Betty made her way toward the desks, Frank's heart unwillingly skipped a beat, and he found it hard to catch his breath.

Betty dumped the bundle of newspapers down on her desk into a sloppy pile and tossed half of the stack over onto Frank's desk, knocking over his strategically placed pencil cup. He watched as his pencils rolled across the top of his desk and spilled onto the floor.

For a moment, Frank just stared at her in disbelief. "You're contemptible."

"I've been called worse." She put her personal effects away, not the least bit bothered by his insult.

Frank stood up from his desk and began gathering his scattered pencils. "And you're late, by the way."

"Oh, am I?" she asked, amused. Betty turned her chair to the side, offering him a view of her profile.

"You told me to be here at eight." He returned to his seat, flustered, and started reorganizing his desk.

"I said YOU should be here at eight. That's got nothing to do with me." Betty leaned back in her chair with a smirk and popped open a fresh newspaper.

"Contemptible. Absolutely contemptible," Frank mumbled under his breath. "What is all this, anyway?"

"Newspapers," she gave a curt answer and continued to scan her paper.

"Yes, well, I can see that, but what am I supposed to do with them?"

"Read them."

"Yes, but why? I mean, what's the point in all this? Why am I reading competing newspapers?"

23

Betty sighed heavily as she rolled her eyes and lowered her paper. "We're looking for a new story to cover. Read through these papers and see if there's anything interesting."

"So you want us to steal someone else's story?"

"It's not stealing. The story is public once it's been printed." She tried her best to ignore him and continue reading her paper.

"Isn't that sort of cheating?"

"It's not cheating if you do it better. Now, stop asking me all these stupid questions and start reading."

"Seems a bit dishonest, if you ask me."

"Listen," Betty snapped and turned to look him sternly in the eye, "I don't want or need an assistant, but nevertheless, here you are. This is how I do things. If you don't like it, you're more than welcome to find another job."

Betty had put Frank in his place and a wave of respect for her washed over him. He picked up a newspaper and with sincere humility and reverence, he simply said, "Yes ma'am."

The two of them sat quietly at their desks for some time, looking over all the local papers. Most of the articles were about the ongoing war; everything else was pretty dull and boring. There didn't seem to be a single story that piqued either of their interests.

"Betty, can I ask you a question?" Frank finally broke the silence between them.

"No," Betty said flatly.

"I'm just not sure what it is that I'm supposed to be looking for."

"That's not a question, Frank." She looked at her watch; it was eleven right on the nose.

Frank said nothing and only stared at her with one cocked

24

eyebrow. He was amused by her, but mostly, she just frustrated him. She truly made it a chore to be the least bit civil toward her.

Betty folded up her newspaper and picked up the receiver on her desk phone. She glanced over at Frank, saw the look on his face, and thought maybe she should stop antagonizing him for just a moment.

"Look," she said with a softer tone as she began to dial, "if you have the instincts for this job, you'll know what you're looking for when you see it." Then she turned her attention to her phone call. "Yes, can I please speak to Officer Matthew Abshire? This is Miss Betty Boudreaux. Thank you."

Frank eyed her secretly from behind the newspaper he was pretending to read.

"Hello, Matthew, how are you?" Her voice light and flirtatious. "I was wondering if you were free for lunch today." Betty twirled the phone cord between her fingers and giggled in a sultry tone. "Wonderful. No, I'm sick of the diner, let's go somewhere nice. Oh, perfect. I can meet you there in fifteen minutes. Alright, dear, see you soon."

And with that, Betty hung up the phone. She took a compact out of her handbag and lightly reapplied her lipstick before gathering the rest of her things.

"You're going on a lunch date?" Frank asked, unable to hide the annoyance in his voice.

"Why? Are you jealous?" she teased as she stood up from her desk, things in hand and ready to leave.

"Well, it's just that you got here an hour late and all we've done so far is read our competitors' papers. I thought we were going to do some actual work today," he challenged her.

Betty shot him a harsh look before she opened up the top

drawer and pulled out a stack of handwritten notes. "Here," she said, flopping it onto his desk. "Type this up."

"What's this?"

"Work." She grinned before strutting away.

Frank caught himself watching her swaying hips walk out the door.

He couldn't put his finger on it, but something about her made him feel like himself again.

* * *

Matthew sat in Antoine's Restaurant at a quiet table tucked in the corner overlooking St. Louis Street. He lit a cigarette while he waited for Betty. He was nervous about seeing her today. He had been thinking things over for a while now and he finally made up his mind about the situation. "There's no turning back now," he told himself.

He could hear her heels clicking on the old wood floor before he saw her. Matthew smiled at her with a wide grin and his boyish good looks. He smoothed out his neat blonde hair as he stood to greet her. He always looked exceptionally handsome in his police uniform.

"Hello there, Betty." He gave her a friendly kiss on the cheek and pulled her chair out for her. "You're looking awfully dressed up today."

"Do you think so?" Betty sat down with her usual elegance.

"How's that new assistant of yours working out?" he teased as he seated himself back at the table.

Betty knew where he was going with this and held up her menu to avoid the conversation. "I don't see what that has to do with anything."

"So this get-up has nothing to do with your very attractive new assistant?"

She quickly lowered her menu, her eyes wide and playful. "Oh, I never should have told you that. I swear, Matthew, sometimes I don't know why we're friends." She laughed and resumed looking over her menu.

Matthew took a drag of his cigarette and leaned back in his chair. "Well, we aren't friends now, are we, Betty?"

"What are you talking about, of course we're friends." Betty looked up and saw that he was being quite serious. "Matthew, what's going on?"

"Oh, come on Betty, you've been blackmailing me for years." He leaned forward over the table. As he stamped out his cigarette, he shifted his eyes around the room to see if anyone was in earshot. In a hushed whisper, Matthew continued, "Ever since you found out that Robert is more than just my roommate, you've held it over my head to get inside information for your articles."

"That was before I knew you," she protested. "You know I would never out you."

"Oh, do I? Everybody knows you're an unscrupulous bitch who would do anything for a good story." The moment the words left his mouth, he instantly regretted it. He saw the heartbreak in her eyes, but he had gone too far and there was no backing down now.

His harsh words cut deep. Betty couldn't believe that this was what her best friend thought of her. But he was right. She would do anything for a good story, and she did blackmail him once, although she never intended to follow through with the threat.

Her instinct for self-preservation kicked in. She took all her emotions, wadded them up in a tight little ball, and shoved them down deep. Her voice turned formal and empty. "I'm sorry you feel that way. I've come to think of both you and Robert as good friends."

Matthew laughed. "If this is the way you treat your friends, I'm surprised you have any."

Betty didn't want to admit to him that he and Robert were her only friends. "Well then, since you've made yourself perfectly clear, I suppose we're done here." She began to get up from the table, but Matthew stopped her.

"Hold on a minute, Betty. I'll still give you what you want, but you're going to have to start paying me for it. And trust me, you're going to want to pay for this story, because sweetheart, have I got a doozy for you."

* * *

Betty and Alan were at it again, and although everyone around him went about their business as usual, Frank found it impossible to ignore the commotion coming from Alan's office. He turned his chair all the way around to watch the spectacle through the big picture window.

Betty gestured her hands wildly, pointing her finger in Alan's face. Alan stood stoically with his hands on his hips until finally he had enough, and smacked his thick, meaty hand down on the desk, putting a firm end to the argument.

"Don't mind them, Mr. Martin." Mary Ann decided to stop by Frank's desk on her way out for the day, to try her hand at a little flirting. "They do this all the time. You'll get used to it." She ran her finger along the edge of his desk and batted her eyes at him.

Frank barely glanced at her, his eyes glued to the scene. "She sure does seem upset about something."

"I wouldn't worry too much about it. Betty always gets her way in the end." A deep sourness coated her voice. "Anyway, some of us are going for drinks around the corner if you'd like to join us." She tried to pull his attention toward her with no luck.

"No thanks, Mary Ann. Maybe some other time." Frank was aware that she was flirting with him, but he found that in situations such as this it was best not to encourage it. After all, he was a married man.

"Suit yourself." She got the hint and went on her way.

Betty stormed out of Alan's office and slammed the door behind her, rattling the window with her rage. When she reached her desk, Frank whirled his chair around to face her.

"What was all that about?" His curiosity had gotten the better of him.

"What time is it?" She ignored his question.

"Quarter past five."

"Perfect, just in time for cocktail hour." Her voice was muddled with anger and defeat. Betty grabbed her handbag and quickly made her way out the door.

"Wait!" Frank called after her as he jumped up from his seat and followed her out into the street. The war wound in his leg began to ache and it took him several painful strides to catch up with her. "Aren't you going to tell me what happened?"

"No," she replied sharply as she continued her brisk walk to the bar. "Come on, Betty," he whined.

"Look," she whipped around, "I've had a terrible day, both personally and professionally, so I'm not really in the mood to play with you right now, Frank."

Before he had a chance to respond, she vanished from the street corner into the bar. He stood there for a moment, immersed in a twinge of guilt. He couldn't help but feel responsible for contributing to her bad day. Frank had always prided himself on being a gentleman and when he thought about it, his behavior today wasn't quite up to par. He felt he needed to apologize and redeem himself.

Frank scanned the room for Betty as he walked inside the bar. He saw Mary Ann and a group of their coworkers sitting at a little table toward the back of the room, but Betty wasn't with them. He found it odd that instead, she was sitting alone at the bar with her drink. Nevertheless, he made his way across the lounge and took a seat next to her.

"I'll have what she's having," Frank said to the bartender.

"Double whiskey on the rocks, coming right up."

Betty delicately sipped her drink in silence, while Frank waited quietly for his whiskey. The bartender returned and handed him his drink. Frank swirled the ice around in his glass before sampling it. "I really am a good guy, Betty."

"I know you're a good guy, Frank, that's what makes you so annoying." She took a sip.

Frank snickered. "Are you always so cross?" He really did find her to be funny, he just wished she'd stop aiming her humor at him.

"Not always," she took yet another sip, "but my defenses are up today."

"Do you want to talk about it?" he asked.

Betty's initial reaction was to tell him to get lost, but Matthew's words from lunch were still ringing in her ears. She realized that she wasn't in a position to turn down friends.

Perhaps it was the whiskey, or perhaps it was his charming smile, but either way, Betty let herself become vulnerable, just a little.

"Well, since you asked," she started, "I have dedicated my entire life to this job. I have sacrificed everything else in my life to be the best at this, to the point where there is nothing else. This is it; this career is all I have. And yet I still don't get the respect I deserve." She glanced over at the table where Mary Ann and the others were sitting. "In fact, I'm thought less of and looked down on because of it." She took a less delicate swig of her whiskey.

Frank looked back at his coworkers, and he understood now what Betty was fighting against. "Betty," he turned to her, "they treat you that way because they're jealous. You're a fantastic journalist." He looked down at his drink and then back at her. "You deserve more than that, and I'm sorry if I disrespected you today. I want you to know that I do hold you in high regard."

Betty was moved by his words and felt them profoundly. It was the very thing she needed that night.

"I was reading what you asked me to type up this morning," Frank continued, "about the car theft ring. And I have to say, it's brilliant, I mean really brilliant. How did you manage to figure it all out?"

Betty smirked at him as she leaned on the bar and rested her chin on the back of her dainty hand.

"You know that little exercise we did this morning when we read all those newspapers? You remember, the one you were complaining about." She gave him a playful smile.

"Yes, I remember." Frank shyly returned her grin.

"Well, that's how. You see, because not every paper is going

31

to cover every car theft and since no one reads every paper, it all just seemed like random acts happening all over the city. But because I *do* read every paper, when I sat down with everything that had been printed over the last several weeks, it was clear to me that there was an order to it all. A pattern in where and when the thefts were taking place. So long story short, I did a little digging and found out what was really going on." Betty moved gracefully as she took a sip of her whiskey, never even leaving a lipstick stain on the glass, a little trick she picked up in finishing school.

And that was the thing about Betty: she looked as though she'd be the Perfect Little Woman, but in reality, she was a Bombshell, ready to blow up anything that stood in her way.

"Wow," Frank said, tilting his head to look at her. "I never would have thought of that." He saw her deeply and gave her a crooked smile. "You're impressive," he said, in awe of her.

Betty felt illuminated by his praise and she realized that maybe she misjudged him. "You know, Frank, I think I owe you an apology, too. I haven't exactly made things easy for you. It's not really about you, but more about what you represent," she said, opening up to him a little more.

"And what is it that I represent?" He leaned in closer to her and their eyes danced over one another.

"That Alan doesn't trust me to do my job on my own."

"What happened today with Alan, anyway?"

Betty rolled her eyes and took the last taste of her drink. "I got a lead on an amazing story, and he killed it."

"What's the story?" Frank finished his whiskey and pulled a pack of cigarettes out of his pocket, setting them on the bar.

"May I?" Betty asked, grabbing one from his pack. She cupped her hands around the flame as Frank lit her cigarette for her. Their hands hovered uncontrollably close to each other, not touching but wanting to.

"You ever hear of Ville Morte?"

Frank shook his head no, lighting himself a cigarette before signaling the bartender for two more drinks.

"It's this small Cajun village about two hundred miles from here." She took a drag of her cigarette. "Anyway, a couple of months ago, they discovered a body on Lover's Lane by the swamp. It was a teenage girl, Suzy Quibodeaux, found raped and murdered in her boyfriend's car."

Frank listened intently as he smoked his cigarette.

"But her boyfriend, Bobby Fontenot, was nowhere to be found. So, of course, the whole town thought he did it, until about two weeks later when his body turned up in the exact same spot as Suzy. It was mutilated almost beyond recognition. But here's the kicker," Betty leaned in closer to Frank, "last week, another girl was found in the same area, raped and murdered, and her boyfriend is still missing."

"Why would Alan kill that story?" Frank asked, astonished.

"He said it was too dangerous."

In the background of their conversation, the bartender reappeared and placed each of their drinks in front of them.

"I suppose you pitched it to him going alone."

Betty dipped her finger in the glass and whirled the ice around, then she stuck her finger in her mouth and gently sucked the whiskey from it. "Of course I did."

Frank leaned back and pondered for a minute. "What if I went with you?"

Betty scoffed. "Oh please, Frank, do you really think your wife would allow that?"

He smiled, curiously. "I never told you I was married."

33

"I'm an investigative reporter. I wouldn't be very good at my job if I didn't notice you were married." She pointed to his gold wedding band. "Besides, you're a good guy and good guys are always married."

Frank looked down at his ring and spun it a couple of times before he looked up at Betty. "I can handle my wife." He smiled softly at her, but Betty's skills were sharp, and even though he tried to hide it, she saw a deep sadness in his eyes.

"I'm sorry Frank, but no red-blooded American woman is going to let her husband go out of town with some strange lady."

"Good thing my wife is French."

"Oh well, la di da," she teased him.

"I'm serious, Betty. If I were to go with you, do you think Alan would agree to let us cover the story?" Frank took a deep drag of his cigarette.

Betty paused, watching the smooth flow of smoke drift from his full lips. "Yes."

"Well, it's settled then. First thing tomorrow morning, we'll talk to Alan, and if he agrees to the story, you'll come over for dinner and meet my wife. Then you won't be some strange lady."

"Sounds like a perfect plan, but why wait? I'm sure Alan is still at the office. We can finish our drinks and talk to him tonight."

"Even better. Listen Betty, I think we got off on the wrong foot. What do you say we start over? Friends?"

"Friends," she agreed.

They raised their glasses in a toast to a newfound friendship. Their eyes locked together and, in that moment, a flicker of something more passed between them.

Chapter 5

Betty turned her house key in the lock and stepped inside her dark duplex apartment. She had left a lamp on, but the bulb must have burnt out while she was away. The only thing she hated more than coming home to a dark house was coming home to a messy one.

She flicked the overhead light on to illuminate her lush and elegantly furnished living room. She had decorated in jewel tones to match the authentic Tiffany-stained glass lamp sitting in the middle of her fireplace mantle. The lampshade was amber with images of green vines and oversized blooming red roses.

All of her windows were covered by thick, ruby colored drapes, which complemented her rich emerald green settee, both in velvet. On either side of the fireplace were a pair of deep yellow wingback chairs and curled up in one of the seat cushions was a sleeping Calico cat.

"Hello there, Miss Edgar," Betty greeted the cat and walked over to pet her.

Miss Edgar popped open her bright green eyes and hissed softly at Betty. She jumped out of the chair and quickly scampered off toward the kitchen.

"Well, that's a fine how do you do," Betty said out loud to no one as she went to fetch a new lightbulb for her lamp.

That lamp was special. It had been a gift from her parents after she graduated college, and she never turned it off. Somehow it made her feel safe.

As she changed the bulb out, she glanced over at the photograph next to her lamp. She hadn't really looked at it since the last time she changed out the bulb. It was a picture of herself with her parents and younger brother at the Arceneaux family's annual Christmas party. It was a fancy affair that they all looked forward to every year. The champagne always flowed freely and most of Baton Rouge society was in attendance, dressed in their best holiday outfits.

Betty realized that she was wearing the same red peplum dress she had on in the photo and remembered that she had bought it specifically for that party. She had just come from her job interview at *The New Orleans Post*, and they had offered her the position. Filled with hope of a bright new future, she strolled down Canal Street and spotted the dress in a department store window display. It would be perfect for the upcoming Christmas party. She walked right in and bought the dress for herself. It would become her favorite, not because it looked spectacular on her but because for Betty, it represented her ability to be her own provider; a testament to her hard work. She couldn't wait to show it off and share the news of her success.

Betty knew her family would be so proud of her.

The four of them were standing in front of an oversized, ornately decorated Christmas tree. They were all laughing, no doubt at some witty joke her brother made, unaware of what was coming for their family. It had been the last joyful holiday they ever shared together. Not long after, her father died of a heart attack, and within that same year, her brother soon followed.

She stared at the picture and keenly felt the emptiness in her soul that she oftentimes feared would overtake her. Betty closed her eyes and took several deep breaths before she made her way to the kitchen. She grabbed her favorite lowball glass, then grabbed her bottle of whiskey and poured herself a stiff drink. She swallowed it in one gulp, hoping that would be enough to keep her ghostly memories at bay.

Betty took her shoes off and carried them to the bedroom at the back of the house. She put them in their original shoe box and tucked them away at the bottom of her armoire.

She finished undressing, and in nothing but a silk beige slip, walked to the kitchen and began rummaging through her cupboards, pulling out ingredients to make pie crust. Betty loved to bake, especially when she was mulling over a situation, and tonight, she had quite a few things to sort out.

First, there was planning out the details for the trip to Ville Morte. Alan had agreed to sign off on the project as long as Frank went along.

Then there was the phone call she was dreading but knew she would have to make. However, she decided to avoid that particular issue for now, and settled to come back to it later. Afterall, maybe she'd come up with a solution so she wouldn't even have to make the phone call. In any case, she'd have to figure it out by tomorrow afternoon; it wasn't something she could leave town with unresolved.

And last but not least, there was the dinner party at Frank's house tomorrow night, which was why she was baking a pie in the first place.

Betty set out all her supplies on the dining room table and was ready to get started on her pie crust.

Miss Edgar jumped up on the table and sat on the edge of the workspace. She put her tiny paw up to her mouth and began pulling at her nails with her teeth, sharpening her claws into razor points as she stared down Betty.

"You've decided to help me, I see," Betty said to the cat as she poured the flour, sugar, and salt into a large mixing bowl and began whisking it all together. "Turns out I was right," she continued. "Frank is married. And to a French woman, no less." She dropped the butter and shortening into the bowl and with a fork started to mash everything together. "A man like that can have any woman he wants. I bet she's exotic and sophisticated." Betty let out a little sigh. "I'm sure my little apple pie won't live up to her fancy French expectations, but there's no way I'm showing up empty-handed. Can you imagine what Mama would say? I can hear her now: 'Betty Jane Boudreaux, I did not spend all that money to send you to finishing school just for you to show up at that woman's house behaving uncouthly.'"

Betty's heart ached when she thought of her mother. And suddenly she found herself lost in a distant memory of an argument they had over Betty's going to finishing school. The two of them were standing in the parlor of their family home. Her mother, Marie, was insisting that she attend one year of charm school before going to college.

"Betty," Marie said to her teenage daughter, "you will learn things there that they just can't teach you in college."

"Like what?" Betty argued. "How to fold a dinner napkin?"

Marie Boudreaux pursed her lips and took a deep breath as she sat down on the chaise lounge. "Take a seat, my darling," she instructed with a firm but gentle tone.

Betty plopped down on the chaise lounge next to her mother.

"I would never dream of trying to deter you from the life you want," Marie began. "You know that I support your decision to be a career woman, and I do want you to attend university. But having a career means having to navigate through many social circles, most of which will be dominated by men. I know how much you love kicking in the proverbial door," she smiled, "but sometimes a little charm and grace will open the door for you. And that, my sweet girl," she took Betty by the hand, "is all I want for you: nothing but open doors."

Oh, how Betty missed her mother. But she just didn't have it in her tonight to open that box and everything that came with it. So she brought her mind back to the present and locked the box back up.

Miss Edgar tilted her head to one side while looking at Betty and swooshed her tail around with her usual angst.

"Oh, don't give me that look." She slowly drizzled the cold water into her mixture and gently folded it in to form the dough. "I do not have a crush on Frank."

The cat curled her tail around her legs and let out a soft meow.

"It is not a crush. It's less than a crush. Which, when you think about it, is really actually nothing."

Miss Edgar slowly lifted her paw and pushed the bag of flour off the table, spilling it all over the floor. She jumped down into the pile of flour and trotted off to her favorite chair for a nap, leaving a trail of little white paw prints across the house.

Betty looked at the mess and shook her head. "I should have

gotten a dog." She grabbed a broom and began to clean up.

The truth was, Betty loved that mean little cat. She had come to her on one of the worst days of her life. Having just returned home from her brother's funeral, completely broken and devastated, she found the small kitten sitting on her front steps. It followed her into the house and when she picked it up, it started to purr. She decided to keep the cat and named her after her brother, Edgar.

Betty knew it was stupid, yet she couldn't help but feel that Miss Edgar had been sent to her from Heaven, although it didn't take her long to revise her statement, saying that the cat was sent from Hell. Yet, as much trouble as Miss Edgar was at times, she always managed to make Betty laugh. And over time, she began to realize that she and that cat were more alike than she cared to admit.

Betty continued making her pie crust. She cut the dough into two equal parts and, with her rolling pin, flattened each half into a nice, neat circle. Every now and again, she would pause to write down another chore on her to-do list for tomorrow. When she finished, Betty wrapped the flat dough up in wax paper and put it in the refrigerator to chill overnight.

She meandered over to the living room and sat down on the settee , lighting herself a cigarette. She rubbed its velvet arm with the tip of her fingers and anxiously stared at the telephone. Now that everything else was done, she could no longer avoid the dreaded phone call.

Betty looked at the clock on the wall. It was a few minutes past eight. She wondered if it was too late to telephone, so she just sat there smoking her cigarette and tried to make up her mind. But the longer she sat there, the later it got. Finally, she decided that it was indeed too late to call, but it wasn't too late to make more pie crust. She took the last drag of her cigarette and went back to work in the kitchen.

It was nearly midnight by the time Betty crawled into bed. After finishing up with a third pie crust, she cleaned the kitchen and then washed herself up.

As she lay there alone in the darkness, she began to think of the city and how big it was. She wondered how many people were actually living there; hundreds of thousands, that was for sure. All those different people, living all sorts of lives.

And she realized that of all those hundreds of thousands of people living in New Orleans, not one single person actually loved her; no one cared about Betty. A chill ran through her blood as it dawned on her how alone she truly was, and for the first time in her adult life, she was afraid.

* * *

It was eleven o'clock on Tuesday morning and Matthew couldn't imagine loving anyone more than he loved Robert. He leaned in the doorway of their kitchen and watched as Robert, unaware that he had an audience, danced around the space. He swayed his hips and hummed along to the soft sounds of the radio. Robert had it turned down low, and knowing it was Matthew's day off, he didn't want to wake him. Matthew was going to be working the night shift for the rest of the week, and he needed his day off to adjust.

Robert, however, had been up since about five o'clock. Even though he didn't have court today, being a defense attorney, he always got up early. He loved the quiet stillness of the early mornings and used the time to sit on their back patio

41

with a cup of coffee and a good book before the overbearing humidity set in for the day.

He was right in the middle of making a fresh pot of French press coffee when Matthew walked up behind him. He put his hands on Robert's hips and gave him such a fright that he jumped and sent coffee grinds flying through the air, showering down all over the kitchen.

"Oh!" Robert let out a little scream. "Matthew, you startled me," he laughed. "Goodness, look at this mess." He turned and faced Matthew.

Matthew wrapped his arms around Robert's waist and pulled him close. "I'm sorry, darling, I didn't mean to frighten you. You just look so adorable today." He looked deep into Robert's eyes. "Is that my shirt?"

Robert draped his arms around Matthew's neck. "Yes. All I have clean are sweater vests and it's too hot to wear those."

"It looks good on you." Matthew leaned in and gave the love of his life a long, sweet kiss.

Just then, there was a knock at the door. Both men froze as they shared a moment of panic.

"Are we expecting anyone?" Matthew asked nervously. "No," Robert answered with equal concern.

"Are the curtains drawn?"

"The curtains are always drawn," Robert said with a sad softness. He grazed Matthew's cheek with the back of his hand and put him at ease. "I'll get the door. You clean up this mess." He waved his hand, gesturing to the coffee grinds.

As Robert walked away, Matthew gave him a little smack on the rump.

Robert looked over his shoulder and returned a flirtatious smile.

"I want my shirt back," Matthew teased.

"Wrestle me for it." Robert winked and strutted down the hallway.

As he made his way to the front door, the jolt of panic he received from the unexpected visitor began to twist itself into a knot in the pit of his stomach. Neither of them was ashamed of who they were, and both men hated having to hide away that part of themselves. Robert wanted nothing more than to be able to walk down the street and simply hold Matthew's hand. Matthew wished that he could marry Robert and introduce him to everyone as his husband. But that was not the reality of the world they lived in, so they resolved to just make do living with the curtains drawn.

He opened the front door and was greeted by the smell of fresh baked apple pie. Betty stood there, stiff and nervous, holding the bubbling hot pie.

"Hello there, Betty. What a pleasant surprise," Robert said gleefully, and all the tension faded away when he saw that it was Betty. "And you brought pie, too." He opened the door wide and stepped aside to let her in. "Your timing couldn't be better; we just put the coffee on."

"Oh, I don't want to impose," she said in a tone that Robert found to be unusually formal.

"You're not imposing. Come in and have some coffee and pie with us."

"I couldn't possibly. I just came by to ask for a favor." She looked down at the pie she was still holding and was unable to meet Robert's eyes. "I understand that in light of things, it probably isn't the best time to be asking for any favors, but there's no one else for me to ask." She found the courage to look up at him before she continued. "You see, I'm going out of town for a few days on business and I need someone to peek in on Miss Edgar while I'm away."

Robert could see how uneasy she was, but for the life of him, he couldn't understand why. "Sure, I don't mind looking in on the cat. But Betty, in light of what things?"

Her nerves got the better of her again and she looked away from him. "Matthew made things perfectly clear over lunch. And truly, I don't blame either of you for feeling that way."

"Feeling what way? When did the two of you have lunch?"

"Yesterday. He didn't tell you?" Betty was surprised; she had assumed that Matthew must have talked the whole thing over with Robert.

"He most certainly did not. What on earth did he say to you?" But he knew Matthew better than anyone and had a pretty good idea of what he must have said.

"Maybe you should let him explain it. I really don't want to start any trouble." She could see that Robert was starting to get angry with Matthew and she couldn't have felt more uncomfortable. Betty wanted to end the conversation as quickly as possible before she said something else that might stir things up. "So you'll look in on Miss Edgar for me, then?" She shoved the pie toward him.

"Of course I will," he said and gently took the pie from her.

"Splendid." Betty started backing away from the door. "I leave tomorrow morning, so just pop in every couple of days and make sure she hasn't burned the house down," she tried to make a little joke. "Thank you again, Robert. And enjoy the pie." She didn't wait for his reply as she quickly turned and walked away; she couldn't get out of there fast enough.

Robert watched Betty rush off down the street before he went back inside. He marched straight to the kitchen, determined to get to the bottom of this mess. He found Matthew standing at the counter, pouring two cups of fresh hot coffee.

"Is that apple pie I smell?" He turned to Robert and gave him a smile.

"It sure is," Robert said as he flopped the pie down on the counter. "Miss Betty Boudreaux's famous homemade apple pie."

Matthew let out a heavy sigh and hung his head.

"Do you care to tell me why she thinks we're no longer friends?"

Matthew took a big slurp of his coffee as he tried to think up a suitable answer.

"Put the coffee down, Matthew," Robert instructed while he crossed his arms over his chest. "What happened yesterday?"

Matthew put the coffee down like he was told and sheepishly answered, "I may have called her an unscrupulous bitch."

"You did what?! Why the hell would you say something like that?"

"Robert, the woman has been blackmailing me for years," he replied in his own defense.

"Oh, for God's sake, Matthew." Robert threw his hands up in the air. "We settled that years ago. You know damn good and well that Betty would never out us."

"No, just milk me dry for information."

Robert narrowed his eyes and rested a fist on one hip. "She's been a good friend to both of us over the years and she's more than made up for her indiscretion."

"I'm just trying to protect us," Matthew said, slightly raising his voice.

"Oh bullshit. This isn't about protecting us." Robert raised his voice over Matthew's. "This is about that car theft case."

This struck a deep nerve with Matthew, and he went silent.

Robert continued, "She didn't give you the lead she promised, so you didn't get the promotion and now you're pissed."

"She made a fool of me, Robert. She just couldn't help herself; Betty had to be the big hero of the day and left me in the lurch."

"Matthew, there will always be more opportunities at work. But Betty is one of the only people in our lives who we can actually trust and who we can actually be ourselves around, and I will not lose that."

"I don't understand why you're so upset about this. Betty's a tough cookie; she'll get over it and everything will go back to normal in a couple of weeks."

"She's not as tough as she pretends to be and you know it. When she gets back from her trip you better make things right with her. Until then," Robert snatched the pie off the counter, "no pie for you." And he stormed out of the room.

Chapter 6

Ava stuck her head in the oven. She was not at all pleased that Frank had sprung this dinner party on her last minute, and she had spent the entire day running around trying to get the house ready for guests. She had been so busy that she hadn't even had a moment to get herself presentable and now she was going to have to serve dinner with unwashed hair.

Ava took her frustration out on the oven door and slammed it shut. There were still about ten minutes left on the roast chicken. She checked the potato-leek soup, gave it a quick stir, and turned the fire down low. She felt utterly ridiculous serving soup in the middle of summer, but there hadn't been time or money for much else.

Ava grabbed the dinner plates and the silverware from the cupboard and set them down on the table in a large stack. She bustled back and forth across their tiny kitchen that also doubled as the dining room, trying to get everything ready for dinner on time.

Frank was leaning against the doorway to the kitchen watching her. "Come on, Ava, please don't be sore with me," he tried to reason with her.

"*François*," she only ever called him *François* when she was being serious with him, "you give me no time to make a party."

"It's not a party; it's just dinner with one extra person. Betty's great. I'm sure you'll love her." Frank was too busy checking his watch to see the look Ava shot him.

She was certain that she would not love Betty. She was already so sick of hearing about Betty.

When Frank looked up at her, she was busy setting the table and making her feelings known by lightly banging the dinnerware down on the table. He started to question his decision about waiting until after dinner to tell her about the trip.

It surprised him just how upset Ava had gotten when he told her that Betty would be joining them for dinner. He wasn't quite sure how she would take the news that he was going out of town for a few days and didn't want to chance angering her further. Thinking that she would be in better spirits after a nice dinner with a bottle of wine and good company, he decided that later would be the best time to bring it up. He certainly couldn't bring it up now; Betty would be there any minute.

Frank checked his watch again before walking over to her and with a light touch, placed his hands on her shoulders. "I'm sorry I upset you. But we can't change things now. All we can do is put a smile on and enjoy the evening." He tucked his finger under her chin and lifted her face up so that their eyes met. "Will you do that for me?"

His sweet and gentle nature caused her resolve to weaken. Ava was hopelessly in love with him and whenever he touched her, there was nothing she would deny him. In that moment, she made a promise to herself that she would not embarrass her husband and would be a perfect wife for the evening.

"*Oui*[3]." She looked up into his big blue eyes, hoping for a kiss, but he gave her a hug instead. Frank held her close but released her from his embrace as soon as he heard a knock at the door. He left her standing alone in the kitchen, feeling disappointed and unsatisfied.

Betty stood outside Frank's house on the front porch holding one of her apple pies. She didn't fully understand why, but she was excited to see him. She knocked on the door and as she waited, butterflies danced around in her belly, a feeling she hadn't felt since she was a teenager.

The doorknob turned clumsily this way and that before it opened wide. Standing there in a little white nightgown was Frank's daughter, Avril. She looked up at Betty with bright curious eyes.

Betty stood there, surprised. She wasn't aware that Frank had a child and for a moment, she wondered if she had the wrong house.

"Well, hello there," Betty said to the girl.

Without a word, the toddler swung the door shut and it slammed in Betty's face. Confused as to what just happened, Betty stood there stunned for a moment before the door reopened and Frank's face appeared. "I'm so sorry, Betty. Come on in."

"It's quite alright," she said with a smile.

Avril was hiding behind Frank and clinging to his pant leg. "She forgot she's not supposed to answer the door," Frank looked down at her with raised eyebrows, "but when she heard me coming, suddenly she remembered and slammed the door

---

[3] Oui: Yes

49

in your face. Again, I'm so sorry."

Betty smiled at Avril, "That's okay, I forget my manners all the time"

Avril smiled back at Betty and peeked out from behind Frank.

"Betty, this is my daughter, Avril. Avril, this is Miss Boudreaux."

"It's a pleasure to meet you, Avril." Unable to shake the child's hand because she was still holding the pie, Betty gave her a little curtsy.

"Avril, can you apologize to Miss Boudreaux for slamming the door in her face?" Frank asked his daughter firmly.

"I'm sowwy," Avril said with a happy grin. Her big blue eyes gave her away as Frank's daughter.

"Alright, Sunshine, run along to bed."

"Wead me a stowy, Daddy."

"I've already read you two bedtime stories, now it's time to go to sleep."

Avril looked up at him with sad watery eyes and her lip began to quiver. She knew how to tug at his heart strings and Frank was about to give in when Betty intervened.

"Avril, do you like sweets?"

She nodded her head *yes* in a grand gesture.

"Well, you know," Betty said, "if you listen to your father, I bet I can convince him to save you a slice of this apple pie."

Avril's eyes lit up as she turned to Frank for confirmation.

"She's right, Sunshine. If you go to bed now, I promise to save you a slice. I might even let you have some for breakfast."

She gasped with delight and finally let go of Frank's pant leg.

Avril ran down the hall to her room, all the while repeatedly screaming, "Oh boy, pie for bweakfast!"

"Oh Frank, she's darling."

"She's the light of my life," Frank said proudly.

He looked at the pastry Betty was holding and snickered a bit.

"Is there something amusing about my pie?" Betty asked playfully.

"I just didn't take you for much of a homemaker." When he looked at her, he could not stifle the grin that spread from ear to ear.

Betty took a step toward him and handed the pie to him. "I assure you, Frank, my pie is quite delicious," she said in a tone that made Frank blush and look down at his feet. But when he turned his gaze back to her, he gave her a steamy look that her heart fluttered in unexpected ways.

"I have no doubt your pie is exquisite." He reached for it and lightly grazed his fingers over hers. The touch sent a tingle throughout their bodies.

The two were beaming at each other so intently that neither of them noticed Ava standing there. She watched with knots in her stomach as her husband openly flirted with this woman in their living room. Her angry heart thumped deep in her chest, and she clenched her hands into tight fists that caused her fingernails to dig into the soft flesh of her palms. She witnessed Frank look at Betty in a way that he had never looked at her.

Ava wanted to shove *la putain*[4] right out the front door, but she remembered her promise to herself to be a good wife, and so her duty to Frank overrode her impulse. Besides, she

[4] la putain: the bitch

51

knew getting angry would only push him further away; if she wanted to get closer to him, she'd have to be perfect.

Finally, Frank realized that Ava was standing there, "Oh Betty, this is my wife, Ava."

"It's a pleasure to meet you. You have such a lovely home," Betty said with perfect manners and shook Ava's hand as if she hadn't just been gawking at her husband like a lovesick teenager.

"Merci[5]," Ava replied in a tiny voice and tried to conceal her anger. Betty was exactly what she had expected. She was stunning, a classic American beauty. And when the inevitable look of bafflement that always accompanied her introduction as Frank's wife flashed across Betty's face, Ava had never felt smaller.

Ava, however, wasn't at all what Betty had expected. She was surprised that Ava was so plain and meek. She assumed Frank would have a wife that matched his own good looks.

Well, Betty thought to herself, *she must have a dazzling personality*. But she was wrong on that account, too. Ava was practically mute during dinner, while Frank and Betty sat across from each other, chatting away like old chums.

"So, Frank, I'm curious, what made you decide to pursue journalism?" Betty asked as she cut into her chicken.

"Well, I don't know if you read *The New York Herald Tribune*, but they have a fantastic war correspondent, Marguerite Higgins."

"You're familiar with Marguerite Higgins?" Betty asked enthusiastically.

"Of course. She's the best correspondent out there."

---

[5] Merci: Thank you

"Oh, I agree. She's such an inspiration," Betty proclaimed.

"She's surely been an inspiration to me. I've always planned to be a journalist and reading her work really lit a fire in me to go after it," Frank explained, and he found it exhilarating to talk to someone who shared his passion.

"Did you read her article on the liberation of the Dachau concentration camp?"

"Yes," Frank responded with elation. "It was brilliant and moving."

"The work she's doing is unparalleled."

Ava was having a hard time keeping up with the conversation.

In an attempt to be included, she silently placed her hand over Frank's. He pulled his hand away and reached for his wine glass. Ava didn't think it was possible to feel more insignificant than she did at that moment. She was deflated and shrank into herself.

Betty realized how left out Ava must have felt and tried to steer the conversation in a different direction.

"Ava, this potato-leek soup is simply to die for."

"Merci," Ava said with a forced smile. "Where in France are you from?"

"Champagne."

"Oh, so not far from Paris. Have you ever been? To Paris, I mean."

"Only once." Ava turned to Frank and looked at him with mournful eyes.

Suddenly Frank was reminded of everything he tried to forget. The shame, the guilt, and what he owed her. The familiar sensation of being a disappointing husband overcame him.

"I've always wanted to go," Betty went on. "My favorite aunt lived in Paris for years and she used to tell me stories about all her adventures. Only God knows why she decided to move back to Ville Morte, of all places. But it's actually very convenient for us, Frank, because she still lives there."

Frank held his breath as his entire body tensed up at the mention of Ville Morte. It was then that he realized he had made a terrible error in judgment by not telling Ava about the trip earlier. And he had been so enamored with Betty this evening that he forgot to tell her not to bring it up. He went white with panic, and his eyes grew wide as he tried to quickly think up a way to change the subject.

Betty saw his reaction and misread it completely. "Oh, don't worry, we won't be staying with her while we're on our trip. The paper is paying for our room and board. I just meant she'll be a great resource, she knows everyone in town."

Ava's heart stopped. The look on Frank's face told her that she had not misunderstood.

"*Quoi? Un voyage, François?*"[6] She was too flustered to even attempt speaking in English. "*Quand?*"[7]

Betty didn't speak much French, but she knew enough understand what Ava was saying. She was shocked that Frank hadn't told his wife he was going out of town; had she known, she never would have spilled the beans. Her eyes darted back and forth between them as she sat frozen in her chair.

"Um, well," Frank stammered, "you see, Betty and I are going on a work assignment out of town, to Ville Morte. We're leaving tomorrow morning."

---

[6] Quoi? Un voyage, François? : What? A trip, Frank?

[7] Quand?: When?

The tension grew with an awkward silence that filled the tiny space. Ava stared down at the table in disbelief.

How could he do this to me, she thought to herself. She had spent the entire evening doing her best not to embarrass him, even though he had treated her as if she were the maid instead of his wife. She felt mortified and was heartbroken that all her efforts went unnoticed.

A storm of emotions brewed inside of her, and she knew she could not contain it. No matter how much she tried, she simply didn't matter to him.

"Pardon," her voice cracked. Ava pushed herself away from the table and quickly left the room with tears in her eyes.

Betty stared at him from across the table and lit a cigarette. "Oh Frank, you didn't tell her?" It was clear that she was disappointed in him.

Frank leaned his head back and let out a defeated sigh. "Well, I intended to."

"When, as you were walking out the front door?" she said, giving him a hard time.

Frank smirked at her. "What about you?" He leaned forward and lit a cigarette for himself. "When were you going to tell me you're from Ville Morte?"

"I'm not from Ville Morte." Betty took a long drag off her smoke. "My parents are from Ville Morte. I grew up in Baton Rouge. I used to spend summers out there with my aunt. I haven't been back since I was sixteen. But don't try to change the subject, Frank. You told me you would handle this."

"I'll take care of it, don't worry."

"I am worried." Betty turned serious. "Listen, your personal life is none of my business, but when my business is affected by your personal life, then we have a problem. Alan will go ballistic if I go out there without you."

"You'd really leave without me?" Frank smoked his cigarette.

Betty laughed at him. "What makes you think I wouldn't leave without you?"

Frank thought about it for a moment and then chuckled, "Nothing, actually."

"I suppose in addition to not telling your wife that you haven't packed either. So I'll let you get to it." She put out her cigarette and stood up from the table.

"I'll walk you out."

Frank walked her through the house and to the front door.

Before leaving, Betty turned to him. "I'm counting on you Frank."

"Like I said," he took a step closer to her, "I'll take care of it. Just meet me at the diner in the morning like we planned."

For a brief moment, they stood in silence, looking at each other and feeling inexplicably drawn together.

"Goodnight, Frank," she said softly.

"Goodnight, Betty."

And then she walked out the door, leaving him to clean up his own mess.

Frank walked to their bedroom and found Ava sitting on the edge of the bed in the dark. She looked up at his shadowy figure standing in the doorway and wiped the tears away from her face. His heart broke when he saw her. He hated that she was in so much pain, and he hated that he was the cause of it. Slowly, his self-loathing crept in.

"Please don't go away," she softly cried.

"Ava," he said with gentleness in his voice, "I have to go, it's for work."

She began to sob. "You can't leave. You can't leave."

Frank knelt down in front of her and held her hands in his. "I'm sorry. I really am. But please don't do this, Ava," he pleaded with her. "I need this job. I need this."

She looked into his sad eyes, and she could not find it within herself to deny him this one thing. Even if she tried, she knew she could not stop him from going. Reluctantly, she nodded her head *yes*.

Frank wrapped his arms around her and held her tight against his body.

"Thank you," he whispered.

Ava tried to compose herself, but deep down, she couldn't shake the feeling that something terrible was on the horizon.

* * *

It was an eerie night on the bayou as the full moon hung low in the sky. An unsettling stillness engulfed the stale summer air around the old, abandoned homestead. It had long been forgotten and lay hidden in a grove of trees just beyond the murky waters of the swamp. Even the odd creatures that made the bayou their home kept away from there; they knew that whatever went in wasn't likely to come out.

There wasn't a fleck of paint left on the outside of the shack. Damaged by years of extreme Louisiana weather and total neglect, the exposed wood turned a dull gray and began to rot away. The front porch had leaned to the left for years before it finally gave way and collapsed in the overgrown weeds that threatened to consume the ramshackle dwelling.

Mirroring the collapse of the left side of the porch, the roof had caved in on itself toward the back of the structure. The rest of the rusty tin roof was speckled with large holes that let downpours of subtropical rain leak into the house. Over years of its desertion, the daily summer rain showers caused the floorboards to decay, and one wrong step could sink anyone that dared to embark inside that forsaken place.

Crumpled in the corner of the back room with the sunken ceiling was the dead body of the missing teenage boy, Timothy Babin. He lay naked on the floor in a puddle of his own congealed blood among the trash and refuge of the home's current inhabitant; a man known only as No Face. All four of Timothy's limbs were broken and twisted to unnatural angles that protruded out in all directions. Evidence of the torture he endured presented itself in the form of deep slashes and bruises along his torso. Every part of the boy had been destroyed.

By now, the flies had begun to gather in droves. The smell of the sweet blood of youth intoxicated the flies as they danced around in pools of Timothy's blood. They buzzed around the decomposing body and crawled inside his open wounds to lay their eggs.

The gash across his throat that nearly severed his head from his body was being devoured by a family of rats who, unable to resist any easy meal, braved their way into the shack. They squealed with delight as they gnawed away at him with their sharp rodent teeth.

Using their claws, the rats tore and scratched at the soft bits of flesh around his neck to get deeper inside for a hardier dinner.

But No Face paid no mind to what was going on in the back room. He had finished with the boy hours ago and was now preoccupied with his real work. Just a few more stitches and he would be done.

Among the things that had been abandoned along with the house was an old vanity. No Face sat intently in front of its mirror that had begun to oxidize over time. His naked body was covered in the dried blood of his victim and with filthy hands, he plunged a rusty fishhook deep into his forehead. A thick stream of his own blood flowed down into his eyes. He grunted at the disruption but continued on without wiping it away. He didn't want slick fingers; not now, this was the last stitch.

He pulled the Spanish moss that was attached to the end of the fishhook through his skin and fastened it off. No Face leaned back and looked at himself carefully in the mirror to get a better look at his work.

A wicked grin spread across his lips and he let out a demented laugh that echoed through the empty house as he admired his new masterpiece.

Chapter 7

I t was a little past nine in the morning when the diner on Carondelet Street began to slow down from the breakfast rush. Betty sat at a table near the counter, waiting for Frank to arrive. She had a large road map spread out across the table and in between bites of her eggs benedict, she studied the route they would be taking on their journey to Ville Morte.

The bell over the front door chimed and behind her, Betty overheard two waitresses whisper loudly to each other.

"Oh, my word, Lucy, looked what just walked in," gasped the redhead who went by Sue.

"Well, there's a catch if I ever saw one," replied Lucy. She was a young waitress and had taken the job a few months back with the hopes of meeting an eligible bachelor. Sue told her that a lot of businessmen frequented the diner, and she would have a good chance of meeting Mr. Right.

Betty looked up to see what all the fuss was about. To her amusement, she saw Frank standing at the door with his suitcase in hand. She smiled and waved him over.

"Good morning." Her voice was unusually light and cheerful.

"You're awfully chipper this morning," Frank replied as he

sat down across from Betty.

"Nothing like the thrill of hunting down an intriguing story," she remarked. Mischief twinkled in her eyes as she sipped her coffee.

Frank watched her from across the table. He couldn't help but remember how, in a moment of weakness, he had been thinking of her in the shower earlier that morning. He felt himself blush with embarrassment. Frank knew he shouldn't be thinking of her that way and immediately pushed those thoughts out of his mind.

"Hi there." Lucy the waitress appeared at their table. She looked Frank up and down with lustful eyes. "What can I get for you, sir?" She handed him a menu and gave him a flash of her best smile.

"Nothing for me, thanks."

"You sure, hon? Not even a cup of coffee?" Lucy put her hand on the back of Frank's chair and leaned forward just enough so that her full breasts were inches from his face.

Betty leaned back in her chair and began folding up the map as she glared at Lucy.

What a hussy, Betty thought to herself. She was not at all impressed with Lucy's technique; she thought it made the girl look cheap and obvious. Betty's face grew hot, she could feel her emotions rise up inside of her.

"Look, Frank," she started, "I don't plan on stopping once we get on the road, so if you wanna eat, you better do it now." Her words came out sharper than she intended them to. Suddenly she became aware of just how territorial she felt over Frank, even though she knew she had no claim on him.

"It's alright." Frank smiled at Betty. "I had about half of that apple pie for breakfast."

"Oh, well, honey, if you like pie, we have a delicious pecan pie that goes great with the coffee," Lucy chimed in.

"No, thank you," Frank responded as he handed the menu back to her while trying to avoid the breasts that were being shoved in his face.

"Suit yourself." Lucy was a little disappointed. She walked away, swinging her hips a little too wide in one last attempt to get Frank's attention, but he couldn't take his eyes off Betty.

Despite having one bite left on her plate, Betty pushed it away. She leaned back in her chair and lit herself a cigarette. "Well, she was quite taken with you, wasn't she?"

"I suppose she was." Frank grinned.

Betty took a soft drag of her cigarette and let the smoke flow out her mouth in a smooth stream. "I'm impressed," Betty ashed her cigarette, "most men would flirt back. Your wife's a lucky woman."

Frank let out a deep sigh. "I don't think she'd agree with you at the moment."

"She's still mad?"

"You could say that. But I don't really want to get into all that right now. I'm ready to go when you are."

"Sure." Betty stamped out her cigarette and left some cash on the table.

As they walked out, Betty turned to Frank. "I need to make a quick stop on our way out, if you don't mind."

"You're the boss," Frank replied.

* * *

Frank had no idea what caused the sudden change in Betty's

mood, but she hadn't spoken a word since they left the diner and the tension in the car was palpable.

Betty turned the car onto Magazine Street and pulled up to a large three-story brick building that was surrounded by a high wrought-iron fence. She parked the car on the street and then just sat there in silence. She stared straight ahead, frozen, with her hands in a tight grip around the steering wheel.

Without looking at Frank, Betty broke the silence. "Normally, I would tell you to wait in the car, but it's extremely hot today and I can't in good conscience ask you to do that. So it's up to you if you want to come inside."

Frank had no idea where they were or what they were doing there, but something inside that building had Betty shaken. A profound urge to protect her came over him. He wasn't sure where it had come from; they had only known each a few days. But he felt he needed to be there for her, and he couldn't let her face whatever this was alone.

"I'll come in with you."

As they made their way past the gate, Frank noticed a plaque on the fence post that read:

St. Vincent's Asylum for Women

That was not what he was expecting and now he had more questions than ever. But he knew better than to start asking them.

They walked up the steps and through the front door. The lighting inside was dim and all was quiet except for the faint sound of a radio program playing in the distance of an unseen room.

"Hello. How can I help you?" asked the soft voice of the nurse sitting behind a small desk.

"Yes, I'm here to see Marie Boudreaux. My mother," Betty

answered.

Frank wasn't sure what to think as the bigger picture of Betty's life began to take focus for him.

"Certainly," replied the nurse. "If you both sign in, then you can go on up." She smiled and handed them a large registry book.

After they each signed their names, Frank followed Betty down the hall to a staircase. They walked up to the second floor and rounded the corner down a long corridor. They went through a set of doors that led them outside to a covered walkway that overlooked a courtyard garden, then went through another set of doors, bringing them back inside to the second-floor nurses' station.

"As I live and breathe, is that Miss Betty Boudreaux?" called out the nurse sitting behind the desk. She rose from her seat and greeted Betty with a hug. She was a plump older woman with gray hair and a warm smile.

Betty lit up at the sight of her. "Oh Nurse Clara, I was hoping you would be working today." The two women embraced, and Frank could see Betty begin to relax. "Nurse Clara, this is my assistant, Mr. Frank Martin. Frank, this is Head Nurse Clara."

"It's a pleasure to meet you." Frank shook her hand.

"Nurse Clara, I hope you don't mind, I baked an apple pie for Mama, it's her favorite."

"Oh, I don't mind at all. It might entice her to eat something. Your mama eats like a little bird."

"Oh shoot," Betty exclaimed. "I must have left it in the car. Frank, would you be a dear and run down and grab it for me?"

"Of course."

"Meet me in room 207 when you get back."

The two women watched Frank walk down the hallway. "Oh Betty," Nurse Clara whispered. "He is a looker."

"He is." Betty sucked in her breath and finally peeled her eyes away from Frank as he disappeared around the corner. "And very married."

"They always are," Nurse Clare sighed with a shake of her head.

"So how's my mother been? I'm sorry I haven't been in a while. Work and all." Betty shrugged, disappointed in herself.

Nurse Clara smiled and put her hand on Betty's shoulder in a comforting gesture. "She has her good days and her bad days, but most days are okay days."

They turned toward Marie's room and walked down the hall side by side.

"And today?" Betty asked anxiously.

"Today's an okay day. But I'm sure your visit will turn it into a good day."

They reached room 207. Nurse Clara knocked twice and opened the door.

"Miss Marie, you have a visitor."

Marie was sitting in a wicker rocking chair and staring out the only window in her small room.

Betty was shocked when she saw her mother. Her beautiful dark hair had all gone gray. Her face was hollow and wrinkled. The hourglass figure that Betty had inherited from her was gone; she was nothing but skin and bone. Marie, once a vibrant and strong woman, now seemed small and frail. Betty couldn't help but feel responsible for her mother's decline and her guilt swarmed around her.

"Hello, Mama." Betty forced a smile.

"Oh Betty!" Marie exclaimed joyfully. "Oh, my sweet, sweet

girl.

What a wonderful surprise. Come sit."

Betty walked over to the window and sat in the matching rocking chair.

"I'll let the two of you catch up. If you need anything, I'll just be down the hall." Nurse Clara took her leave of them without closing the door.

Betty grabbed her mother's hand and gave it a gentle squeeze. "How've you been, Mama? I'm sorry it's been so long since my last visit. I've been terribly busy with work."

"I know, sweetheart." Marie reached over and stroked her daughter's cheek. "I'm so very proud of you."

"Have you been eating, Mama? You look so thin."

Marie clicked her tongue, "The food here is terrible."

"Well, I baked you an apple pie. Your special recipe, just like you taught me. So now you don't have an excuse to not eat."

Marie gave a faint smile but said nothing, her eyes drifted past Betty and wandered out the door of her room.

"Well, in any case, I need to talk to you about a matter." Betty could see she was losing her mother's attention.

"Oh!" Marie gasped suddenly, startling Betty. "Oh Betty! You did it, you found Edgar."

"W-what?" Betty was completely bewildered. "No, Mama. Edgar's...he's gone."

But Marie didn't hear a word she said and rose from her chair quickly. Betty turned around to see Frank standing in the doorway holding the apple pie. He was frozen in perplexity as Marie approached him with outstretched arms. He looked to Betty for some sort of clarity, but she was just as perplexed.

"Edgar," Marie called out to him, but she stopped short

once she got close enough to get a good look at his face. "Oh. You're not Edgar." She took a step back. "No. No, you couldn't possibly be Edgar," she said quietly, irritation and confusion hiding behind disappointment.

Betty stood beside Marie and put her hands on either side of her shoulders. "No, Mama, this is Frank Martin. He works with me."

"Oh. I see. It's nice to meet you, Mr. Martin," Marie said. She walked away, not waiting for a response from Frank, and with a blank stare, she stood by the window looking out at nothing, lost in her mind's chaos.

Frank set the pie down on the nightstand. "Is she okay?"

"She's just tired." Betty tried to downplay the situation.

"Is there anything I can do?" Without thinking, he grabbed her hand. He was genuinely concerned and wanted to help.

Betty looked up at him with a sad smile. "No. But thank you." She squeezed his hand. "Just wait for me at the nurses' station. I should be done here in a few minutes."

He was reluctant to leave her. Frank knew she could handle things on her own, but he wanted to be there for her, just in case. Regardless of those feelings, he respected her request and left the room. Betty closed the door behind him.

"Mama, are you okay?"

But Marie didn't answer; she was a million miles away.

Betty continued, even though she wasn't sure if Marie would hear her. "What I was trying to say earlier is that I'm going out of town on a business trip. To Ville Morte."

Still Marie said nothing.

"I know your people are there. Is there anyone in particular you would like me to call on and give your regards to?"

Marie gave her nothing but silence as she stared absently

out the window. It was clear that she was in a deep haze and there was nothing more that Betty could do for her.

"Well, I guess I'll leave you to your thoughts then." Betty turned to walk out of the room feeling defeated, but on second thought, she turned back around. "Mama, I'm sorry. I didn't know you thought I was still looking for Edgar." She waited but there was no reaction from Marie. She gave up and moved toward the door to leave.

"Don't go, Betty."

A sense of relief washed over her; she didn't want to leave things this way. "I can stay a few more minutes."

"No. I mean don't go to Ville Morte." She turned away from the window and faced Betty.

"Whyever not?"

"If you leave, Betty, you won't come back." Marie moved closer to her.

"Of course I'm coming back, Mama. I promise I'll stop by here first thing when I get back into town."

"No!" Marie said forcefully and she grabbed Betty by the wrist hard. "No. You'll be taken from me." Her eyes were wide and wild. It was a look Betty had never seen before on her mother, and it frightened her.

Marie's voice grew louder, "You'll leave me a childless mother." Her eyes glazed over, and she was no longer looking at Betty, but looking through her. Marie tightened her grip on Betty's wrist, her fingernails digging deep into her daughter's skin.

"Mama, you're hurting me," Betty pleaded and yanked her wrist back.

Marie lost her balance and crumpled to the floor on her knees. She crossed her arms over her chest and began to rock back and forth. She let out a heavy sob and began to wail, "My baby! I can't find my baby! My sweet baby boy."

Betty knelt down beside her. "Mama, you're upset. Come on, let's get you into bed." She grabbed her mother's arm and tried to pull her up, but Marie refused to move.

"No!" she screamed like a child throwing a tantrum and pushed Betty away from her. Betty fell backward on the floor.

"I want my baby! Where's my baby?" Marie screamed in between desperate sobs.

Betty was stunned. She had never seen her mother like this before.

Just then, the door flew open, and Nurse Clara came rushing in to help. She sat down on the floor next to Marie. Speaking in a soft voice she asked, "What's wrong, darlin'?"

Marie sniffled, "I can't find my baby boy."

"Oh, I know, sweetie." She wrapped one arm around Marie's shoulders and pulled her close, rocking with her.

A male nurse approached the door with a syringe full of barbital, but Nurse Clara held up her free hand to signal to him to wait at the door. She continued rocking Marie and humming a gospel tune. Marie finally began to calm down and took a deep breath.

"You know," Nurse Clara began, "maybe you can find him in your dreams."

"I think I've seen him there before," Marie said hopefully.

"Oh yes, darlin,' you can find all sorts of things in your dreams." Nurse Clara motioned for the male nurse to come into the room, and he knelt down on the other side of Marie.

"This will help." The male nurse took Marie's arm and plunged the syringe into her vein. Her body immediately started to relax.

"Alright Miss Marie, let's get you into bed. We can't have you sleeping on the floor now."

They worked together to get her in the bed and Nurse Clara tucked her in. Within seconds, Marie was asleep. Nurse Clara turned to Betty, who was still crouched on the floor with her mascara running down her face.

"Miss Betty, are you okay, darlin'?" Nurse Clara helped her into one of the rocking chairs.

"I've never seen her like that before."

"I know. It's hard to see your mama that way. But she's alright now."

"Is she often like this?"

"From time to time. Grief is a strange thing and Lord knows your mama is lost in it."

"Do you think she'll ever get better?"

"Well honey, only time can answer that. For now, all we can do is let her rest." She helped Betty up out of the chair. "Now, there's a bathroom right down the hall, why don't you go and splash some cold water on your face."

"Thank you." Betty walked out of the room and rushed down the hall. Frank called after her, but she didn't acknowledge him. The last thing she wanted was for him to see her this way.

* * *

Desperate to stop her mind from getting carried away, Betty kept her eyes focused straight ahead on the two hundred miles of flat highway that stretched out before them. She and Frank had been driving down LA HWY 2 for about twenty minutes. Neither spoke a word since leaving the city, and with every mile that passed, the silence grew louder, more uncomfortable.

Frank could no longer stand it. "Betty, who's Edgar?"

She realized, suddenly, that had been waiting for him to ask. And with the release of her breath, the story of Edgar came pouring out of her.

III

Baton Rouge, LA Spring 1942

Chapter 8

I suppose the whole mess started in the spring of '42. It was mid-morning on a Friday, and I was right in the middle of sewing a pair of red velvet curtains for my new apartment when the phone rang.

"Betty, it's Mama. Are you still coming down to visit this weekend?" Her voice sounded tired, as if she had just woken up. I was relieved that she was finally getting some sleep. My father had passed away a few months prior, in January, and she hadn't been sleeping much.

"Of course I'm still coming. I'm all packed, I just need to finish with my curtains, and then I'll be on my way."

"Oh good. How is the new apartment?"

I looked around at the bare space. "It's coming along. There's a lot of potential. I just bought the most gorgeous red velvet fabric to make curtains. I think you'd really love it."

"That's wonderful," she responded, although it didn't really feel like she was listening to me, but rather waiting for her turn to speak. I wasn't wrong. "Listen Betty, do me a favor and stop by The Camp[8] on your way in."

"Why? Is there something wrong with The Camp?"

We owned a fishing cabin on the Amite River. It wasn't anything fancy, just a small rustic cabin. But somehow Mama made it feel homey.

"Well, no, nothing's wrong with The Camp. It's just that your brother went out there about a week ago and he hasn't been back." She paused to take a deep breath before letting out a heavy sigh. "I have a feeling, Betty."

Mama used to get what she called *"feelings,"* and they were usually *"bad feelings"* in which case she would become convinced that something terrible happened. She would call up everyone she knew to make sure no one had died. No one ever did, of course.

"Mama, I'm sure Edgar's fine. You know your *'bad feelings'* never amount to anything."

"I beg your pardon? Just because the *"gift"* skipped you doesn't mean you have the right to dismiss it. Please just do this for me, Betty. I'm really worried. It isn't like him to be gone for so long."

She was always the nervous type, fretting over this or that.

Daddy was always able to calm her down. I guess he just made her feel safe. I had never met two people more in love than my parents. They got each other through everything. Mama was trying hard to get through his death, but Lord knows she was a complete mess without him.

Edgar and I decided that since he was already living in Baton Rouge, he would be the one to look after Mama. Being the

---

[8] The Camp: Cajuns refer to their recreational hunting and fishing cabins as The Camp

more sensitive of the two of us, Edgar was always better at those kinds of things. Besides, it meant that I wouldn't have to give up my career to move back home.

I had been working for *The New Orleans Post* for less than a year. Back then, Alan had me writing puff pieces. To be perfectly honest, I didn't mind. I was still grieving the loss of my father and the loss of my family as I had always known it.

"Okay Mama. I'll stop by on my way in."

* * *

I pulled my car up to The Camp just as the sun was beginning to set behind the cabin. The sky was burning with vibrant pinks and oranges and reds. Normally I loved watching the sunset here, but there was something ominous about it that day. I think it was the stillness. There were no birds chirping, there was no breeze rustling through the trees, there was nothing except complete silence.

I stood in the front yard looking around. Edgar's truck wasn't there. I walked onto the front porch and found that the door was cracked open. It let out a low creaking moan as I pushed it open, and an odd feeling of dread washed over me.

I was afraid of what I might find inside, but everything was exactly as it should be. Nothing was out of place, but everything *felt* different.

The Camp had always been a happy place for us. Daddy loved to take the whole family out here on weekend adventures. Mama would pack a lunch, and we would all load up in the boat and spend the entire day out on the water. Then we'd have a fish fry with what we caught and spend the evening playing cards. My memories of The Camp were always filled with joy and laughter, but that day, there was an unease in the air that made my skin crawl.

I was so overcome with this feeling of heaviness that walking down the hall felt like walking through mud. The setting sun cast eerie shadows throughout the cabin and as I reached the door to the back bedroom, my heart began to thump deep in my chest. I didn't know what I was about to discover behind that door. I flung it open and found… absolutely nothing.

But the whole room was filled with a violent sadness and an urgent feeling to get the hell out of there. I couldn't explain it, but I had a *bad feeling* that something terrible happened.

* * *

It was well past supper time when I arrived at Mama's house. The whole house was filled with the aroma of crawfish étouffée. Somehow it comforted me. Being home with my mother and the familiar smells of childhood made me feel safe, even though I could feel it in my bones that everything was about to come undone.

I found her in the kitchen, standing at the sink.

"Something smells good." I was trying to keep my voice light. I didn't know how I was going to tell her that Edgar was missing.

"Oh Betty, you had me worried half to death. I was expecting you much sooner." She rushed to me and embraced me in a tight hug. "Are you hungry, baby? There's food on the stove. I already ate but help yourself."

"I'm starving. I haven't eaten since breakfast." I grabbed a plate out of the cabinet and scooped a pile of rice in the middle before opening the lid of the cast iron pot. The étouffée was still bubbling hot. For a moment, I forgot the bad news I had to deliver, and all seemed right with the world as the étouffée dribbled over the rice and a heap of fat juicy crawfish covered my plate.

I sat down at the table across from Mama. She was smiling but I could see the worry in her eyes. I pushed my food around my plate, trying to avoid her gaze.

"Will Edgar be joining us?" she probed.

I took a big bite and chewed slowly, savoring every bite as I tried to buy myself some time to find the words to explain what I couldn't.

"Betty, out with it," she said firmly. Mama always could see right through me.

"He wasn't there." I paused to swallow and let the flavor dance around my tongue. "His truck wasn't there, he wasn't there, and it didn't look like anyone had been there."

"But that's where he told me he was going. He wouldn't lie to me." Panic began to rise up in her voice. "Why would he lie to me?"

"I don't know, Mama."

"Well, we have to find him." She stood up quickly, unsure of what to do next.

"Mama, sit down, I already went to the police." She sat back down in her seat.

"They said there wasn't much that they could do since he's an adult. But they assured me that they would be on the lookout for his truck."

"Nineteen is hardly an adult. He's still a teenager, for God's sake." Mama pulled a handkerchief out of her pocket and dabbed her eyes. "If your father were here..." She was too choked up to finish her sentence and took a deep breath to compose herself.

I reached across the table and took her hand in mine. "I'll find him, Mama. I promise you, I'll find Edgar."

She squeezed my hand as she held back her tears. "I think I need to go lie down. Will you bring a glass of water to my room, please?" She left the table before I could answer. She didn't want me to see her cry. Mama hated it when people saw her cry.

When I got there, she was already in bed. I handed her the glass of water and watched her take two pills from a bottle on the nightstand. After Daddy died, she had trouble sleeping. It had been decades since she slept alone. No matter how busy she tried to keep herself during the day, at night she couldn't escape the fact that the love of her life was gone.

Edgar told me she would stay up all hours of the night cleaning like a maniac. Finally, he made her go see a doctor and she was given a prescription for barbiturates. Now, it seemed all she did was sleep.

I turned the light off in her bedroom and shut the door before heading down the hall to Daddy's old study. He always used to say it was the quietest room in the whole house because it was all the way in the back. When he was alive, he used to keep a bottle of whiskey hidden in the bottom drawer of his desk. I hoped it was still there; I needed a little something to settle my nerves.

The room still smelled of him, old books and tobacco. I breathed in the scent as deeply as I could; my God, how I missed him. He would know exactly how to handle this situation, how to keep Mama calm. I tried to think of what he would do and wondered if I had what it took to step into his shoes. The need for that whiskey was stronger than ever.

I said a silent prayer as I sat down in his leather desk chair and tried the bottom drawer. The damn thing was locked. So I stuck my fingers in my hair and pulled out my lucky bobby pin. It had been a gift from a boy I dated in college. The pin came apart in two pieces and was meant for picking locks. He had always been impressed that I knew how, an unexpected trick I picked up in finishing school, and had it custom-made for me.

I was in luck; sitting in the bottom of the drawer was half a bottle of whiskey and Daddy's favorite drinking glass.

As I lifted them out to pour myself a double, I noticed a small brown leather journal. It was engraved with Edgar's initials; it had to be his. I opened it and tucked inside the pages were letters from Ruby Baptiste.

She had written me a letter after Daddy died to give her condolences; apparently, she had written one to Edgar as well, and then some. Ruby was the granddaughter of our former nursery maid, a colored woman named Miss Mabel. She looked after Ruby during the summertime and the three of us children spent every summer together. She was my first and best childhood friend. But eventually, we got too old for a nursery maid and Miss Mabel went to work for another family. Like many childhood friendships that are separated by time and distance, not to mention the unfortunate divide that society had put between our races, we lost touch with Ruby.

I had no idea that they had been in touch. This could be the very thing I needed to help find him. Without hesitation, I began to read through the pages of his journal, Edgar's privacy be damned.

* * *

January 11th, 1942

I have just received a letter from my dear old friend, Ruby Baptiste. I have thought of her often over the years. I was surprised at how my heart fluttered upon reading her letter; apparently my boyhood crush has been lying dormant all these years.

I can't seem to recall when I met Ruby for the first time, but I always thought she was the prettiest girl I ever saw. I used to follow her and Betty around like a lost puppy and would play whatever girlie game they were playing just to be around Ruby.

I remember her being bright and thoughtful, and she absolutely hated any game that would get her clothes dirty. Whenever we played hide and seek outside, we could count on finding her hiding somewhere clever inside the house, curled up with a good book.

I am so glad that after all this time she has written me. My spirit has been dark since Dad passed away a few weeks ago. But her letter brought me such joy, and, dare I say, hope. My heart gave me no other choice but to write her back. And to my great pleasure, she responded and has invited me to have lunch with her and Miss Mabel. How wonderful it will be to see them both again!

January 16th, 1942

I have just returned from lunch at Miss Mabel's. What a wonderful time we had. I was so nervous standing at the front door, *fidgeting and sweating through my shirt, even though it was a chilly day. I wanted to make a good impression; what would Ruby think of me now that I am grown?*

Then the door opened and there I stood, like a fool unable to speak, the very sight of her took my breath away. What a beauty she had become!

Finally, I came to my senses and spoke. "I brought an apple pie." I handed the pie over to her.

She smiled and my heart melted. "Thank you, Edgar. Did you make it yourself?"

"Oh no. No. I wouldn't do that to you, Ruby. This is one of Mama's pies."

She laughed. "That's right, your Mama always did have the best pie in the parish."

"Yeah, she's taken to baking a lot since Dad died."

We stood there for a moment, taking each other in. I blushed when she smiled, which made her smile wider.

"Y'all, don't just stand there. Ya lettin' all the flies in," Miss Mabel called from the kitchen.

Ruby shook her head with a silent laugh. "Come on in, Edgar."

I was instantly taken back to my childhood at the smell of Miss Mabel's cooking.

"Something smells delicious," I said as I walked over to the stove where Miss Mabel was standing over a pot.

"Red beans and rice with corn bread. That was always ya favorite as a little boy," she said proudly.

I leaned over the pot and pretended to stick my finger in, like I did as a boy. She swatted my hand away playfully.

"Look now, just 'cuz ya grown don't mean I cain't still throw ya over my knee." She sprinkled in some pepper and gave the pot a stir.

"Grandma, be nice. Edgar is our guest."

"Listen," Miss Mabel said to Ruby, "I helped raise that boy. He ain't no guest, he family." She set her spoon down and turned to me. "Now come child, let me get a good look at ya." We gave each other a long hug.

"My goodness," she continued, "ya sure not a little boy no more."

"No, ma'am. I'm nineteen years old, all grown up now, and I'm studying at LSU, just like my dad."

"Oh yeah? Whatcha studying, baby?"

"English. I want to teach poetry."

"You always were a good boy, Edgar. Even when you wasn't, you was." Miss Mabel placed her hand on my cheek. "Now y'all go set the table. Lunch be just about ready."

We spent the rest of the afternoon reminiscing and catching up. I learned that Ruby is a schoolteacher, which came as no surprise. She attended Xavier University in New Orleans and after graduation, she moved back to Baton Rouge.

"Did you enjoy living in New Orleans?" I asked her while the two of us sat in the living room sipping coffee.

"I loved it."

"Why didn't you stay?"

"As much as I loved it there, I felt that it was more important to give back to the roots from which I've sprung. I've received so much from my community. My need to be here is bigger than myself. I'm here to help it grow stronger and hopefully the next generation can build on that, and so and so forth."

"For what it's worth, I sure am glad you're back."

She is truly a spectacular woman. Not only is she smart and elegant, but she laughs at all my stupid jokes. And not just obligatory laughs, but real ones. She has the most beautiful laugh I've ever heard. What I would give to spend my life making that

84

exquisite woman laugh. I do believe I am smitten.

January 18th, 1942

My Dearest Edgar,

It was so wonderful to see you again. Grandma says you're welcome over for lunch anytime so long as you bring us more fresh pie from your mother's kitchen. I do hope that I will see you again soon. You have such delightful and funny stories. Despite the roles that society says we must play, I would very much like to be friends.

Yours truly, Ruby Baptiste

January 31st, 1942

There is no denying it, I am in love. I am in love with the enchanting Ruby Baptiste. She makes my heart sing; I can't get enough of her. Her smile, her laugh, her mind. She is incredible. We've been spending time together on the weekends. We sit out on her back porch, just the two of us, and talk all afternoon over coffee and pie.

We were sitting on the porch swing as usual when Ruby turned to me. "Please tell your mama I said thank you for all the pies you've been bringing over. She really doesn't have to go through all that trouble."

"It's no trouble. She doesn't even know I've been bringing 'em over."

Ruby cocked her head and wrinkled her brow in confusion.

"Well, what I mean is, ever since my dad died, she's been... different. She stays up all hours of the night just baking pies for no reason. You should see our kitchen. There's pie everywhere. So I just grab some and bring it over."

"Edgar! You mean to tell me you've been feeding me stolen pie?"

I panicked. Had I offended her? "No. No, not stolen."
She laughed. "I'm just teasing you."
"Oh." I relaxed. "You really had me going there for a second."
She took a sip of her coffee. "You miss him, your daddy?"
"Everyday."
"You know Mr. Amos was the one who taught me how to read."
"Really? I didn't know that."

"Yeah, I was about five or six. I was sitting in the study one day and I had pulled a bunch of books off the shelf and put them in a big pile all around me. Then your daddy walked in, and I thought I was going to be in a world of trouble for messing with his things. But he just smiled at me and asked me what I was reading. I told him, 'Nothing, I can't read yet.' He laughed and asked if I'd like to learn. I said, 'Yes sir, I sure would.' That summer, he sat Betty and me down in his study every day after lunch and gave us reading lessons. He said it would give us a head start when we started school. And he was right. Your daddy was a good man, Edgar, I'm sorry he's gone."

Her kindness and warmth stirred my heart. I never felt that way before, so connected and seen.

"May I kiss you, Ruby?"

She gave me a soft smile. "No. But not because I don't want you to. If Grandma saw you kissing me, she would come out here and smack you upside the head with her cane. And then we wouldn't be able to see each other anymore. But you can hold my hand, if you like."

It wasn't what I was hoping for, but somehow it was better.

February 5th, 1942
I was unable to have lunch with Ruby this week because she was

attending a church picnic. I decided to go to the park and surprise her. I knew it was a risky move; she may not want me there. A lot of people in both our communities likely wouldn't take kindly to our relationship. But I couldn't go two whole weeks without seeing her.

I saw her sitting on a picnic blanket surrounded by her students, who were listening to her read them Bible stories. I walked past her at a respectable distance and gave a little whistle to get her attention.

She looked up at me and my heart soared when she smiled. I walked behind a grove of trees, hoping she would follow me and waited for what seemed like ages. Finally, she came around the corner.

"Edgar?" she whispered.

I rushed to her and hooked one arm around her waist, pulling her close to me. She smelled like roses. She wrapped her arms around my neck and drew my face down to hers. Then and there we shared our first kiss. It was full of love and passion. I knew then that I never wanted to kiss any other woman.

My whole body was on fire as she ran her fingers through my hair. "You are everything," I whispered in her ear.

She leaned into me and kissed me once more. "I need to get back before someone sees us."

"Let them see." I pressed my forehead to hers and we swayed together to the rhythm of the breeze.

"You're trouble, Edgar Boudreaux." She laughed.

"Well, I can't be the cause of my lady's trouble." I rubbed my thumb across her cheek. "I won't keep you from your picnic. I just had to see you, even if only for a moment." I kissed the back of her hand and started to leave. I turned to face her as I walked away, "I love you, Ruby Baptiste."

I left before giving her a chance to respond, for fear that the declaration of my heart would go unrequited.

February 7th, 1942

My dearest Edgar,

You left the park so quickly that you didn't give me a chance to say, I love you too, Edgar Boudreaux. I cannot fight it. I cannot deny it. You have my heart. I have never loved another and I can only count the days until I see you again.

Always Yours,

R.B.

February 16th, 1942

Valentine's Day, what a splendid holiday. I wanted to do something special for Ruby, but we couldn't exactly celebrate our love with a night out on the town. So I took her to The Camp.

I filled the place with four different kinds of roses, her favorite flower. We had a candlelit dinner of catfish courtbouillon, not the most romantic dish, but it's the only thing I know how to cook. And of course, there was wine and chocolate.

She was quiet over dinner, clearly contemplating something. I began to wonder if I had done something wrong. "Is everything alright, Ruby? You're awfully quiet."

"Edgar, this is all lovely, but I'm curious. What exactly are you expecting tonight?" The softness faded from her face; she was all business now.

"I'm not quite sure what you mean, Ruby."

"I'm a respectable woman and I have been saving myself for

marriage. I intend to keep it that way. I can't afford to make any mistakes. It's not the same for us as it is for white girls. We have to hold ourselves to a higher standard, work twice as hard just to be seen, if we're even seen at all. I love you, but I will not compromise myself for you. So, if you had plans on taking me to bed, I suggest you reevaluate." She was very firm and direct in her convictions, which only made me love her more.

I reached across the table and took her hand in mine. "Ruby, I cherish you. This is all to make you happy. I would never do anything to make you feel uncomfortable or tarnish your reputation. I belong to you, I'm here to protect you and make you feel safe. You're in charge here, it's what you want."

"I don't think a man has ever asked me what I wanted before." The softness had returned to her face. "I want to sit on the sofa, hold hands, and talk."

And talk we did. We talked about what life would be like if we could get married. What our children would be like. We decided to have three, two boys and a girl. They would all be whip smart and we would live on a farm in the country. She would have a giant library filled to the brim with every kind of book you can imagine. And when we're old and gray, we'll sit on our front porch in our rocking chairs, drinking mint juleps and watching our grandchildren play in the yard. We spent the entire night dreaming up a future we both know we can never have. My heart is filled with such deep sorrow, for I have never wanted anything more.

March 1ˢᵗ, 1942

I am devastated. Ruby and I had a fight.

Over the last few weeks, we have been spending time together at The Camp. At her request, our relationship has never become more physical than kissing, and I have been more than happy to oblige. But when faced with the question of our future, I am at a loss. I no longer want to keep our love hidden. I want to marry her, but she insists that it's not possible.

"We could run away together."

"And just where do you think we'd run to, Edgar?"

"I don't know, Paris? I have an aunt who used to live in Paris, and she said that it's nothing like America for colored people."

"Paris?! Really, Edgar?" She threw her hand up. "I'm not sure if you're aware, but Paris is under Nazi occupation at the moment. I don't think we'd be welcome."

Disconcerted, I ran my fingers through my hair. "All I know is that I love you. I want to be your husband. There has to be a way. There has to be somewhere we can go."

"We have people who rely on us, we can't just leave. What about my grandmother and your mother? We can't abandon them."

"So we're just to keep doing this for the rest of our lives? Sneaking around and hiding as if we have something to be ashamed of? Because I'm not ashamed." I took a deep breath to compose myself and moved closer to her. "I want a life with you. A real life," I pleaded as I stroked her cheek. "I want to give you children and build you your dream house, with the library and the wrap-around porch."

She leaned her face against the palm of my hand as tears welled up in her eyes. "Edgar, I don't think you know what you're asking of me."

Frustrated, I turned away from her, and to my deep regret, I raised my voice. "I don't think you know what you're asking of me! I don't want to keep you a secret any longer. It's all or nothing, Ruby."

She stared at me with fire in her eyes and I could see that she was seething. "Perhaps our relationship has run its course. It's probably for the best."

I was crushed. We have not spoken another word to each other. Even as I sit here now, I cannot find the words to express how heartbroken I am. She is the sun, and I have been banished from her orbit.

Chapter 9

The smell of fresh coffee woke me. My neck and shoulders ached from sleeping hunched over the desk. I had fallen asleep in the study reading Edgar's journal. Still trying to process everything I had read about Edgar and Ruby, I made my way to the kitchen.

I found Mama at the sink furiously washing dishes. "You left a whole plate of uneaten étouffée out last night," she said with a short fuse.

Normally I would have been sassy with her, but I knew how much she was going through, so I held my tongue. "Everything okay?" I asked as I poured myself a cup of coffee.

"Oh yes, everything is just fine. My husband is dead. My son is missing, and my daughter is…" She, too, held her tongue.

"I'm what, Mama?" I gave her a stern look that dared her to finish her sentence.

She softened. "A blessing. You've been nothing but kind and helpful." She looked at me and smiled. "You're all grown up now. I'm so proud of you, Betty." She went back to abusing the dishes and I leaned on the counter, sipping my coffee, while I waited for her to tell me what was really bothering her.

"The police came by this morning," she huffed, "said they found Edgar's truck."

"Where is it? Did they find him, too?" I was overhasty in my hope.

"No." Her voice was sharp. "They didn't find him. Although they think they did. They said they found his truck in the middle of a sugarcane field on the outskirts of town. It was burnt up, like it had been set on fire." She wiped a glass dry and put it in the cabinet, slamming the door shut.

"What was he doing out there?"

"It wasn't him," she snapped at me. "They said it was him but it's not him." She took a deep breath and let it out in a heavy sigh. "Apparently, there were two bodies found in the truck. They got burnt up, too. It was a man and a woman, but you see it couldn't be Edgar; he doesn't have any girlfriends. Someone must have stolen his truck. He's probably out there somewhere, stranded and trying to get home."

She was desperate, grasping at straws, trying to find any way she could to rationalize that this wasn't Edgar. I began to wonder just what those sleeping pills might be doing to her brain.

In the state she was in, I didn't have the heart to tell her that Edgar did, in fact, have a girlfriend.

"It isn't him, Betty. It can't be." Her voice cracked. I put my arm around her and held her close to me.

"I'll go down to the police station and get it all sorted out."

"You have to find him, Betty. You just have to." She began to cry.

"I will. I'll find him, I promise."

She pulled back. "I'm sorry Betty, but I think I need to go lie down." Mama left the kitchen in tears. Despite her conviction, we both knew that Edgar was gone.

* * *

I went down to the police station with a heavy heart. Unable to face the situation head-on as Edgar's sister, I decided to face it as a reporter. I could get all the facts I needed and keep my emotions in line.

An officer brought me to a small room where we could speak in private.

"Listen, Miss Boudreaux," he sounded frustrated, "we've already explained all this to your mother. We found his truck burnt out and unfortunately, his body was in the truck at the time of the fire, along with an unidentified female."

"How can you be sure it's my brother?"

"Again, miss, we already explained all of this to your mother and she asked us to leave."

His rudeness left me dumbfounded. "I'm sorry for the inconvenience, but you'll have to explain to me as well."

"We were able to match his dental records. We have confirmed that the body recovered in that truck was in fact your brother, Edgar Boudreaux."

I felt the crushing weight of his words as my last bit of hope was destroyed.

"And the young woman?" I asked.

"It's not likely we'll be able to get any dental records; *it* was," he squirmed uncomfortably in his chair and cleared his throat, "a Negro girl."

My sadness shifted to anger when I heard him refer to Ruby as *it*. "I believe I know who *she* is," I corrected him. "Miss

Ruby Baptiste was a friend of the family."

He shuffled some papers on his desk with little interest in anything I had to say. In fact, he looked downright bored.

My fury was building up inside of me, but I knew an outburst would not help me at this moment. I clenched my jaw and, with as much composure as I could muster, said, "I trust that you'll do everything you can to find whoever did this to my brother and my friend."

He looked up at me with complete indifference, "Well, Miss Boudreaux, we don't believe there was any foul play here."

"What do you mean? His truck was set on fire." I was beginning to lose the grip I had on my composure.

"The scenario that the evidence points to is that the two of them had too much to drink and when they passed out, one of them was smoking a lit cigarette that caught the truck on fire."

"You can't be serious." The idea was so ridiculous that I almost laughed in his face. "There was no reason for the two of them to be all the way out there."

"We see this kind of thing often with working girls."

"*I beg your pardon.* Miss Ruby Baptiste was a schoolteacher."

"You'd be surprised."

I was infuriated and he could see it.

"Miss, we've looked into it and as far as we're concerned, the cause of death was accidental. Case closed."

I glared at him. I had never hated someone more. "I want to see his body," I demanded.

"Miss, I don't think…"

"I really don't give a damn what you think"—now was the moment to use an outburst to my advantage—"I want to see my brother's body."

* * *

Mama rushed to greet me as soon as I walked into the house. "Oh Betty, please tell me you have some good news." She was hopeful until she saw my face. I couldn't look her in the eye and tell her that her only son was dead. I heard her catch her breath as I stared at my feet.

"Betty, please."

I looked up at her, the tears falling down my face. She could see what was coming and stepped back from me.

"No." She shook her head. "No. Don't say it."

"Mama." I tried to speak gently.

"Don't. Don't say it."

I stood there in silence and watched the light fade from her eyes.

"I think," she said with ragged breath, "I need to go lay down."

She turned away from me and stumbled her way down the hallway, overtaken by darkness. Mama was never the same after that day.

I needed a drink now more than ever, so I headed to the study for a whiskey. I couldn't get the image of Edgar's charred body out of my head. The sister part of me wished that I had never gone down there, but the reporter side of me was glad that I did.

What I saw was undeniable proof of murder. A bullet wound to the neck. The coroner, that son of a bitch, tried to tell me it was self-inflicted, that Edgar had realized he was trapped inside the car and shot himself in order to keep from burning alive. But I knew enough to know one does not shoot themselves in the neck when attempting suicide.

I feared that I would be overcome with grief, but I couldn't let myself be distracted by it. I needed to stay focused. It was clear that the police weren't going to be of any help. They were lazy and indifferent at best.

I had to do something; I couldn't just sit back and let this happen. So, I did the only thing I knew how to do: write. If the police weren't going to investigate, then I would, as a reporter. They were murdered and I intended to prove it.

* * *

"Mama."

No response.

"Mama," I tried again and shook her to wake up. "Mama, we have to go soon, or we'll be late for Edgar's service." The curtains were drawn, and the room was dark.

She grunted at me and rolled over. I stood over her bed, looking down at her. She had taken to her bed days ago and refused to do anything but sleep. Now she was about to sleep through her son's funeral.

I felt like I was facing all of this alone. It wasn't fair. None of this was fair. It seemed as if I was losing my entire family.

I grabbed the bottle of sleeping pills off her nightstand. I wished that I could sleep it all away, too, and convince myself this was all just a bad dream. But not facing the truth would only prolong the pain.

It was worrisome how fast she was going through those pills, and I feared she was becoming too reliant on them. I opened up the top drawer in her nightstand and found a pile of empty pill bottles. I took one out and put two pills from the current bottle in the old one. I put the full bottle in my purse and the other on her nightstand. I didn't want to leave her without any.

I tried to wake her again, but it was no use. So I left her bedroom, locked up the house, and made my way alone to my brother's funeral.

* * *

I felt numb as I looked down into the hole that was Edgar's grave. He was buried next to Daddy. Someday, Mama would be buried there, too, and eventually so would I. In that moment, everything felt meaningless. What was the point if we all just ended up bones sleeping inside of beautiful caskets?

I couldn't let myself give in to the emptiness, or I would surely drown in it. So I willed myself to become filled with determination. There was work to be done. If anything was to have meaning, it would be to uncover the truth about what happened to Edgar and Ruby.

Alan and his wife Judy were the only other people there. Daddy and Alan met in '23 when they were both attending LSU. They were great friends and Alan was like family; that's probably why he gave me a job at *The Post*.

Judy rested her hand on my back. "Have you cried yet?" She was tall, thin, and a real no-nonsense type of woman, which made her kindness all the more genuine.

"No." My voice was tired and stoic.

"I'm not much of a crier myself. But I can tell you this much, don't fight it when it comes. Allowing yourself to feel it is the key to not getting stuck in it." She gave my hand a gentle squeeze before turning to Alan. "I'll be waiting for you in the car, darling." Judy gave him a quick kiss on the cheek and left the two of us alone.

Alan moved closer to me, "How you holding up, kiddo?"

"By a single thread."

"I know you're going through a lot, so you take all the time you need. Your job will be waiting for you when you get back."

"But Alan, how will the paper ever get by without the latest appliance reviews?" I joked.

"Good to see you haven't lost your sense of humor." He chuckled. "But I think we can manage."

"Actually, there is something I'd like to talk to you about, but there's somewhere I need to be right now. Can we meet at LaFleur's Tavern, say around seven o'clock? It's the big pink building on Government Street."

"Anything you need, Betty."

"Thank you, Alan."

"Sure thing, kid."

I walked through the graveyard and across the parking lot to my car. I leaned my back against the driver's door and closed my eyes, feeling the weight of my sorrows.

Suddenly, the hairs on the back of my neck stood up and a shiver ran down my spine. All my senses went on high alert; I could feel eyes on me. I turned to get into my car when I saw him.

Across the parking lot, there was a man sitting in a light blue truck smoking a cigarette. He glared at me with cruel hateful eyes and my blood turned cold as a claircognizance came over me. I knew, truly knew, that this man murdered Edgar and Ruby.

I jumped into my car and locked the doors. Quickly, I

searched the glove box for a pen and paper to write down the license plate number, but when I looked up, he was gone.

* * *

"Well, I'll be, if it ain't Betty Boudreaux." Miss Mabel smiled instantly when she saw me. We hadn't seen each other since I was a girl. "I'd recognize those mischievous eyes anywhere. Come on in, baby." She opened the door wide to invite me in. I followed her to the kitchen, and we sat down at the table. She tried to hide her sorrow, but I could see she was just as miserable as I was.

"I was wondering when ya was gonna come see me."

"I'm so sorry about Ruby. Did you already have a service for her?"

"Yesterday." She fidgeted with the edge of her tablecloth. "And Edgar?" She cleared her throat, sniffled. I could tell she was trying to keep from crying.

"We buried him a couple of hours ago."

"This all so senseless." She slapped her hand against her thigh.

"Miss Mabel, I don't know what the police told you, but I don't think this was an accident. I believe they were murdered."

She leaned back in her chair and smacked her lips, "Baby, you ain't tell me nothing I don't already know. A white boy and a colored girl running around together. Something like that bound to get the attention of the wrong person."

"Do you have any ideas about who that might be?"

She got up from the table and stood at the kitchen sink and

looked out the window. "I got me a few ideas."

"Any of them tall, blond, and drive a light blue truck?"

"That be Lloyd West. He from Texas." She narrowed her eyes as she gazed out the window and mumbled under her breath, *"Les maudits texiens."*[9]

"He was watching me at Edgar's funeral."

"He musta followed ya here. He parked outside my house right now."

"What?" I rushed to the window. Sure enough, there was his truck parked across the street. "He did it, Miss Mabel, I know he did."

"Betty, just leave this alone."

I was shocked by her request. "He's a murderer, I can't just leave it alone."

"Leave it be, Betty," she said firmly.

"But Miss Mabel…" I began to protest.

"Dammit, Betty, just leave it be! Lord, child, you never could just let things be. I don't need no white woman coming up in here trying to save the damn day. Ya don't know what ya messing with. Ya just gonna stir up more trouble. Just go on and tend to ya own family."

It had been years since I had a scolding from Miss Mabel and every word stung just as deep as it had when I was a child. I knew better than to backtalk her, and my lip quivered as I tried to hold in my emotions. But then I realized I wasn't eight years old anymore and was allowed to speak my piece.

"They were my family," I said with composure. *"You* are my family." I wiped a rogue tear from my cheek. "I understand that you want me to leave it alone, and out of respect for you,

---

[9] Les maudits texiens: the damned Texans

I'll do my best to keep you out of it. But I'm going to fight for Edgar, and I'd like to fight for Ruby too, if you'll let me."

We stood in the kitchen for a moment; neither of us had anything left to say. I couldn't read her, so I walked out of the house and to my car. The light blue truck had once again vanished.

* * *

Inside LaFluer's Tavern, it was dim and smoky. Besides two older men sitting at the far end of the bar, the place was empty. Alan wasn't there yet, so I sat down at the bar to wait for him.

"What can I get for you, miss?" the bartender, a clean-shaven middle-aged man, asked.

"Double whiskey on the rocks."

He returned with my drink and lingered. "Haven't seen you in here before, you new in town?"

"Just passing through." I wasn't in the mood to make friends. I took a sip of my whiskey, let it burn down the back of my throat. On second thought, perhaps this bartender might be helpful, so I asked, "You know a cowboy by the name of Lloyd West?"

"Yeah, he's in here all the time stirring up trouble, usually with his buddy Cole. But Cole ain't been around lately."

"They ever start trouble with Edgar Boudreaux?"

"Not that I can recall. But you can ask Lloyd yourself, he just walked in."

I looked over my shoulder, toward the door, and there he was, just standing there, staring at me. I turned around and tried to play it cool, but my heart was beating faster than a racehorse. He sauntered across the room, smoking a cigarette, and sat down next to me. He smelled like stale smoke and cheap whiskey.

"Lloyd," the bartender said as he poured a beer, "I don't want no trouble from you tonight. You understand me?"

Lloyd took a heavy drag of his cigarette. "No sir, no trouble from me." He had a thick Texas twang. Smoke billowed out of his nose, and he continued to stare at me, practically burning holes into me with his gaze. He was trying to frighten me, and it was working, but I'd be damned if I let it show.

"You sure are a pretty young thing, ain't ya?" He grazed my forearm with the back of his index finger.

My entire body tensed up, a mixture of fear and anger. "Don't touch me," I said through a clenched jaw.

"What's wrong, sweetheart, I'm not your type?" He blew his smoke in my face and leaned in close to me. "Yeah, I bet you like them Negros, just like your brother did." He tucked my hair behind my ear and leaned in even closer, inches away from my face, and whispered in my ear, "Maybe I'll get to see what your insides look like, too. I'm an excellent shot."

I shook with fury. My fists were balled up so tight that my fingernails were tearing into my palms. I was on the verge of losing all self-control, about to pick up my whiskey glass and smash it against the side of his face, when Alan appeared behind me.

"What's going on here?" Alan asked in his commanding voice.

Lloyd jerked back from me. "Just having a friendly little chat." He lifted both hands in surrender.

"It didn't look very friendly." Alan glared at him.

I grabbed Alan's arm. "Get me the hell out of here," I hissed.

He took me by the arm and led me through the door. Outside, relief washed over me and then I began to breathe heavily as the realization of what just happened hit me. I clutched my waist and doubled over, trying to catch my breath.

"Jesus Christ, Betty, are you alright?" Alan asked, concerned. "Who was that?"

I stood up and looked around the parking lot. "Come with me." I led him to my car. "Get in. I don't want anyone to overhear us."

"Betty, what the hell is going on?"

I lit myself a cigarette. "Edgar's death wasn't an accident."

"What?" He looked at me, confused.

"I saw the body, he had a bullet hole in his neck. He was shot and then set on fire to cover it up."

"Why haven't the police done anything about it?"

"Because he was in a relationship with a colored lady. And they don't think that either of their deaths are worth investigating."

Alan sat silently and contemplated my words. "You're gonna need solid evidence to prove an accusation like that. Do you have any?"

"Not yet. But I can get it. That's what I wanted to discuss with you. I want to investigate for *The Post*."

"No, Betty, it's too dangerous. Your father would never forgive me if something happened to you."

"Well, Daddy's dead," I snapped. "And so is Edgar. And Mama's lost her goddamn mind. I'm the only one left. Who else is going to fight for my family?"

"Betty, it's too risky."

"That man practically confessed to me. He threatened me

because I'm on to something. I'm doing this with or without your help, Alan."

He paused to think, rubbing his forehead. "Goddamn it, I know. Listen, you have to be smart about this." He pulled out a notepad from his front shirt pocket and scribbled something down. "This guy might be able to help. He's a police officer." Alan tore the paper from his notepad and handed it to me. "He's done some favors for the paper before."

"Thank you."

"Don't make me regret this, Betty." He got out of the car and leaned in through the door. "I'm gonna follow you back to your mom's, make sure you get home safe." He closed the door and left.

I unfolded the paper he gave me and read the name: Officer Matthew Abshire.

* * *

My whole world had changed within the span of a week, and I had only packed enough underwear for the weekend. Besides the fact that I needed fresh clothes, I was desperate to enlist the help of the officer Alan had suggested.

I was in my childhood bedroom packing my suitcase to head back to New Orleans, when I heard a knock at the front door. Startled by the unexpected interruption, I cautiously made my way through the house to answer the door; who knew who might be on the other side?

"Miss Mabel." I was surprised to see her there. We hadn't spoken since our disagreement a few days before. "I wasn't expecting company. Please, come in."

She stepped inside the foyer and looked around, nostalgia written all over her face. "My goodness, it's been a long time since I been in this house."

"So what brings you by, Miss Mabel?"

"I heard ya mama ain't doing too good. Thought I'd drop by and check in on her."

"Well, I'm afraid that's true, she isn't doing well." I couldn't help the sigh that escaped me. "In fact, she's still in bed. I can't promise she'll be up for seeing visitors, but you can certainly try."

She followed me to Mama's room. I knocked softly before opening her bedroom door. "Mama, someone's here to see you."

Her back was to the door, and the bedcovers were pulled up to her chin. "Tell them to come back later. I'm not feeling well."

"Oh, come on now Marie," Miss Mabel stepped inside the room, "I done come all this way to see ya."

Mama shot up in bed, her face lit up like I hadn't seen in months. "Mabel!" she called out to her with outstretched arms. Miss Mabel rushed over and sat on the edge of the bed.

I watched as the two women who raised me embraced in a tight hug and wept with each other. They didn't need words; they understood each other's pain. Mothers of dead children. I felt a bit like an intruder standing in the room with them. They were sharing a moment of unimaginable pain. I decided it was best to let them have this moment to themselves and went back to my room to finish packing for New Orleans.

After some time, Miss Mabel found me in my bedroom. "Ya leaving, Betty?" she asked from the doorway.

"Yes ma'am. I need to go back to New Orleans for a bit." I

latched my suitcase and set it on the floor.

"Don't tell me ya givin' up."

"Of course not. You know me better than that. I just have to settle a few things."

"Ya takin' ya mama?"

I scoffed. "I can't even get her out of bed, I don't know how I could manage to get her all the way to New Orleans. I'm just going to have to leave her for a while."

"She needs looking after."

"I know," I sat down on the bed, defeated, "but I don't have any other choice."

"Tell ya what." She sat down on the bed next to me. "I'll look after her while ya gone."

"I can't ask you to do that."

"You can. And ya know why?" She grabbed my hand. "Cuz we family, baby."

I was overwhelmed by all my emotions. Throughout this whole ordeal, I had been trying to stay strong and shoved every feeling down as deep as I could. But sitting there with Miss Mabel, I felt safe enough to finally breathe and it all came flooding out of me. I broke down like a little child. She held me and we cried together, for Ruby, for Edgar, for Daddy, for Mama, for everything.

* * *

I was desperate for help and couldn't leave anything to chance. There was no way I was going to risk Officer Abshire turning me down, so I had to make sure he wouldn't have a choice. I tailed him for about a week, memorized his schedule, and learned as much as I could. I was looking to get some dirt on him, anything really, and ended up uncovering just the ammunition I needed.

I checked my watch. Almost 7:30; he would be getting off from his shift soon. I waited under a streetlamp just outside the police station. It was one of those rare Louisiana nights when the weather is agreeable. Early spring, a chill in the air leftover from winter, but the breeze is warm from summer's approach.

I spotted him walking across the parking lot and called out, "Officer Abshire."

He turned, searched my face for recognition but found none. "Yes ma'am, can I help you?"

"Please, call me Betty."

"Well, Betty," he smiled politely, "I'm off duty so if you need to report something, you'll have to go inside."

"Oh, but I need to talk to *you*."

"Look, I'd love to help you but it's late and I'd really like to get home to my dinner." He turned away from me and continued walking to his car. He was giving me the brush-off and I certainly couldn't have that.

"Eager to get home to the missus?" I followed after him.

"No. No missus." He smirked to himself, thinking I didn't know his secret.

"The mister, then?"

That stopped him dead in his tracks. "What are you getting at?" He whipped around to face me. He was trying to play it off, act tough, but I saw the panic in his eyes, and I knew I had him.

"I'm not one to judge, but I can't speak for your squad. Who knows what they might do if something like that were to get out."

"What is it that you want?"

"I'm in need of your skills. I was told you have experience with undercover work."

He narrowed his eyes at me; I smiled in return.

"There's a diner around the corner. Let me buy you dinner and explain my situation. Besides, it'll be good for your reputation to be seen having dinner with a beautiful woman." I winked at him, but he was not amused.

I gave him an account of everything and reluctantly Matthew agreed, but truthfully, I gave him no choice in the matter.

Several days had gone by, and I was back in Baton Rouge waiting for him at Mama's house. She was asleep, of course, and I was in the study getting ready for Matthew's arrival when there was a soft knock on the study door. Miss Mabel poked her head in. "Betty, ya have a minute to talk?"

"Sure, Miss Mabel. Have a seat."

"Oh no baby, I cain't stay long, my nephew here to pick me up. But before I go, we need to talk about whatcha gon' do 'bout ya mama."

I leaned against the desk and sighed.

"Betty, she cain't be left alone no more. Ya mama needs serious looking after. She be poppin' them pills like they candy. Damn near burned the whole house down trying to cook while she half asleep."

I closed my eyes and rubbed my temples. Maybe if I wished hard enough, this would all go away. But then I realized that burying my head in the sand would make me just like Mama, and that thought scared me more than anything. I opened my eyes to see Miss Mabel staring at me with concern. "Ya alright, baby?" she asked.

"I'll be ok." I gave her a halfhearted smile to ease her worry. "Just one more thing to add to the plate. Here, let me walk you out."

We stood on the front porch and said our goodbyes. "Now Betty, ya call me if ya need somethin', ya hear?"

"Yes ma'am. And thank you again for staying with Mama. I don't know what I would have done without you."

"Prolly let this house burn down," she joked as she got into her nephew's car.

Just as they were pulling out, Matthew's car pulled in. He got out of his car and walked up onto the porch.

"Did you have any trouble finding the house?" I asked him.

He gave me a sideways glance. It was clear he didn't trust me, and I couldn't blame him. "Let's just get this over with."

I led him through the house and into the study.

"You'll need to get him talking," I said.

Matthew sat on the sofa while I poured us a couple of whiskeys.

I handed him his drink and sat down across from him in one of the leather club chairs.

"What makes you think he's going to tell me anything?"

"He's proud of what he did and he's dying to talk about it. He practically admitted it to me."

Matthew took a sip and leaned back. "Okay, so even if he does confess to me, why do you think the police are going to believe my word over his?"

"Two reasons." I set my drink down and explained as I made my way over to the desk. "One, you're a fellow police officer, your word holds more weight, they'll respect you over anyone else. And two," I reached inside the top drawer of the desk, "you're going to record everything he says." I pulled out my Minifon Portable Recorder.

"Wow." He got up from his seat to meet me at the desk. "These things cost a pretty penny." He took it from me and examined it.

"They do, so be careful with it."

"Right. How should I conceal it?" There was an excitement in his voice, and I could tell he was beginning to let his walls down.

"I'm glad you asked." I walked across the room over to the coat rack and presented him with one of Daddy's old jackets. "I've sewn a secret inside pocket that you can put the recorder in. I've already tested it out and it catches sound well enough, just try not to move around too much or it'll get muffled."

He slipped the jacket on. "Well, you've thought of everything, haven't you." There was a hint of admiration in his voice.

"Almost everything." I said and took up my seat in the club chair. "What's your plan once you get to LeFleur's?"

Matthew sat across from me and picked up his drink. "I figured I'd saddle up next to him at the bar, start out with a racist joke or two. Once I get him laughing, I'll feed him a story about a lynching. Since I know all the details from the police report, it'll sound like I was there. Hopefully that will get him comfortable enough to start talking."

I leaned forward in my chair. "How confident are you in this plan?"

"Pretty confident. I deal with scum like him all the time." He took a sip of his drink and then set it down on the side table. "Just for the record, Betty, I would have helped you with this case without the blackmail."

111

"Well, if that's the case, then I don't mind telling you that I never planned on exposing you, even if you had said no." I could see him soften. "Let me make it up to you. When all this mess is behind us, I would love to have you and your boyfriend over for dinner."

A strange look passed over Matthew's face.

"You'll learn to love me," I teased.

He huffed through his nose. "It's not that. It's just odd hearing someone refer to him as my boyfriend."

I leaned back in my chair. "Tell me about him. How'd the two of you meet? I love a good love story."

"Well," he started, "his name is Robert. We met in court. He's a defense attorney."

"A police officer and a defense attorney. What an odd couple."

"That's what you find odd about my relationship?"

"Don't self-deprecate, Matthew. It doesn't suit you. And for the record, I don't think there's anything odd about homosexuals. That's part of what we're fighting for here, the right to forbidden love."

"You're a strange woman, Betty."

"I've been called worse." I looked at my watch. "You better get going."

Matthew stood up. "I'll come straight back here after I talk to him."

"Good luck," I said as I walked him to the door.

On pins and needles, I paced the house for hours, careful not to wake Mama. That night, I was grateful for those sleeping pills. It was almost midnight, and Matthew still hadn't returned from the bar.

I was sitting on the front porch when he finally returned,

and I rushed to greet him. "What happened? Did he talk?" I asked anxiously.

There was a disturbed look on Matthew's face. "Yeah, he talked. He told me every detail. That son of a bitch is a monster."

"Where's the tape? Let me hear it."

He tried to stop me as I reached for the jacket. "No, Betty. You don't need to hear it. Trust me."

"I'm not some dainty little flower; I can handle it." His eyes begged me not to. "Please. I have to know what happened to my family."

* * *

The events of March 15th, 1942, from the perspective of Ruby Baptiste

Hello. My name is Ruby Baptist, and this is the story of my death.

I knew that I shouldn't have been there, but I couldn't stop myself from going to the Boudreaux family camp that night. Even though the relationship with Edgar had come to an end, it wasn't over. My feelings for him—well, they consumed me. I was hopeless, lovesick for him. The mere mention of apple pie had me bursting into tears. I missed him so much that I physically ached. So, against my better judgment, I went out to The Camp to see him.

I stood on the front porch, unsure of myself or what I might say to him and knocked on the door. My heart pounded against my chest while I questioned my own sanity. I was ready to turn tail and run, when he opened the door.

He looked an awful mess. Unshaven, hair sticking up every which way, eyes bloodshot from days of drinking. He was eaten up by heartache, which in turn made my heart ache. He didn't say a word, just stepped aside and let me in.

Before he even finished closing the door, I was pouring out my heart to him. "Edgar, I'm sorry. I'm so, so sorry." My words got caught in my throat. "I don't know, I don't know what to do." I began to sob. "I love you and I want to do the right thing, but I don't know what that is."

He rushed to me, wrapped his arms around me. He smoothed my hair and did his best to comfort me, even though he, himself, was hurting.

"It's okay," he whispered while I cried into his chest. "We'll figure out what the right thing is together." He walked me over to a nearby chair and sat me down. He knelt in front of me and stroked my cheek. Never has anyone looked at me with such pure love. "Let me get you a glass of water." He went to the kitchen to fetch me some water from a pitcher on the counter.

My will began to waiver; running away with him suddenly didn't seem like such a crazy idea. Our love was once in a lifetime. I would be a fool to walk away from someone who made my soul sing like this. There aren't many men in this world who are willing to put aside their pride and hurt feelings to take care of a woman. I didn't know if I could live my life without him. Nothing else seemed to matter; there was no question, I was a fool in love.

I got up from my seat and went to him in the kitchen. I stood behind him and wrapped my arms around his waist, pressing my face into his back. We stood there, silent and still, both clinging to this moment, afraid of what might happen once it passed.

Out of nowhere, the silence was broken by a loud bang on the door that startled us both. Something about that knock was menacing; loud, hard, and slow.

Still holding onto him, I could feel his entire body tense up. "Stay here," he instructed me as he moved away to answer the door.

When Edgar opened the door, two men pushed their way inside. The tall one, Lloyd, had a rifle and the shorter one, Cole, had a pistol. Lloyd slammed the door behind him and casually leaned against it, blocking our only way out.

I was paralyzed with fear.

"Well, well, well. What do we have here?" Lloyd pushed the tip of his cowboy hat with the barrel of his rifle. He had a calm air about him, which was chilling in the most terrifying way.

"I don't know, Lloyd, looks like we caught us a couple of lovebirds." Cole had a wad of chewing tobacco tucking in his bottom lip, and he turned his head and spat on the floor.

"Look, fellas, we don't want any trouble." Edgar moved to stand in front of me.

"Shoulda thought of that before you went and took up with a Negro slut," Cole said and moved in closer to us. He licked his lips as he looked me up and down and spat on the floor again.

"You watch your mouth, you piece of shit." Edgar started to move forward to confront him, but I put my hands on his shoulders and held him back.

Lloyd stepped away from the door and the two men circled us like wolves. This was my worst nightmare, my biggest fear realized. This kind of cruelty was the very thing I had been warned about my whole life. I knew these men meant to kill me. In their minds, I had stepped out of line and that was punishable by death.

"What'd you say, boy?" Lloyd came closer. He towered over us.

Meanwhile, Cole came around from behind and tried to lift my skirt with the end of his pistol. I shrieked and tried to push the gun away. Edgar turned around, trying to defend me. When Edgar took his eyes off Lloyd, he grabbed Edgar by the back of the neck and smashed his face into the counter. Cole hooked his arm around my waist and held me against his body, his free hand groping at my breast.

Edgar was laid out on the floor. Lloyd forced him to his knees and repeatedly punched him in the face with all his might. Blood flew all over the kitchen. The sounds of the bones in his face breaking reached my ears and I found myself screaming in ways I didn't know were possible. I struggled against Cole, trying to get to Edgar, but he just laughed and tightened his grip on me, pinching my nipple. I was trapped and the only thing I could do was scream even louder than before. Lloyd looked up at me with cold eyes. "Shut your whore mouth, bitch." He marched over and, with the butt end of his rifle, hit me in the temple until I lost consciousness.

I didn't know how long I had been knocked out, but when I woke, I found myself in the back bedroom, face down on the bed. I tried to stir but my arms and legs jerked back, and I realized that each limb was tied to a post on the bed frame. Little by little, my senses returned to me, the dirty taste in my mouth from the filthy cloth gag tied around my face, the air on my skin telling me I was naked, the sound of thumps and groans.

I looked around the room and saw the two Texans taking turns kicking Edgar. He was gagged and hogtied on the floor. A muffled whimper escaped my throat, and they turned their attention toward me.

"Oh shit, look who's awake," Cole said to Lloyd, and he wiggled his eyebrows with excitement. "Mind if I go first? I been waitin' for this since the day we caught 'em smoochin' in the park."

My mind raced, I remembered that day in the park, when Edgar surprised me. It was the day we shared our first kiss, the day he told me that he loved me. To think that in the shadows of something so beautiful, evil was lurking.

Lloyd slapped Cole on the back. "Do the honors, my friend."

I could hear him behind me unbuckling his pants. My breath began to quicken. *Oh God, was this really happening?* I tried to think, but there was no way out of this. The mattress sank under Cole's weight as he climbed onto the bed. He was touching himself and rubbing against me. I wanted to fight back but the only part of my body I had control of was my head.

Lloyd lifted Edgar to his knees, and gripped him by the back of his hair. "You better watch this, boy." He yanked Edgar's head up and kneed him in the back. Edgar was tired from the beatings, but he still had fight in his eyes. It was killing him that he could not save me. We locked eyes and I could see he felt everything I was feeling. Pain, fear, shame.

He began to weep. I turned my head away to face the wall. I couldn't look at him while it happened.

Cole rammed himself into me dry. I screamed out but my voice was muffled by the gag. I could hear Edgar's muffled screams too, and then another beating from Lloyd.

"Oh shit, Lloyd," Cole called out from inside of me, "I think we got us a virgin."

"Yee haw, brother," Lloyd answered. "Break that filly in."

The pain was almost as excruciating as the shame. If utter humiliation was what they were after, they hit their mark. The more I screamed out or tried to resist, the rougher he got. And the rougher he got the more, Edgar tried to break free and thus another beating from Lloyd ensued. It was all too much: the sound of the man I loved being tortured, the gleeful cheers of our captors egging each other on, my body being violated.

I shut my eyes and tried to remember that day at the park. Back when everything was still beautiful and full of possibility, before everything came crashing down around us.

When he was finished, Cole spat his tobacco on my back.

He and Lloyd switched places and the nightmare began again. It seemed as though it went on for hours, them taking turns, beating us both in between rounds. They raped me with a vicious brutality found only in humans. When it was over, I couldn't even lift my head off the mattress.

I lay like a broken plaything on the bed. I could feel my body being lifted, dragged across the floor, blood dripping down my thighs. The sound of a door opening, a warm breeze against my naked flesh, dirt under my feet. I prayed that this was finally over, but I could tell by the elation in their voices that this wasn't done yet.

I was tossed on the ground under the pecan tree and fell on my knees. I was too weak to hold myself up and I let my body double over. There was a thud. When I lifted my eyes, I saw Edgar kneeling in front of me. He was unbound and ungagged, like me. The sight of my poor beloved left me breathless. His face, his body, was swollen, bloody, and bruised. I inched my hand forward and touched his fingertips.

"Alright boy, you got two choices," Lloyd stood behind him and aimed the rifle at Edgar's back, "you can sit back and watch us string 'er up." Cole put a noose around my neck and yanked me away from Edgar. "Or two, you can take that there pistol and shoot that whore in the head." Cole tossed his pistol on the ground between us. "'Sup to you, boy."

"Fuck you, you son of a bitch," Edgar mumbled.

Lloyd pressed the rifle into the base of Edgar's skull. "I'd watch that mouth if I were you, boy."

"Edgar, please." It took every bit of strength I had left in me to speak. "Please just shoot me."

"I can't, Ruby. I can't," he said, crying.

"Please," I pleaded with him. "Please Edgar, end this for me. Don't let them lynch me."

Edgar hung his head and sobbed. He stared at the pistol for a moment before picking it up. Then he looked me in the eye one last time. "I love you, Ruby Baptiste."

I closed my eyes and in a flash it was over. All the pain was gone. The heavy weight of life had been lifted and I was free.

Before my body even hit the ground, Edgar aimed the gun and shot Cole right between the eyes. He fell in the dirt and died instantly. Lloyd shot Edgar through the neck, his body tumbled over onto mine, and he bled out in seconds.

Edgar knew he'd never be fast enough to shoot them both. He knew that if he shot Cole before me, Lloyd would kill him, and I'd be lynched. He spared me that pain and gave me a quick death.

"Shit!" Lloyd yelled. He looked around at the three bodies.

He didn't have much time if he was going to get this cleaned up by himself before sunrise.

What happened next was pretty simple. He loaded our bodies into the bed of Edgar's truck. Then, he went back into the cabin and spent the next few hours cleaning every inch of The Camp. Next, he drove the truck out to a sugar cane field about thirty miles outside of town. He buried Cole not far from where he parked the truck. Finally, he placed Edgar and me in the cab, doused it in gasoline, and lit it on fire.

He didn't have much trouble hitching a ride back into town. From there, he walked back to The Camp, retrieved his own truck, and went on as if nothing ever happened.

Betty and Matthew brought the taped confession to the police.

They had no other choice but to arrest Lloyd. He pled guilty to Edgar's murder, but they never charged him with mine since technically Edgar pulled the trigger. They didn't charge him with my rape, either. The District Attorney said, "He's already going to prison, no sense in charging him with the rape of a dead woman." But he really meant a Black woman.

Betty was furious about it, of course, but there wasn't anything she could do, although it wasn't for lack of trying. He got life in prison, so at least there's that, but my family never saw justice for what happened to me.

Chapter 10

The silence hung heavy in the car as Betty and Frank continued to drive down Highway LA 2, past the sugarcane fields and crawfish ponds, through small unnamed towns. It took some time for Frank to process the horrific story Betty just relayed to him. He wanted to offer her some words of comfort, but words worthy of a response escaped him.

She wiped a stray tear from her cheek. "I wish I could say I've made my peace with it, but..." her voice cracked and trailed off. She reached for her purse to get a tissue, and without thinking, Frank grabbed her hand. It was the only thing he could think of to comfort her. His heart raced when he touched her, and he let his hand linger longer than he should have.

"How is it possible to make peace with something like that?" he finished her thought.

"Exactly." She smiled at him and squeezed his hand. For the first time in a long while, she felt a true connection to someone.

"Did you ever write that article?" Frank asked, still holding her hand.

"As a matter of fact, I did. It turned out to be a huge success and I've been an investigative journalist ever since. It was difficult, though, to have my success so intertwined with my suffering. I don't know about you, but '42 was a hell of a year."

Frank glanced out the window. He watched the sun sink below the horizon of the sugarcane fields and illuminate the evening sky with its last bit of dying light. The car whizzed past a sign that read, *"Bienvenue à Ville Morte."* Frank realized that he was still holding her hand and gently let go as his past flashed before his eyes. In that moment, he regretted everything, yet he regretted nothing.

"I can certainly relate. I had my own set of troubles in '42."

"Is that when you hurt your leg?" Betty asked.

Frank nodded.

"Well, go on then. I can't be the only one to share my troubles."

Frank gave her a weak smile, "I think we've had enough talk about troubles for one night, don't you?"

"I suppose you're right." She sighed with disappointment. "But you owe me that story." Betty put her free hand back on the wheel. She began to feel unsure of herself; perhaps he didn't feel the connection that she felt. But then again, if anyone knew how hard it was to let down one's wall, it was her.

Whatever the case might be, she thought it might be best to rein in her feelings a bit. But her curiosity was piqued, and she realized that she didn't really know all that much about Frank.

"Well, if you aren't going to share your troubles, you can at least tell me where you're from."

"Kansas," Frank said, lighting a cigarette.

"Really? I've never met anyone from Kansas."

Betty continued down the road that would lead them into town. They came to a crossroads. A few feet ahead was a small beam bridge, and the sugarcane fields gave way to a forest.

A young boy wearing a straw-hat, high-water britches, and no shoes was fishing off the side of the bridge. Next to him sat a cream-colored dog with pointy ears. The dog caught Frank's attention and as they drove across the bridge, he locked eyes with it. The dog had piercing blue eyes, and despite never having seen her before, Frank felt as if he knew that dog,

"You ever been down here in these parts before, Cajun country, I mean?" Betty asked.

"No. What's Cajun?"

"The Cajuns?" Betty asked. "They're the descendants of the Acadien people who were forcibly removed from their land in Nova Scotia. They ended up settling here, in the southwest region of the state. They're country folk, mostly farmers and fishermen. They've been a pretty isolated community."

"Isolated how?"

"Well, for one thing, they mostly speak French. I mean, they do speak English, but almost everyone is brought up speaking French as their first language. Most kids don't start speaking English until they go to school. They sort of have their own way of doing things. It's very culturally rich down here."

"Sounds like an adventure."

"Welcome to *Acadiana*."[10] Betty looked over at him and

---

[10] Acadiana: Southwestern Louisiana where the Acadian exiles from Canada settled; Cajun country

smiled, *"Laissez le bon temps rouler."*[11]

* * *

Madeline swept the front porch of her large Victorian home. Her new guests would be arriving any minute and she wanted everything to be just right; she was a bit fussy that way. Her boarding house was the only one in town and her reputation for being an impeccable hostess was a source of pride.

The house had been in her family for as far back as anyone could remember, each generation adding on to it until it had become a grand house. Her father left it to her after he died. She carried on the family tradition of opening the house up to anyone who needed a place to stay.

Madeline was one of Ville Morte's most well-informed citizens, although most people called her a busybody and a chatterbox. Her circle often teased her and said that her constant talking was her way of drowning out the ethereal humming that was a near-constant for her. The gift of clairaudience came to her later in life; she was thirty-three when it started. Now she was fifty-eight, and over the years, she learned to manage it properly.

She stopped sweeping and listened. The humming turned to tingling. She heard the faint sound of nervous laughter. Her guests would be here soon.

Madeline set her broom down and hurried through the house to the kitchen. Out of the ice box, she grabbed a pitcher of sweet tea and set it on a tray with three glasses.

---

[11] Laissez le bon temps rouler: Let the good times roll

When she returned to the porch, a car was pulling into the driveway. She beamed with pride as she stood on the front porch, ready to welcome her guests.

"Betty Boudreaux," she called out when she saw Betty step out of the car. "Oh, it's so good ta see ya, *cher*."[12]

"Miss Madeline," Betty smiled and greeted her with a warm hug. "This is my colleague, Frank. Frank, this is Miss Madeline. She's a dear friend of both my aunt and my mother."

"It's wonderful ta meet ya, Frank," Madeline said. She spoke English but her words bent under the weight of her Cajun accent. "Would y'all like some sweet tea?"

"I'd love some, thank you," Frank said.

Madeline was pouring each of them a glass when the cream-colored dog they passed on the road came running up on the porch, wagging her tail and leaving a trail of muddy paw prints in her wake.

"*Oh, mais la,*[13] *Le Bleu,*[14]" Madeline scolded the dog. "I jus' cleaned dis porch."

"What a cute dog," Betty said and reached down to pet her. "Oh my, look at those eyes." Le Bleu looked at Betty with her intense ice-blue eyes. Her pointy ears perked up as she sniffed Betty. "Is she yours?"

"Well, yes and no. Le Bleu is everybody's dog. She runs aroun' town and makes herself at home wherever she pleases. I suppose she picked me for supper tonight."

Le Bleu turned away from Betty and started sniffing at Frank. She sniffed him for a long time before she sat at his

---

[12] cher: darling

[13] Mais la: Cajun phrase meaning *Good grief*

[14] Le Bleu: Blue

feet and stared up at him. Again, Frank had the strange feeling that he knew this dog.

"What kind of dog is she?" Frank asked. "She's very unique."

"Who knows," Madeline answered. "Her line's been aroun' here a long, long time. Most of da pups run off, but da blue-eyed ones always stick around. Soul dogs, ma cousin used ta call 'em. Anyway," Madeline turned to the dog. "Le Bleu, you'll have ta wait for supper, I've got ta give dese people a tour of da grounds."

Le Bleu plopped down on the porch with a groan. Madeline led them inside, chatting away.

"Dis here," she pointed to her left, "is da parlor." It was a large open room with lots of wingback chairs, a couple of chaise lounges, and a telephone bench.

Madeline walked around the room, showing off her furniture. "People like ta sit here and visit or use da telephone. We don't have phones in da cabins. Oh, dat's right, I forgot ta mention dat y'all will be staying in da cabins. After ma late husband, Leon, passed, he left me some money, not a lot of money, ya see, but enough ta do some sprucing up aroun' here. Anyway, I had a few cabins built on the side of da house. Now that Leon's gone, I don't feel comfortable having strangers staying inside da house. I jus' use the rooms in da house in case we're full, which we never are because we don't get dat many visitors here. In fact, you two are my only guests dis week." Madeline rambled on without giving Betty or Frank a chance to respond.

"Dis is da breakfast nook." She pointed to the bay window at the head of the parlor. It overlooked the front yard and had a perfect view of the dock on the bayou. There were three small round tables, each with two chairs, that were set perfectly around so that they all had an unobstructed view. "Breakfast is served here every morning. And over here," Madeline walked briskly across the room, "is da dining room." Behind a half wall, there was a formal dining room with a table that sat ten.

"Now I don't do lunch, but y'all are welcome ta supper any night of da week. I always make extra, ma kids and grandkids are always stopping by, usually unannounced, mind ya, but really it don't bother me, I always love having dem over. Now usually on Sundays, I don't have da guests over for supper because dat's when da whole family gets ta'gether. But you're family, of course, Betty, so ya must stop by."

Betty smiled. "I will certainly try, Miss Madeline."

"Enough of dis "Miss Madeline" business. You call me Tante[15] Mad, same as da rest of my family. And same goes for when ya see Suzette Trahan. Poor thing is so tender-hearted, if ya call her Miss Suzette instead of Tante Suz, she might burst into tears. Now come on, I'll show ya to ya cabins."

Madeline led them out of a side door in the parlor and around the back of the house past the backyard garden. To the left of the main house were four identical stand-alone cabins. Each had a small front porch with a single rocking chair that faced the bayou.

The trio walked inside.

"It's not much, but you'll have everything ya need. There's a little kitchen over dere wit a stove and an ice box. Dere's pots and pans in the cabinets if you wanna cook. And over dere is a bat'room. It's got a tub wit a shower. Na da doors don't have locks, but I promise ta knock. Ya privacy will be respected. Betty, ya cabin is next door." She turned toward

---

[15] Tante: Aunt

the door to leave. "Well, I'm sure ya tired so I'll let ya settle in. Y'all come up ta da main house for supper later if ya feeling hungry." She continued chattering on as she left the cabin.

"She was very friendly," Frank said as he shoved his hands in his pockets and leaned back on his heels.

"Tante Mad does love to chat." Betty laughed and tucked her hair behind her ear.

Frank gave Betty one of his half-smiles. "So does calling her Tante Mad apply to me, too?"

"You can test it out. I'm sure she won't be shy about correcting you." She returned his smile.

They gazed at each other and let the silence fill the room. "I'm pretty beat," Betty looked down at her feet. "I think I'll just head to my room and call it a night. Let's meet for breakfast in the morning and we can work on a strategy."

"Okay, Betty. I'll see you in the morning."

"See you in the morning."

After Betty left the room, Frank collapsed onto his bed and before he knew it, he was out like a light.

Chapter 11

I t was so pitch black when Frank came to that he wasn't even sure his eyes were open. The air was thick and hot; the scent of damp earth overwhelmed him. Beyond the smell and the darkness, it was a tiny, muffled voice that brought Frank to this place. He could hear Avril crying.

"Avril?" Frank called out to her, but she continued to cry softly in the distance without answering him. Maybe she couldn't hear him, maybe she was lost or trapped somewhere.

The impulse to save his child took over and his body sprang into action. He tried to sit up and smacked his forehead on something hard above him, blocking his movement and knocking him back down.

"What the hell is going on?" he mumbled, and as he felt around Frank realized that he was enclosed. He reached in his pocket and pulled out a matchbook. Fumbling in the dark, he struck a match and for a brief moment, his surroundings were illuminated. The horror of his reality seized him. Frank was locked inside a small wooden coffin.

"Hey! Hey, let me out!" Frank yelled and banged his fist on the coffin lid.

He could still hear Avril crying in the distance. "Daddy," she wailed in between sniffles. "I want my Daddy."

"Hang on, Sunshine, I'm coming," he called out to her, but he knew she couldn't hear him.

Maybe, he thought, he could use his legs to push the coffin lid open. He had to get to his little girl; she was scared and she needed him. He tried to move his legs into position, but his left leg wouldn't budge. Suddenly there was a throbbing in his thigh. He lit another match, and to his terror, realized that not only was he nailed inside the coffin, but he was nailed *to* the coffin. A tremendous nail had been driven right through his left thigh.

His breath quickened. He was trapped.

The hot air around him grew hotter still and it became hard to breathe. Panic washed over him. The coffin felt like it was getting smaller with each breath that he struggled to take. The harder his heart beat against his chest, the more intense the throbbing in his leg grew. With a violent force, blood spurted from his wound and pooled around him. All the while, Avril's tiny voice called out for him.

His pounding heart echoed in his ears and the sound formed another voice, a man's voice.

"And now a reading from the book of Revelations," the voice boomed. "I know your deeds, that you are neither cold nor hot. Because you are lukewarm, I spit you from my mouth!" His voice was commanding and steeped with judgment. The biblical reading continued but gradually his words were drowned out by the sound of weeping voices. Frank realized that this was his funeral.

He screamed as loud as he could and pounded his fists against the coffin lid once more. "Help! Help! I'm trapped! I'm still alive down here. I'm not dead yet!"

His voice rang out through the small space. Then he heard a thud on the top of the coffin and then another and another. Flecks of dirt fell on his face. He was being buried alive.

All the while he screamed for help, the blood from his leg was gushing out of him at an alarming rate. The more Frank yelled, the faster the blood filled his coffin. It sloshed around his cheeks and flowed into his ear canal. It crept inside his nostrils and dripped down the back of his throat, causing him to choke. He could taste it on his lips and the tip of his tongue. Just as he was about to drown in his own blood, it all vanished. There was complete silence. No thuds of dirt, no cries from Avril.

Nothingness surrounded him.

All his panic turned to sorrow when he realized he would never see Avril again. She would grow up without him. He wouldn't be there to protect her from the evils of the world, nor would he be there to celebrate the joys of her life. She was so young. Would she even remember how much he loved her?

In an endless eternity, these thoughts looped on repeat in his mind. Time no longer existed. Frank was lost in the void of death.

It felt as if an entire lifetime had passed in just a few short moments, when finally, there was a faint rustling above him. Frank listened intently as the sound grew louder, closer. It was the sound of dirt being cleared away. Someone was digging him up. He was being rescued at last.

The coffin lid swung open. A light blinded him and obscured his savior's face.

Frank awoke with a violent jerk. The bright morning sun pierced the sheer curtains of the cabin window and hit him right in the eyes.

A sense of relief washed over him as he realized it had all just been a bad dream. Much like in his dream, the air in the room was thick, hot, and damp. He had sweated through his bed sheets, which left him feeling sticky and moist.

Frank groaned as he sat up in bed. He couldn't shake the uneasy feeling the nightmare had left with him. He wanted to call and check on Avril, to hear her little voice and know that she was safe. But calling home would mean having to speak with Ava, and Frank was in no mood to put up with her this morning, not with his leg hurting this way. The pain he felt in his leg during the dream had been very real. It ached something awful, a sure sign of coming rain.

He rubbed the top of his leg and decided he would call home in the afternoon once he felt better. Frank pressed down with the palm of his hand and stroked the scar that ran the length of his thigh. There was a certain bumpy texture to it. Scar tissue formed into a keloid, so the skin was thick and raised.

A wave of guilt crashed around him. A good father would call his daughter despite any hardship. A good husband loved his wife. Frank always believed that he was a good man; he strived to be one. But over the last few years, no matter how noble the deed, he always fell short of his expectations. He had become a disappointment to himself. The more time that passed, the less he believed in his own goodness.

He threw his feet over the side of the bed and glared at the cane he had propped up against the dresser. Ava made him pack it "just in case." He hated the damn thing; it made him feel like an old man. He had too much pride to use it and decided that he'd just have to push through the pain. Maybe a shower would make him feel better and help wash off the reminiscence of his nightmare.

Frank hobbled to the bathroom. But a shower did not, in fact, help, and only added to his sour mood. Water from his shower refused to evaporate and the moisture clung to his body due to the deep humidity of a classic Louisiana summer. His clothes smothered him.

Beads of sweat rolled down the length of his back. The shower had been useless. How was he supposed to present himself as a respectable man if he looked like something that just crawled out of the swamp? Finally, Frank gave up and left to meet Betty for their morning meeting.

Frank walked down to the main house and made his way into the parlor through the side door. Across the room, Betty sat at one of the bistro tables in front of the bay window. The table was set for two with coffee and a basket of fresh beignets.

She scribbled away on a notepad, absorbed in her work. The morning sunlight shone down around her and bounced off her blonde hair. It created a golden aura around her.

Frank became very aware of his disheveled appearance, and he felt nervous to talk to her. He stood frozen for a moment, unsure of himself. Then she looked up at him and smiled. His heart stirred, and all of Frank's troubles drifted away.

He walked toward her and with every step, pain shot through his left thigh. "Morning," Frank said and winced as he sat down to join her. He tried to hide it as best he could and was relieved that Betty didn't seem to notice.

"I would ask how you slept but by the looks of you, I'd say not very well." She took a sip of her coffee.

Frank smirked at her joke and poured himself a cup of coffee. "Not well at all. It's too damn hot. How is it that you're not drenched in sweat?"

"Baby powder." She shoved the last bite of the beignet she was eating into her mouth and rubbed her finger together to get the remaining powdered sugar off. "It helps absorb the excess moisture. You can get some at the general store while I interview the police."

"You don't want me to go with you?" Frank leaned back in his chair and crossed his arms.

"I think divide and conquer is the order of the day. You're an excellent listener; you proved as much yesterday on the drive down. I'd like for you to talk to the locals and get a feel for the sentiment about the murders. Plus, you speak French. That'll help with getting people to trust you."

"Hmm," Frank rubbed his chin, "I was thinking it might be better if we keep that under our hat for now."

"Why?" Betty asked, unsure of his idea.

"People might say things to each other in French that they wouldn't say to me directly. Think about it. If you and I were with someone who only spoke French, and we wanted to have a private conversation, we would just speak to each other in English, and the other person would be none the wiser to our schemes."

"I don't know, Frank. We need to get these people to talk to us. I think speaking their own language to them will facilitate that."

"It could give us an advantage in gathering information."

Betty thought about it for a moment. He did have a point, but she wasn't sold on the idea. "What if you can't pull it off?"

"You're going to have to start trusting me at some point." He gave her a disarming smile.

She tried to be hard, but her true feelings peeked through her hidden smile. Even in his unkempt state, he was still the most handsome man she had ever had in her company. There was just something about those goddamn blue eyes staring right through her.

"Fine," she said and took a bite of another beignet. When she lifted her face, she had a dusting of powdered sugar across her nose.

Frank stifled a laugh. She was adorable.

Chapter 12

"*Fils putain!*"[16] Clovis Romero yelled from behind the counter when he saw Father Klein, Ville Morte's new priest, walk into his grocery store.

"Well, good morning to you too, Clovis," Father Klein responded with equal disdain.

They had been a thorn in each other's side since the day they met. Father Klein was not a Cajun, which was precisely why the Church sent him to the area. It was thought that the Cajuns needed some Americanization, and Father Klein was more than happy to oblige. He was unkind, strict, pompous, and arrogant, which won him little respect and fewer friends around town.

"Oh no, no, no, no, no, no. Out, you! You ain't welcome in here."

"Clovis, you're being unreasonable."

"Well, dat may be true Father, but you a thief."

"I beg your pardon, I am no such thing." He was outraged.

"Oh, but you is. You tryin' ta rob us of our culture, you."

"Clovis," Father Klein sighed, frustrated, "there's nothing I

---

[16] Fils putain: Son of a bitch

can do. The order came directly from the diocese. I am no longer allowed to do Mass in French."

"*Mais*,[17] half the people in dis town don't speak uh lick uh English. How dey suppose ta understan' Mass?"

"Simple, they just have to learn to speak English."

Clovis' face turned beet-red. He was a Cajun through and through, with Spanish ancestry on his father's side and Acadian and Native American on his mother's side. Clovis was hot-tempered and loved nothing more than a good fight, except maybe good food…and good music…and beautiful women. "You lucky you a man uh da clot' or I'd pop ya in ya mout' rig't na."

"I need groceries. What am I supposed to do?"

"Go ta uh store dat speaks English. Na get out."

Father Klein narrowed his eyes. "This isn't over, Clovis." He turned to storm out of the store and nearly ran right into Frank, who was stepping through the door. "Watch your step, young man," he barked at Frank and then hurried down the street.

"What's wrong with that fella?" Frank asked Clovis.

"I'd be mad like dat, too, me, if I had uh stick dat far up ma ass."

Frank laughed as he walked over to the counter. He instantly took a liking to Clovis, who was a few years older than Frank.

"You new ta town?" Clovis asked. He eyed Frank with a hint of suspicion. Normally strangers didn't bother him, but since the murders, like everyone else in town, he had become wary of anyone he didn't recognize.

"Yes. Just got in yesterday. I'm staying at the Prejean

---

[17] Mais: But

Boarding House."

"Oh yeah." Clovis scratched his beard. "Madame Madeline is a fine lady an' a damn fine cook, too."

"I've never tasted better beignets than I did this morning."

"She's known for dat, her," Clovis said.

"Frank Martin, by the way." Frank reached his hand out to Clovis for a handshake.

"Clovis Romero. But everybody just calls me Romero."

As Frank shook his hand, he noticed that Clovis was missing his ring and pinky fingers on his right hand.

"Say, ya related ta da Martins down da Bayou?" Clovis asked.

"Doubtful. I'm originally from Kansas."

"Keyawww. Ya uh long ways from home, huh? What brings ya down here?"

"After I was discharged from the Air Corps, I moved to New Orleans."

"Dey sent me home, too, after ma fingers got blew off." He held up his hand and laughed as he wiggled the nubs of his missing fingers.

"What branch did you serve?" Frank was excited to talk to a fellow soldier.

"OSS.[18] Being dat ma French is prolly betta dan ma English, I did a lot uh translatin' and workin' wit dat French Resistance."

Frank felt a slight tightening in his chest at the mention of The Resistance, and it took a great deal of strength to shove those memories and emotions back down.

"Intelligence, huh? That's pretty impressive. You must have some good insight into the murders of those teenagers."

---

[18] Office of Strategic Services

"Whatcha know 'bout dat?" Clovis asked, and he crossed himself.

"I work for *The New Orleans Post*, I've been assigned to cover the story."

"I tell ya what," Clovis opened up like a book, "it's da most horrible thing dat ever happened in dis town. I cain't believe dat something like dat could happen here. Things have changed 'round here since I got back from da war. Dey beat dem kids in school for speaking French. Dey stopped doing Mass in French, and now all dis violence an' murder. I hardly recognize ma own hometown. All dese outsiders comin' in an' changin' things. It's a real shame, if ya ask me."

"So you think these murders were done by someone from out of town?"

"Had ta be, ain't no way it was one of us."

"How can you be sure?"

"It's a small town, we all know each other. We all grew up together. Dose kids was everybody's kids. Nobody 'round here would ever do something like dat ta dem. Here in Cajun Country we all family. Dis all started when outsiders came in and started tryin' to change things. Tryin' ta change our way uh life. But I tell ya what, us Cajuns is stubborn, stubborn and we ain't given up our culture without a fight."

Just then, the bell over the door chimed and a jovial old man dressed in overalls and a straw hat walked in carrying a crate of fresh-picked strawberries. He was tall and lanky with skin that was weathered from a lifetime of working and playing outdoors. Deep wrinkles carved his face and grew more pronounced when he smiled. "Ey Romero," he called out.

"Ey Hebert," Romero returned the call. *"Comment ça va?"*[19]

"Très bien, très bien,"[20] Hebert said as he joined them at the counter. He looked Frank up and down. His fancy city clothes gave him away as an outsider. *"Qui c'est ça couillon?"*[21]

Frank smiled politely and pretended he didn't understand what they were saying.

"Hebert, dis is Frank. Frank, dis is Hebert. He sells me strawberries. He understands English but he don't speak it." He turned to Hebert. "Frank is doing a newspaper story on da murders." Both men crossed themselves.

"Lui as-tu parlé Beaux Guilbeau?"[22] Hebert asked with a little laugh.

"Non, non, non," Romero rolled his eyes at Hebert. *"C'est juste une histoire de fantômes."*[23] Romero glanced over at Frank; something about the way his ears perked up gave him a sneaking suspicion that Frank understood every word they were saying.

* * *

Sheriff Luke Landry sighed heavily. "I'm sorry Father Klein, but there's nothing I can do."

"Well, you can go down there and give him a talking to."

Luke hadn't been sheriff of Ville Morte for very long, and

---

[19] Comment ça va: How are you doing?

[20] Très bien: Very good

[21] Qui c'est ça couillon: Who is this fool?

[22] Lui as-tu parlé Beaux Guilbeau: Did you tell him about Beaux Guilbeau?

[23] C'est juste une histoire de fantômes: That's just a ghost story.

up until now, his job had consisted mainly of settling disputes and keeping the peace among the townsfolk.

"It's his store, he has the right to refuse service to anyone," Luke explained and absentmindedly traced his finger along the edge of the case file he had been looking over before Father Klein had burst into his office. He felt the pressure to find the killer before more teens were added to the list of murder victims. He was doing the best he could, but his little department was ill-equipped to handle such an intense investigation.

"What am I supposed to do? He's the only store in town. I can't walk ten miles both ways to the next town."

"Well Father, people around here are nice, I'm sure someone can help you out."

"I don't know about that. Ever since I got here, people have been pretty rude."

"Nobody likes change, Father," Luke said dismissively as he escorted Father Klein out of his office and down the hall to the front waiting area of the station.

"You're the law around here. Fix it."

"Again, Father," Luke tried not to lose his patience, "Romero is not breaking the law. Now, if you'll excuse me," Luke opened the door and ushered him out, "I have some things to attend to."

Father Klein turned to him with his usual arrogance. He opened his mouth to insult him, but Luke cut him off.

"It was a pleasure as always, Father Klein." Luke immediately swung the door shut before Father Klein had a chance to open his mouth again.

Luke turned to his secretary, Edwina, and shook his head out of frustration. "If you need me, Edwina, I'll be in my office."

"Oh, well, actually Sheriff, there is someone here to see you." She motioned to a chair against the far wall. Luke looked over and his heart stopped beating, his breath caught in his throat. Even though it had been nearly eight years, he'd recognize Betty Boudreaux anywhere.

Betty rose from her seat and stepped toward him with an outstretched hand. "Betty Boudreaux with *The New Orleans Post.*"

Luke stood there dumbfounded for a moment before he shook her hand, "Um, Luke Landry...um, *Sheriff* Luke Landry."

"It's a pleasure to meet you, Sheriff Landry," Betty replied cordially.

A wave of disappointment washed over him. She didn't recognize his name or his face. He gave her a weak smile and nervously shuffled his feet. "How can I help you?"

Edwina's eyes darted back and forth between Betty and Luke. She had never seen him this flustered by a woman before. Women were always vying for his attention. He was one of Ville Morte's most eligible bachelors, and not just because most of the young men were away at war.

Luke wasn't very tall, a common trait among most Cajuns, but he sure was handsome. He had light brown hair, hazel eyes, and a sun-kissed complexion. Luke had a respectable position in the community and came from a good Catholic family. Simply put, he was a catch.

"I have some questions regarding the recent string of murders."

Edwina and Luke both crossed themselves.

Betty looked into his shiny hazel eyes and there was

something familiar about Luke, but for the life of her, she couldn't place him.

"I figured as much," Luke said, and he was able to regain his composure. "Why don't we talk in my office?"

Betty followed him down the hall and into his office, where she took a seat in the chair across from his desk. She watched him pick up the file on the murders and put it away in the top drawer of his desk before locking it. He stood by the open window behind his desk and stared out over Main Street in deep contemplation. Betty waited for him to speak first.

Luke took a deep breath. "I'm sorry to inform you, Miss Boudreaux, that I can't give you any information about the case at this time. Out of respect for the families that have lost their children, it is the Sheriff's department's official stance to not speak to the press until we have caught the person responsible."

"I see," Betty said as she folded her hands in her lap and sat back in her chair. "That is very unfortunate."

"Sorry to disappoint you." Luke took a seat at his desk and lit himself a cigarette. "I have a duty to protect this town. I can't have the press coming in and mudding up the waters of this investigation."

"Oh, but on the contrary, Sheriff." Betty lit a cigarette. "I've noticed that the police department here in Ville Morte is rather small. And while that may be sufficient under normal circumstances, this case is not the norm. Having the press on your side can get the attention of the right people and the right people can help get these murders solved."

"I've asked the state for help but they're dragging their feet."

"That's precisely my point. Once word gets out past the city limits of Ville Morte, and the larger public start demanding a resolution, the state will have no choice but to send the help you need."

"Hmm. That's an interesting point, Miss Boudreaux." He tapped his fingers on the desk while he thought about it. "Alright, you can ask me one question."

There was something about his mischievous smile that was disarming and familiar, but still, she couldn't place him. "Why don't you tell me about that missing boy."

Luke sat forward and leaned on the desk. He let out a deep sigh as he hung his head, "He ain't missin' no more." He stopped to clear his throat. Luke did his best to mask his accent when talking to people outside of Ville Morte. He noticed they didn't take him seriously when he used it, but every now and then it slipped out.

"You found him?"

"What was left of him." He rubbed his eyes. The images of the mutilated body haunted him.

"Was he found like the others?"

"Yep," Luke said, looking down.

"I assume you took photos of the crime scene." "We did."

"May I see them?"

Luke's eyes shot up at her. "No, ma'am, you can't." He was shocked by her boldness.

She gave a little smile. "It would save you the trouble of having to answer all these questions."

"That file is confidential. Now if you'll excuse me, I need to get back at it."

"Of course. Thank you for your time, Sheriff." Betty stood up and shook his hand. When she put her hand in his, that feeling of familiarity came over her once more.

Chapter 13

Betty walked out of the small police station and strolled down Main Street toward her car. When she rounded the corner, she caught a glimpse of Frank leaning against a street pole, smoking a cigarette. Smoke billowed from his mouth. His top shirt was unbuttoned, exposing his undershirt which clung to his muscular body. He glistened with sweat in the hot Louisiana sun. A hungry smile spread across her lips and she noticed a stirring in her loins that made her feel bold.

"Hello there," Betty said, the smile still lingering on her lips.

Frank recognized the look in her eyes and cocked up an eyebrow. "I got you something."

"Did you?" Betty took the cigarette from between his fingers and helped herself. "Well, let's see it."

Frank reached down into the bag of groceries he had at his feet and lifted out a small brown paper bag. "Just a little something to say I told you so." He gloated and handed her the bag before he started to button up his shirt. "Keeping my French a secret just may have paid off."

She playfully rolled her eyes as she took the bag from him. She pulled out a bottle of whiskey and laughed. "Much more appreciated than flowers."

"I thought as much," Frank said, proud that he possessed the ability to please her. He pushed himself off of the street pole and winced in pain as soon as he put his full weight on his bad leg.

Betty noticed and made sure to keep a slower pace as they walked down the street toward the car. They walked together, so close that their hands kept accidentally brushing up against each other. Neither made any attempt to pull away. When they approached the car, Betty just kept on walking.

"Where are you going?" Frank asked.

"We've got to do something about that leg."

"My leg is fine." He looked away, embarrassed.

"Your leg is not fine. You've been limping all morning. Clearly, you're in pain."

"It's just the weather. Whenever the pressure drops, my leg hurts. It'll pass as soon as the rain does."

"Frank," Betty stopped to look him in the eye. "This is Southern Louisiana, it rains every day in the summertime. We need to take care of your leg."

Frank grinned and leaned over, bumping his shoulder into her playfully. "Betty, are you concerned about me?"

"No." She flirtatiously pushed him away. "I'm concerned about the article. What did you find out?"

"It may be nothing, but I overheard the grocer, Romero, talking to his friend about a man named Beaux Guilbeau. I'm not sure how useful it will be; they did refer to him as a ghost."

"Hmm, that is odd, but we have to start somewhere. I didn't get much out of the police. But I think the Sheriff can be persuaded to help us."

Betty stopped in front of a wood building painted blue

and white with a large front porch. There were two small bay windows on either side of the front door. Each had a mannequin display, one with women's fashion and the other with men's fashion. A large sign hung that read *La Corde à Linge*.[24] Betty stopped to admire a dress in the window.

"Just exactly how is a dress shop supposed to help my leg?"

"I guess you'll just have to trust me." Betty gave him a half-smile.

Inside, there was a woman sweeping the floor. She was in her late fifties but still retained a youthful glow. The skin around her face was taut except for a few crow's feet around her piercing green eyes. Her hair was a rich brown that was beginning to gray at the temples, and she wore it swept up in a loose French twist. She was a little wider in the hips than the last time Betty had seen her, but she still maintained her hourglass figure.

The woman looked up when Betty and Frank walked in and she broke out into a wide smile. "I knew I was gonna have visitors today. I was hoping it would be you." She set her broom down and embraced Betty in a hug.

"*Tante*[25] Viv," Betty exclaimed. "I guess Madeline told you I was in town."

"No, *cher*,[26] it was the Gift. And who's your friend?" Vivian eyed Frank curiously.

"Oh, this is my colleague, Frank. Frank, this is my Aunt Vivian."

As Frank shook Vivian's hand, he could feel her eyes looking

---

[24] La Corde à Linge: The Clothes line

[25] Tante: Aunt

[26] cher: darling

into his soul, as if she knew all his secrets, even the ones he kept from himself. He felt naked and exposed.

Vivian gazed at him with pity in her eyes. *"C'est la vie,"*[27] she said, mostly to herself. "Nothing a good cup of coffee can't fix. Y'all come on in the back, I just put on some coffee."

They followed Vivan through a door that led to a parlor in the back of the shop.

"Have a seat, *s'il vous plaît."*[28] Vivan motioned for them to sit in the loveseat. "I'll go get the coffee," she said and then disappeared from the room.

Betty looked over at Frank. He was staring down at his hands folded in his lap. "Is everything okay? You seem a bit tense."

"Yeah. It's just your aunt, is um…"

Betty shook her head. "Tante Viv has that effect on people. She has a way of making you feel vulnerable. She's a bit psychic."

"I'm better known as a *traiteur."*[29] Vivian reappeared in the room, carrying a tray topped with three full cups of coffee and bowls of sugar and cream. She set the tray down on the coffee table. "Help yourselves." She grabbed her cup and sat down in a cozy chair across from them.

"So, Tante Viv, I was wondering if you would tell us a little about your time in France. I've been curious about that lately."

"Oh yes. I lived in Paris for almost five years. I did some modeling, if you can believe that." She laughed at the memory of her youth. "I studied dress design. Shamelessly ran around

---

[27] C'est la vie: That's life

[28] s'il vous plaît: please

[29] traiteur: folk healer

the Latin Quarter with my artist friends. I loved it."

"Why on earth did you ever come back?" Betty asked.

"Well, Madeline, who you both know, has always been my closest friend. I received a letter from her one day. Her cousin passed away." Vivian paused and closed her eyes. She let the memory of him come to the forefront of her mind. A faint smile shrouded in sorrow formed on her lips. "He and I were close for a time. I wanted to give him a proper goodbye and pay my respects." Heartache wrapped itself around her voice like a snake strangling its prey. "When I came back from France, I found your mother, Marie, who is actually my second cousin, on the verge of blossoming into a young lady. Her mother had died when Marie was a little girl. I could see her father needed help. Poor fool had no clue how to raise a daughter. I took it upon myself to help bring her up. I owed her mother at least that much." A reflective sadness passed through her eyes. "How is your mama, by the way?"

"Not well, I'm afraid." Betty took a sip of her coffee.

Vivian let out a heavy sigh. "I figured as much. That poor girl has had more than her fair share of hardship and loss."

"Sometimes I think we might be cursed."

"I certainly know how you feel," Vivian responded. "Anyway, how are you? How's life in the big city? Do you still enjoy working for the paper?"

"Oh yes, I love it. I couldn't possibly imagine doing anything else."

"That's wonderful. And what about you, Frank, tell me about yourself."

"There's not much to say. I'm afraid I'm not that interesting."

Vivian leaned back in her chair and eyed him carefully. "Oh, I very much doubt that."

149

"Well, I'm originally from Kansas, I just moved to Louisiana about ten months ago with my wife and daughter and this is my first assignment for the paper."

"That's actually why we're here," Betty interjected. "We're covering the story about those young people who were murdered."

"Isn't it just so sad? Those poor kids, they were just babies. It's all anyone can talk about."

Betty turned to Frank. "What was that name you heard this morning?"

"Beaux Guilbeau. Someone in town may have implicated him in connection to the murders."

"Do you know anyone by that name, Tante Viv?"

Vivians eyes grew dark, her body tensed up, and she got very serious. She took a sip of her coffee before answering. "We don't talk about Beaux, out of respect for Suzette. You'll remember her, Betty, she's my business partner and a dear friend. Beaux was her brother...and he's been dead for a very long time. Now that's all I'll say on the matter."

Just then, there was a low rumble of thunder in the distance. "Guess it's about time for the afternoon rainstorm," Vivan said, changing the subject.

"Oh, that reminds me, Tante Viv, Frank is having some pain in his left leg. Do you think you can help?"

"I'm sure I can do something. What happened to it, if you don't mind my asking?"

"War," Frank replied.

"Aah, well I've helped many a soldier in my day. Come with me, I'll fix you up."

Frank followed Vivian down the hall and around the corner into a small dark room. Inside it smelled of sage and eucalyptus. Across from the doorway, there was a tiny window, the only source of light in the room. Outside, the storm clouds blocked the sunlight; it gave the room an eerie ambiance.

The walls were lined with rows and rows of shelves, cluttered with glass bottles all stuffed with herbs, or salts, or oils. Thunder rumbled low overhead and reverberated through the room. The jars on the wall vibrated; they seemed to come alive and clink around with the hopefulness that they would be chosen.

Pushed up against the left wall was a small worktable. The shelves and drawers around it were full of curious tools and instruments. Half-spent white pillar candles were placed at each corner of the tabletop.

Vivian struck a match and lit all four candles. She gestured to a large wooden exam table in the middle of the room. "Remove your trousers and lay down on the table, s'il vous plaît," Vivian instructed. "The blanket is for your modesty." She turned her back.

Frank took off his pants, lay down on the table, and covered all of himself except for his left leg.

"And what's the nature of the injury?" Vivian asked, her back still turned.

"Broken femur and some shrapnel."

"Very good. Now, I need you to stay quiet and relax. Try to focus your mind on something pleasant."

His first thought was of Avril. But the thought brought up unsettled feelings. He could feel his body tense up as his mind turned to Ava and the shame of his marriage.

"Pleasant feelings, monsieur," Vivian said.

Frank took a deep breath and released his family. It almost

surprised him when the image of Betty came forth in his mind. It was a memory from earlier that morning. She was smiling at him with powdered sugar on her nose. He could feel himself begin to relax and he heard Vivian chuckle quietly to herself.

Her hands moved quickly around the shelves, pulling down jars. She poured some of the contents of each carefully chosen jar into a mortar. Another clap of thunder. Using the pestle, she crushed her ingredients together. Then she took a dollop of lard from a tin canister and plopped it into a clay bowl. Vivian rubbed the herb and salt mixture from the mortar between her fingers and sprinkled it into the lard. With an eye dropper, she added a fragrant oil and mixed everything together.

She walked over to the exam table with an armful of things. Thick rain drops began to spatter against the window. With her left hand, she waved a smoldering sage bundle over his leg. In her right hand, she waved a hawk feather to direct the smoke. The wind outside picked up. She set down her tools and laid hands on him.

Vivian chanted in French that Frank could not understand. He could feel heat coming off her hands. It seeped into his leg, wrapped itself around his bone, and swirled through him. After her third incantation, she scooped out a glob of the lard mixture and massaged it into his thigh. Once it was absorbed into the skin, she paused for a count of three and then repeated the ritual twice more.

The storm raged outside. Thunder boomed. Wind gusted and howled. Rain beat down on the tin roof.

As the third and final round of the ritual came to an end, he felt alleviated from his pain. It was so vivid that he could almost see it leave his body, like mist dissipating in sunlight.

Vivian took some muslin cloth and wrapped it around his thigh. "There, that should hold. You need to come back in three days so we can do it again." She smiled down at him.

"It already feels better." Frank was shocked that it worked so well. His leg hadn't felt this normal since the injury. Perhaps Vivian did possess a gift.

* * *

Once the storm had passed, Frank and Betty headed back to the boarding house. When they pulled up, Madeline was sitting on the front porch.

"Hey, how y'all doing?" she called out to them as they got out of the car. "I got some fresh sweet tea if y'all want some."

"That sure does sound nice, thank you, ma'am," Frank said when he stepped up on the porch. He poured a glass and handed it to Betty, who was right behind him.

"No, thank you," she said, and Frank kept the glass for himself. "So, Betty," Madeline began, "have ya been by ta see ya Tante Viv?"

"Yes, actually we just came from there."

"Dat's good. I know she misses ya."

Just then, Luke Landry walked out of the house, wiping his hands with an old rag.

"Sheriff Landry," Bettey exclaimed, "what are you doing here?"

"Oh, dis is my grandson, Luke. You remember don't ya, Betty? The two of ya spent damn near everyday together dat summer you came ta visit."

Suddenly the memory of the summer she turned sixteen

came flooding back to her. "Luke Landry, of course I remember now. Why didn't you say anything earlier?"

"Oh, I figured it would come back to you sooner or later." He smiled and gave her a playful wink. "Well Maw Maw," he turned to Madeline, "dat leak in the kitchen should be all fixed now. I got ta get back ta work." He leaned in and gave his grandmother a kiss on the cheek.

"Alright baby, you come by Sunday for supper."

"Yes, ma'am." Luke put his hat on and then turned to Betty. "Miss Boudreaux, it was a pleasure, as always." He tipped his hat to her and walked off the porch.

Betty touched her finger to her lips and remembered all the stolen kisses they had shared. She wondered how she ever could have forgotten about Luke Landry and their summer romance.

Frank saw the smile Betty gave to Luke as he drove away. There was no use denying it, he was downright jealous.

Chapter 14

The sun had not yet fully risen on that early Friday morning. It left the kitchen on Eleonore Street dark. Ava sat at the dining table and glared at the telephone on the wall. The ashtray was full, the wine bottle was empty. She spent all night watching the phone and willing it to ring. One by one, she chewed her fingernails down to the quick, only stopping after she tasted blood.

Ava lit herself a cigarette.

Why hadn't Frank called? Had she done something to upset him? Of course she had, she shouldn't have been so clingy when he left. She shouldn't have cried. Damn it, why did she have to cry? She was always so weak when it came to him. Why couldn't she just be stronger? Ava cringed at the memory of herself on her knees, tears and snot running down her face as she sobbed and begged him not to leave, grasping at his pant leg like a desperate child. But she wouldn't have to resort to such tantrums if only he showed her the slightest bit of regard or affection. He starved her for love. What else could she do but cause a scene? It was the only time he ever paid any attention to her. It was his own fault that she behaved this way.

How dare he treat her like this? After everything she had done for him. She was the mother of his child, his precious Sunshine, and still, he left her to rot in the shadows.

But it was odd that he didn't call to speak to Avril. He didn't just promise Ava that he would call every day, he also promised Avril. He rarely broke a promise to his daughter, only in instances in which it couldn't be helped. Perhaps something terrible happened. He was chasing down a murderer, after all. Or maybe there had been a car accident, it was a long drive. Ava conjured an image in her mind of Frank's mangled body lying dead on the side of the road somewhere. *Oh mon dieu,*[30] no, not that. She loved him so much. She would die if something happened to him.

She couldn't live without him. Something was keeping him from calling. Deep down, she knew there was only one reason…Betty. That whore was trying to get her claws into her husband. She had been causing trouble since the day she came into their lives. And now Frank was trapped with that vile woman. What sort of tricks was she using to get at him? Would Frank be dumb enough to succumb to her schemes? What man wouldn't fall for her charms? Betty was beautiful and smart and fashionable, everything Ava was not. But no, no, Frank was a good man. He was flawed and difficult at times, but he was a good man and true to his word, even if it meant his own downfall.

Ava lit herself a cigarette.

Why hadn't Frank called? Had she done something to upset him?

---

[30] Oh mon dieu: Oh my god

* * *

Miss Edgar pinned her ears back and let out a deep growl before hissing and swatting at Robert. She was crouched on top of his bookshelf. Robert jumped back and spilled the saucer of milk he was trying to give her down his shirt.

"I am just trying to be nice to you, you old mean thing. I could have just left you in that dark apartment all by yourself." He walked back to the kitchen to pour some more milk in the saucer.

"Who are you talking to?" Matthew asked.

"The cat," Robert said sharply. He swung open the refrigerator door and grabbed the bottle of milk.

"What cat?"

"Miss Edgar. We agreed to watch her while Betty was away, remember." He was careful not to look at Matthew as he poured the milk into the saucer.

"No, you agreed to look in on her, not bring her here."

"She was lonely all by herself."

"Robert, you have literally brought evil into our house." He tried to lighten the mood by making a joke.

"She's not evil," Robert snapped and set the milk bottle down on the counter with a thud, "she's just scared." He left Matthew in the kitchen alone to bring the saucer of milk to Miss Edgar.

Matthew sighed deeply. He was at his wit's end trying to make things up to Robert, but obviously he was still upset about the Betty situation.

"Goddammit!" Robert yelled and then there was a loud crash.

Matthew rushed to the living room to see what all the

commotion was about. Robert was standing there with blood running down his hand. Spilled milk and a broken saucer lay on the floor. Miss Edgar was still atop the bookcase, tucked tight against the wall, her fur standing on end.

"Lord almighty, are you alright?" Matthew asked and tried to examine Robert's hand. "Here, let's wash it."

Robert pulled away. "No, it's okay. I can do it." He walked to the kitchen with Matthew trailing behind him.

"Are you still mad at me?"

Robert didn't answer, he just ran his hand under the cold water.

"I don't want to fight with you anymore." Matthew's voice was soft and low.

Robert hung his head. "I don't want to fight with you anymore, either. I hate it when we fight."

Matthew took a step closer. "Then let's not fight. Kiss and make up?" He stroked Robert's arm.

Robert looked up and gave him a coy smile, then leaned in and kissed him. Matthew wrapped his arms around him. He pulled Robert close and held him tight. Matthew cradled the back of Robert's head and ran his fingers through his hair. "I love you," he whispered in Robert's ear.

"I love you too." Robert replied. He stepped back so he could look Matthew in the eye. "And I know you're sorry. It's just, well, I can't shake this feeling that I'll never see Betty again. That's why I brought the cat here. That way she'll have to see us to pick her up."

Matthew put his hands on Robert's shoulder and looked him deep in the eyes. "I promise you, I'll make things right with Betty. Whatever it takes. Don't worry, you'll see her again."

* * *

Ava stood outside the office of *The New Orleans Post*. She wondered if she was crossing a line coming here, but Frank left her no choice. She hadn't heard a word from him since he left.

When she walked into the bullpen, it was busier than she expected, and yet not one person acknowledged her. She clutched her purse to her chest, feeling lost and out of place. People moved around her as if she wasn't even there. Ava was practically invisible.

"Can I help you?" She heard a squeaky woman's voice call out to her. Ava whipped her head around and saw Mary Ann sitting behind a desk and smiling at her. Ava scurried over to the desk.

"Yes. I am Frank Martin's wife. Has he called here?"

"You're Frank's wife?" Mary Ann said with a forced smile. "Have a seat." She pointed to a chair in front of her desk. "I haven't heard anything and most of the calls come through me but let me speak to Alan and see if he's heard from them. I know they're out of town." Mary Ann got up from her desk and walked into Alan's office.

Ava sat there, still clutching her purse. She wasn't sure what she was hoping for. If he had called here, it would mean he deliberately hadn't called her. If he hadn't called, it might mean something bad happened to him. She started chewing her fingernails.

Mary Ann reappeared and sat back down in her seat. She gave Ava a tight smile. "I'm sorry, Mrs. Martin, but neither of them has called to check in. He didn't leave a number where you can reach him?"

Ava shook her head.

"They didn't leave one with us, either." Mary Ann looked around to make sure no one was watching and slipped Ava a piece of paper. She leaned in, and in a hushed voice said, "Don't say you got this from me, but here's the address for the boarding house. Maybe an operator can help you find the phone number with this. Between you and me, I'd be worried too if I were you. That Betty Boudreaux is trouble."

Ava's heart dropped into the pit of her stomach. Her fear had been confirmed. She wasn't crazy, after all.

Chapter 15

Betty turned her car down an unpaved road. Gray storm clouds gathered overhead in the distance and blocked out the sun. It cast a gloom over the countryside. The wind kicked up and swayed the sugarcane growing tall in the fields along the road.

"How far out do they live?" Frank asked.

"They're cattle farmers, Frank. They live in the middle of a cow pasture."

"You sound like a snob, Betty."

"I resent that. I am not a snob."

"Take it from someone who grew up on a farm, you sound like a big city snob. You might want to rein that in before you ask them for an interview."

Betty looked at Frank and smiled. "I didn't know you grew up on a farm."

"Yeah, my family grows wheat out in Kansas."

"Well, aren't you full of surprises? Does that have anything to do with your troubles of '42? Let me guess, a bitter family dispute over the rights to the farm. You lost, causing a rift in the family and that's why you moved to Louisiana. Am I close?" Betty teased.

Frank cocked his head to one side and gave Betty a cheeky smile. "Not even a little bit."

"You know you still owe me that story."

"All in good time, my pretty, all in good time," Frank misquoted *The Wizard of Oz*.

They finally pulled up to the little farmhouse. It had a timber frame and sat on cypress blocks about two feet off the ground. The gable roof sloped down low and hung over the front porch. It was a classic Acadien-style home.

Chickens scattered around the front yard to avoid the car as Betty pulled in. They could see Mr. Quibodeaux working in the field nearby. She parked the car and shut off the engine.

"We can use your farm experience to our advantage. So, here's what I was thinking: we'll talk to the parents separately. I'll speak with Mrs. Quibodeaux, as I can relate to her about the murder of a close family member. And you can talk to Mr. Quibodeaux. Your way in with him can be fatherhood. And farming, apparently," Betty joked.

"You're the boss," Frank huffed. He gazed out the window and cocked his jaw.

"Is there a problem here, Frank?"

"Gee, I don't know, Betty, the man's daughter was just raped and murdered. I'm not sure how keen he's going to be on talking about farming with a stranger."

"Do I need to remind you what it is that we're doing here, Frank?

This is the job, getting people to open up about some of their most horrific experiences. Talking to them when they are at their most desperate and vulnerable."

"I know that, Betty, but you don't have to be so cavalier about it."

Betty leaned back in her seat and took a deep breath. "I'm not trying to be cavalier," she said softly. "But sometimes I have to turn down my feelings in certain situations. If I allowed myself to fully experience everything I felt in this case, I would never be able to get the job done. Do you understand?"

Frank turned his blue eyes to her. "I can understand that."

"It's sweet, though," Betty placed her hand over his, "that you care so much about these strangers."

Frank grazed the top of her hand with his thumb. They sat there for a moment in silence. There was a force between them, pulling them together. It felt inevitable.

Betty looked away first. "Okay then, let's be quick about it. I want to leave before the rain starts, otherwise the car is likely to get stuck in the mud."

They got out of the car and gave each other one last look before going their separate ways.

Frank walked off into the field toward Mr. Quibodeaux.

Betty stepped up onto the front porch and knocked on the door.

Mrs. Quibodeaux answered and gave Betty a puzzled look. "Can I help you?"

"Yes, my name is Betty Boudreaux and I'm with *The New Orleans Post*."

A sadness shifted into Mrs. Quibodeaux's eyes. "I see. I suppose ya wanna talk about Suzy."

"If that's alright with you?" Betty asked kindly.

"Come on in."

Betty followed her into the sitting room and took a seat. Mrs. Quibodeaux sat across from her.

"Can I get you somethin'? I can put some coffee on." It was an automatic response, years of instilled Southern manners.

163

"Oh no, don't go to any trouble on my account."

"You said ya name was Boudreaux, ya have any relations down here?"

"Yes. Amos and Marie Boudreaux are my parents."

"Oh," Mrs. Quibodeaux let out a breath. *"Mais* yeah, I rememba ya mama. She was a lil bit olda dan me. I used ta follow her aroun' like a lost little puppy. I wanted ta be jus' like Marie when I was growing up." She looked down at her hands. "Seems she and I got a lil bit in common dese days. I was very sorry ta hear about ya brother."

"Thank you." Betty gave her an uncomfortable smile. "Why don't you tell me about Suzy," she encouraged Mrs. Quibodeaux to keep talking.

"She was a good girl, a real good girl. Suzy never gave no trouble. An' so beautiful. She won da Miss Magnolia pageant last year." Tears welled up in her eyes. "You know dey give da winner college money now."

"No, I didn't know that," Betty said in a soft voice.

"Suzy was gonna be da first Quibodeaux ta go ta college. She wanted ta be a nurse. She wanted ta spend her life helpin' people." Her lip quivered. "She loved helpin' people." Mrs. Quibodeaux's voice cracked, and her composure broke. "I jus' don't understand." She let out a deep and heavy sob. "I don't understand why it had ta be my child dat died." She covered her face in her hands and wept. Mrs. Quibodeaux tried to regain her composure, but her voice was still shaky, her face red with emotion. "If you'll excuse me, Miss Boudreaux, I think I will go put dat coffee on, after all."

"Yes, of course."

As Mrs. Quibodeaux left the room, Betty leaned her head back and stared at the ceiling. She let out a deep breath. It was heartbreaking to watch. This scene was all too familiar, the suffering all too real. Betty tried to remain professional but sitting across from this grieving mother brought up the pain from her past. She couldn't help but see her own mother in this woman. All her old wounds threatened to rip themselves open. She had to get out of there. Betty sat up and began to gather her things, but when she glanced around the room, she saw a young girl, around twelve, standing in the hallway, looking at her.

"Hello," Betty said.

"Hello," the girl replied as she stepped farther into the room. "I'm Jacqueline, Suzy's little sister."

"It's nice to meet you, Jacqueline. I'm Betty."

"Sorry about Mama, she hasn't been herself lately. I mean she is, but not really." Jacquline sat down next to Betty on the sofa.

"I know what you mean. When my brother died, my mama took to the bed and never really left."

Jacqueline searched Betty's eyes and saw her own pain reflected back at her. "How did he die?"

"He was murdered."

"Like Suzy." Tears danced in Jacqueline's eyes. "She was my best friend."

Betty reached out and held Jacqueline's hand. Jacqueline took a deep breath, "I just keep thinking that she'll walk up on the porch any minute." She took out a handkerchief and wiped her nose. "I know she won't, but still..."

Betty knew the torment that this young girl was going through.

All the anger of losing Edgar came rushing back to her and with it came the fire of justice. She vowed to herself that she would stop at nothing to catch this monster.

"Listen, Jacqueline, I want to help. I'm here to help find who did this to your sister."

"Oh, I know who killed my sister. It was that *mataille*[31] No Face."

"No Face? Who is No Face?" Betty's curiosity was piqued.

"Well, I've never seen him, but some of the older kids who hang out at Lover's Lane say they've seen a man out there before. There's something wrong with his face, like it's melted off or something. Nobody knows who he is. I always thought it was just something they said to scare us younger kids. I didn't believe he was real until now."

"Did you tell this to anyone?"

"None of the adults believed me. They said that it's just a ghost story."

"Thank you, Jacqueline. You've been very helpful. If you need anything, come find me, I'm staying at the Boarding House."

"Does it ever go away? The sadness, I mean," Jacqueline asked as Betty stood up to leave.

"No. Eventually you'll stop feeling it in everything you do and after some time, it won't sting quite so much. But deep down the loss is always there."

* * *

Frank walked across the pasture to where Mr. Quibodeaux was unloading hay bales.

---

[31] tataille: monster; boogeyman; scary creature

"Excuse me, sir, are you Mr. Quibodeaux?"

"I am. And you are?"

"I'm Frank Martin, I work for *The New Orleans Post.* Do you mind if I ask you a few questions?"

"No. I'm busy."

"You look like you could use a hand."

Mr. Quibodeaux stared at him blankly.

Frank rolled up his shirtsleeves. "I grew up farming. I could help."

"If I wanted help, I woulda asked ma neighbors." He stood on the bed of the truck and looked down on Frank.

"I don't mean to bother you at a time like this, it's just that my boss..."

"I don't give a damn about ya boss. Ma girl is dead. An' ya wanna put dat in ya paper for everybody ta read about."

"I know that this is a hard time for you and your family."

"You don't know shit, boy." He jumped down from the truck and puffed his chest out.

Frank braced himself. He thought for sure this man was going to punch him in the face. And rightfully so, in his opinion.

Mr. Quibodeaux glared at Frank with rage in his eyes. All he felt these days was rage, and deep sorrow. He did want to punch Frank in the face, not so much because Frank had upset him, but because he just wanted to take it out on someone. He could see that Frank wasn't going to put up a fight, which took the wind out of his sails. Mr. Quibodeaux took a step back, sat down on one of the hay bales, and pulled out a flask. He took a big swig and then handed it to Frank.

"You got kids, Frank?"

"Yeah." Frank smiled, thinking of Avril. "A daughter." He

had a small sip from the flask and then handed it back.

"How old?" He took another swig.

"She's three."

"Take ma advice, tell her dat ya love her every day. Spend as much time wit her as you can. Believe me when I say, nothing else matters." He fought back his tears. "Because you never know what kinda monster might steal her from you." He drained his flask. "Excuse me, I need ta go check on my wife. She hasn't been well."

He got up and left Frank to ponder how he might feel if he were in Mr. Quibodeaux's shoes. Dark storm clouds brewed overhead and a single fat raindrop fell from the sky.

Frank sat down on a hay bale, wishing he had more of whatever was in that flask. The helplessness of Mr. Quibodeaux was palpable, and Frank felt every inch of it in his soul. He couldn't imagine losing Avril that way. He couldn't imagine losing her at all. Then it dawned on him that he hadn't called home since he had been in Ville Morte.

What kind of man didn't call his family for four days? Four days was an eternity to a child.

He was startled out of his spiral when he felt a cold nose on the back of his hand. There sat Le Bleu, and she cozied up to him, easing his discomfort in a way that only a dog can.

"Hey there, girl," he said and scratched her on the head. She let out a groan of satisfaction and looked up at him with her ice-blue eyes. It was as if she could read his mind. The weight of his own judgment lay heavy on his shoulders. He knew he couldn't put off calling home any longer. His family deserved better.

Chapter 16

Frank glanced at his watch. He had enough time for a quick call home before he and Betty planned to leave for the *fais do-do*.[32]

He left his cabin and walked to the main house to use the phone.

He picked up the receiver, took a deep breath, and dialed the numbers. He would have to explain himself; Ava would be upset that he hadn't called sooner. It rang a couple of times.

"Hello?" a strange voice answered his phone.

"Hello? Who's this?"

"This is Bridget Riley. Who is this?"

Frank relaxed. Bridget was his neighbor who sometimes watched Avril. "Bridget, it's Frank."

"Oh," she laughed. "Frank, how are you? How's your trip going?"

"Splendid. How are things back home?"

"Your girls miss you, that's for sure. I'm afraid Ava isn't home right now, she had to run out. But she should be back any minute."

---

[32] fais do-do: weekend dance

Frank felt the tension leave his body. "Um, that's alright. Can you put Avril on?" Frank could hear her in the background, begging for the phone.

"Daddy!" she squealed when she came on the line.

"Hello, Sunshine." It hit him just how much he missed her when he heard the sound of her voice. As she babbled on about important toddler business, Frank's mind couldn't help but wander over to thoughts about Mr. Quibodeaux. It was overwhelming to think of such a loss. "Avril, my sunshine, I want you to know that I love you very much and I miss you terribly."

"I love you, too."

Frank got all choked up. It was the first time he heard her pronounce the letter L properly. He looked at the clock on the wall; it was time to go. "I have to go now but I want you to promise me that you'll behave while I'm away."

"Yeth, Daddy," Avril promised and handed the phone back to Bridget.

"Thanks for watching her, Bridget." The clock in the front hall struck six. "Um, tell Ava I called." He looked up just in time to see Betty glide through the front door. Everything flew right out of his head.

"Wait," Bridget was still on the line. "I think I hear Ava now." She saw Ava coming down the hall. "It's Frank," she mouthed and pointed to the phone.

Ava rushed over and grabbed the phone from her. "Frank?" He didn't hear her; he was already hanging up.

"Frank!"

Click. The line went dead.

"François!" she yelled into the receiver, but it was too late. She lost him. Ava slammed the phone into its cradle. She leaned her forehead and palms against the wall. Her shoulders shook as she wept silently. Everything she had been feeling bubbled up to the surface. All the worry, all the distrust, even all the hope, folded in on itself and alchemized into rage. Ava beat her hand against the wall. She was so tired of being invisible.

Betty looked stunning in her dark green dress. It had cuffed short sleeves that were rounded and pleated at the shoulders. It hit right at the knee and had a free-flowing skirt. She paired it with a matching marigold yellow belt and heels, which complemented her hair that was done in soft curls that framed her neck.

The kitchen door groaned when Madeline pulled it back. She peeked through the crack to spy on Betty and Frank. There was nothing she loved more than watching romance blossom. She couldn't wait to get to the *salle de danse*[33] and tell Vivian and Suzette all about it.

"Well, don't you look handsome." Betty smiled and adjusted Frank's tie for him. She smoothed it out and let her hand run down his chest.

"You look…" Frank let his words drop as he looked her up and down. "Perfect."

"Almost perfect," Luke said as he appeared at the front door.

"Oh, *mais la*," Madeline mumbled to herself when she saw Luke.

He would spoil the moment between them for sure. Madeline knew how he felt about Betty; poor fool hadn't stopped talking about her since she got to town. She loved Luke, he was her favorite grandson, but Madeline knew the difference

---

[33] salle de danse: dancehall

between true love and first love, although she wasn't sure Luke did.

Luke walked into the house holding a single short-stemmed peony. "I was hoping to run into you." He strutted over to Betty and gave her a kiss on the cheek. "This is for you." He tucked the flower behind her ear. "Now you look perfect."

Betty felt flattered. "Thank you. That's so sweet." She returned his kiss on the cheek.

Frank glared at Luke. He felt a flash of anger and his face grew hot. Who the hell did this guy think he was? Frank hoped that Betty wouldn't fall for such a cheap trick. If this joker knew anything about Betty, he would know that she preferred whiskey to flowers. He realized then that was privileged information and his anger turned to smugness, his glare to a smirk.

Madeline burst through the kitchen door. "Oh good, Luke, ya here. We should get a move on if we're picking up Vivian and Suzette."

"Save me a dance, Betty," Luke said as Madeline rushed him out the door.

At the last minute, Madeline leaned in toward Betty and whispered, "There's an open bottle of muscadine wine in the kitchen. Help yaself." She gave Betty a wink and flittered out the door.

Betty turned to Frank. "Shall we have some wine before we go?"

"Sure." He watched her hips sway as he followed her into the kitchen. "So," Frank uncorked the wine on the counter while Betty grabbed two clean mason jars from the cabinet. "What's going on between you and that sheriff?" Frank probed.

Betty set the glasses down in front of him. She observed

him as he precisely poured the content of the wine bottle evenly into each glass. Concentration looked sexy on him. "Nothing." She smirked. "Luke is just an old friend."

Frank leaned in to hand her the wine. "You might want to tell him that." He cocked his eyebrow and gave her a half smile.

Betty took a sip of wine. "Careful Frank, you sound jealous."

He rested his forearms on the counter and looked up at her. "What if I was?" Mischief shone in his eyes.

Betty took a sip of wine to hide her blushing face. She shouldn't feel this way about him.

Frank knew he shouldn't be flirting with her, but the way she looked tonight, he couldn't help himself.

They hid their growing feelings behind small talk and finished their wine.

"Shall we?" Betty asked.

"After you." Frank held the door open and followed her out of the kitchen. He was mesmerized by the rhythm of those hips.

* * *

Nestled in a field, Thibodeaux's Tavern was located on the far end of Main Street in an undeveloped part of town. The outside of the building wasn't much to look at; it was an old barn that had been converted into the local *salle de danse*.

Tonight was the first *fais do-do* since the murders. After two and half months of foregoing the weekly Saturday night dance, everyone in town agreed it was time to reinstate it. The proceeds from tonight were going to the families of the victims, and all of the townsfolk of Ville Morte were more than happy to come together for their neighbors. There would be plenty of food and music and drink and dancing. The whole town would be there tonight.

Betty and Frank approached the entrance to the *salle de danse* and stood in line to get inside. A warm breeze sent over the aroma of hot jambalaya. Frank's mouth began to water.

"I want whatever that smell is," he said.

Betty hadn't realized how hungry she was until now. "Me too."

They got to the front of the line and paid the dollar entry fee. An old woman with a long silver braid over her shoulder took their money.

"Excuse me," Betty asked, "where is the food line?"

The woman looked at her, confused, and shrugged her shoulders.

"I don't think she speaks English." Frank stepped up. *"Manger?"*[34] he asked her.

Her face brightened. "Ah, *manger!*" She pointed in the direction of the food.

"Merci beaucoup,"[35] Frank replied.

"Pas de quoi."[36] The old woman smiled wide; she didn't have a single tooth left in her head, but her eyes had the *joie de vivre.*[37]

They stepped inside the building and were hit with a wall of thick muggy air, but the whole place was alive with the spirit

---

[34] Manger: to eat

[35] Merci beaucoup: Thank you very much

[36] Pas de quoi: You're welcome

[37] joie de vivre: joy of life

of community and culture. A lively song boomed from the stage. The band moved along to the music they were playing from the soul.

Frank recognized Clovis Romero on stage playing the fiddle. Even though he was missing two fingers, he never missed a note.

The dance floor was a square in the middle of the room framed by a wooden rail to separate it from non-dancing areas. It was packed with people of all ages dancing a fast step. Men danced with their wives and girlfriends. Female friends danced together without reservation, and a few danced only with themselves.

To the left of the stage was a wooden platform packed with teenage boys. Above the platform hung a hand-painted sign that read *La cage aux chien.*[38] In an attempt to cut down on trouble-making, young men weren't allowed to roam the dancehall freely, except when they were dancing or asking for a dance.

The wall right of the stage was lined with tables for people to eat and watch the dancing. Sitting at a table with Madeline and Vivian, a woman with a round face and rosy cheeks threw her head back and let out a hearty laugh while fanning herself with a paper fan. Betty knew her as Suzette Guilbeau Trahan. *Tante* Mad must have said something funny because *Tante* Viv was doubled over laughing and clapping her hands together.

"Let's sit with the *Tantes.*" Betty pointed out their table. Frank nodded in agreement, and they each grabbed a plate of jambalaya and a bottle of beer.

"Betty!" All three *tantes* called out in unison when they saw

---

[38] La cage aux chien: the dog cage

her. "Betty, you remember your *Tante* Suzette?" Vivian asked.

"Of course I do." Betty smiled and wrapped her arms around Suzette in a tight hug. She was a few years younger than Vivian and Madeline, but the three of them were inseparable.

"Dis mus' be ya friend Frank." Suzette wiggled her eyebrows at Betty.

Betty blushed. "Yes, this is my friend Frank."

"Y'all sit down, *cher*." Madeline scooched over to make room for Betty. "We passin' a good time over here." She held up a flask and took a small sip.

Frank sat down next to Vivian and across from Betty, who sat between Madeline and Suzette.

"How's your leg, Frank?" Vivian asked him.

"It's amazing. I haven't had any pain since I saw you."

"*Très bien.*[39] I expect to see you back in my shop on Monday."

"Yes, ma'am," Frank replied as he took his very first bite of jambalaya, ever. A burst of flavor flooded his mouth and took over his senses. He couldn't focus on anything other than how good the food was. The rice was tender and plump from cooking in a thick savory broth. Fats from the chicken and smoked sausage blended together to give the dish a rich taste. It was spicy enough to make his nose run but not spicy enough to stop eating.

"How do you like it?" Betty asked.

Frank looked up at her with wide eyes. "It's the best goddamn thing I ever put in my mouth."

The women laughed as he continued to shovel spoonfuls of jambalaya into his mouth.

The song finished playing and Romero stood on the stage.

---

[39] Très bien: Very good

He commanded everyone's attention. "Listen up, y'all. I jus' wanna say thank y'all for coming out tonight. I know we been goin' through it lately wit' all da tragedy dat's befallen dis community. But it's times like dis dat we got ta come together and help support each other. Even though it's dark times, we gonna pull through because we got community. So let's embrace each other and shine our light together so we can make it through da dark times. Na Ima take me a lil break, but don't worry, da music's gonna continue wit out me."

There was a round of applause as Romero left the stage, and a new fiddler replaced him. Frank watched him walk across the dancehall to the bar.

Frank looked at Betty from across the table. "I need another beer, how about you?"

"Yes, please." She smiled.

They let their eyes linger a moment too long before Frank left the table.

Frank walked over to where Romero was waiting for his drink.

He was laughing through a conversation with the bartender. "And den Le Bleu comes runnin' 'round da corner wit a pair of *caneçons*[40] in her mout'. And who ya think I see?" He slapped his hand on the bar. "Thibodeaux, chasin' behin' dat dog, butt ass naked." He laughed so hard he nearly fell off his barstool. Clearly, he had been drinking on stage.

"Hey, Romero." Frank took a seat next to him.

"Eey, Frank."

"I enjoyed your speech. It was uplifting."

"Aah, *merci*," Romero said as he reached for his drink on

---

[40] caneçons: underwear

the bar. He took a sip and regarded Frank for a moment. "Ya know, I mite talk dumb, but I don't think, me. And ya know wut I think, Frank?" He was a little drunk. "I think ya speak French jus' fine. Na I cain't help but wonder why ya would keep dat secret."

"Like you said, you're not dumb. You know why."

"I do know why, cuz dats exactly wut I'd do if I was tryin' ta get information. So wut kinda information ya after, Frank?"

"What can you tell me about Beaux Guilbeau?"

Back at the table Suzette giggled, "Oh child, he's a dish."

"What I would give to have a man look at me like that again." Vivian sipped from the flask and passed it to Betty.

"Yes, well, he's married." Betty sipped, then passed to Suzette.

"*Mais*," Madeline said, "he don't seem too married ta me." The more she drank, the more her accent came out.

"Y'all are terrible." Betty laughed.

"She manipulates him," Suzette blurted out. Her eyes were closed, and they danced back and forth behind her eyelids. "She manipulates him with her tears."

"You can see dat?" Madeline asked.

Suzette popped her eyes open and looked at Madeline. "Mais yeah, I can see dat. He carries it around on his shoulders everywhere he goes. Ya tellin' me ya can't hear dat?"

"No, I been blockin' it out lately. I can't handle it right na wit everything dats been goin on around town."

"I felt it," Vivian spoke up. "I felt it when he came in for a healing."

"What are you all talking about?" Betty looked at each of them, confused.

"I know ya mama told ya about da gift, *cher*," Suzette

answered.

"The Gift." Betty rolled her eyes. "A lot of good that did our family," she scoffed.

Everyone grew quiet and a sadness fell over the table.

Each Tante put a hand on Betty to comfort her, and she could feel the power of these women vibrate through her body.

Then Madeline started to laugh. "Do y'all remember the time that Marie and Babette got caught sneaking into the bar?"

Suzette and Vivian started laughing as well.

Their laughter began to lift Betty's sadness. "I don't think I've heard this story."

"Vivian, you tell it," Suzette said between giggles.

"Well," Vivian began, "your mama and her cousin Babette were about fourteen at the time. And it was at a Saturday night *fais do-do*, much like this one tonight. Back then, the bar was separate from the dance floor. Well, Marie's daddy told her that she was not to ever go on that side of the curtain. He didn't want her drinking or to be around a bunch of drunk *coonasses*.[41] Your mama was a good girl, but Babette was wild, always gettin' into trouble. She wanted to go to the bar, so she convinced Marie that they could sneak over and have one drink without getting caught. So off they went. Now, I was sitting there and saw the whole thing. They ordered drinks and sat down at a table. I could see that Marie was nervous as can be. I don't think she really wanted to do it. But Babette was lovin' it, she loved trouble more than anything. So, there they were and just as Marie went to take her first sip, outta

---

[41] coonasses: a slur referring to Cajuns

nowhere her daddy comes up an' knocked that glass right out of her hand. He had been sitting in the corner, watching the whole time. Oh, he was so mad, he didn't even have to say a word, he just glared at her. He marched her straight outta there by the ear. She never touched a drop of alcohol ever again."

Betty laughed. "Mama never told me that story."

"*Mais,* I imagine she wouldn't," Suzette said. "She was pretty *honte*[42] 'bout dat."

"*Pauvre bête,*[43] her daddy whooped her behind so bad she couldn't sit for a week," Vivian said.

"Keyaww, y'all remember how mad she was at Babette?" Madeline took her turn with the flask.

"Did Mama stop being friends with Babette? I've never heard her talk about her before."

The three women exchanged glances. "Sometimes I wish we had." Suzette sighed.

"She had a spiteful heart," Vivian said.

"Trouble followed her wherever she went," added Madeline.

Suzette took a gulp from the flask. "She took up with my brother, Beaux. They brought the worst out in each other."

Vivian and Madeline exchanged glances and tensed up.

Suzette had a tendency to have loose lips when she drank. Vivian reached over and gently placed her hand over Suzette's to quiet her. Betty could feel the tension between them.

"And where is Babette now?" Betty asked.

"Shreveport, last anyone heard," Madeline said. "But that's enough of that talk. Here comes Luke."

---

[42] honte: embarrassed

[43] Pauvre bête: Poor thing; poor fool

Luke walked up to the table. "Hope you don't mind, but can I steal Betty away for a minute?"

"By all means, don't let us stop you," Madeline said.

"What can I do for you, Luke?" Betty flirted as she stood up from the table.

"Well, I was hoping to buy you a drink and then to have that dance you promised me."

"That sounds nice." Betty linked her arm in his and they walked to the bar.

"I'm glad to see you're still wearing my flower," Luke said. "I do love peonies." Betty smiled.

"I remember."

"So," she leaned on the bar, "have you given any more thought into giving me an official statement for my article?" Betty shamelessly batted her eyes at Luke.

"I've given it quite a bit of thought, but I haven't made up my mind about it yet."

"I understand. But you should know that the article is getting written whether we have your help or not."

"We, as in that fella Frank?" Luke pointed to Frank, who was at the other end of the bar chatting with Romero.

Betty looked over her shoulder. Frank was watching them. She turned back to Luke. "Yes, as in Frank."

"Is he your fella?"

"No," Betty blushed, "he's my assistant."

"Well, ain't you fancy," Luke teased.

"I don't like to brag."

"That don't sound like the Betty Boudreaux I remember." He laughed.

"That was a long time ago."

"Not that long ago." Luke looked into her eyes, hoping to

see that old spark rekindled.

"You know you don't have to give me a statement, you could just let me have a look at the file."

"Betty, I'm not letting you see that file," he said with a condescending laugh.

His tone rubbed Betty the wrong way. "And why not, exactly?"

He took a step closer and grabbed her elbow. Lowering his voice, he said, "Trust me, Betty. A woman shouldn't see that."

"That's awfully presumptuous of you, Luke." She yanked her elbow away from him.

Suddenly, Frank was at her back. "Do you have this, Betty?"

"I have it." She leaned against Frank's chest. Being close to him made her feel calm.

Luke narrowed his eyes. "You got some nerve, Betty Boudreaux, coming back here after all this time and demanding shit from me." He couldn't help but feel like she had been toying with him. "Y'all have a nice night." He shook his head and walked off.

"What was that about?" Frank asked.

Betty watched Luke storm off. "Nothing. But I think it's safe to say the police won't be helping us." She knew she needed the details of the crimes to move forward. She turned her attention back to Frank. "What about you? Did you get anything out of Romero?"

"I was trying to work the Beaux Guilbeau angle. Romero said he doesn't remember much, he was just a little boy when Beaux was around. What he did remember was that Beaux had been a local accordion player, but he died mysteriously about twenty years ago. Said Beaux is buried out in the old cemetery. He remembers going to the funeral with his family.

People say his ghost still haunts the bayou. So I'm pretty sure it's a dead end."

Betty lit a cigarette. "I don't know, my gut tells me there's something more to the story. It came up in conversation with the *tantes* and they all got real nervous about it." She handed Frank the cigarette and he took a puff.

"I think we're wasting our time on this lead."

"Maybe. But it might be worth a trip out to the cemetery."

Frank handed her the cigarette and cocked his eyebrow. "And what, you plan on digging him up?"

"Hmm, that does sound like me," she joked.

"Whatever you want, Betty." He looked in her eyes and smiled. "You're the boss."

"Well, what I want is to dance. You do dance, don't you, Frank?" She took a drag.

Frank chuckled. "I do. But I've never danced to Cajun music before."

"It's been awhile for me but I think we can stumble our way through it." She stamped out the cigarette. "I may even let you lead."

Frank took her by the hand and led her to the crowded dance floor. The band began to play a slower song, "Jolie Blonde."[44]

"Oh, I love this song," Betty proclaimed, and Frank pulled her close.

"Pretty blonde," he translated and looked down at her with soft eyes. He didn't expect that holding her in his arms would make him feel this way. It was electric and he was helplessly drawn to her. He had never met a force like Betty.

---

[44] Jolie Blonde: Pretty Blonde

Betty studied his face as they danced: his jawline, his cheekbones, those full lips and blue eyes. Frank truly was beautiful. A beautiful, tenderhearted man. She felt things for him that she knew she shouldn't; after all, he belonged to someone else. But no one had ever looked at her the way he did.

As they moved across the dance floor, everyone else seemed to fade away. It felt like they were the only two people in the room. They both knew that they couldn't be together, but they could at least have this moment.

A loud commotion off the dance floor broke the spell. Betty looked around and found it jarring to see so many people when just a moment ago, she had felt as if she were alone with Frank.

They turned around just in time to see Romero punch Father Klein square in the jaw, sending him backward into a table. Jambalaya and beer went flying everywhere. Father Klein tried to stand up, but Romero rushed at him and tackled him to the ground.

One bystander got pushed into a woman, her husband got upset and shoved the other man. After a few heated words, they soon began fighting and someone else was pushed, and so on and so forth until a small brawl had erupted.

Betty watched as Luke and the other deputies rushed to break it up. "That's it," she said more to herself than to Frank.

"What?" Frank asked.

"Come with me. I have an idea."

Chapter 17

"Betty, this plan is insane."

"Don't be such a ninny, Frank," Betty said as she crossed the street and walked over to the empty police station.

"You can't just break into the police station and steal a case file." Frank followed after her.

"We're not stealing it, we're just borrowing it." She trotted over to the side of the building where Sheriff Landry's office was. "We'll put it back after we've had a good look at it." She approached the window to his office and pushed up on the glass. It opened without hesitation. None of the windows had locks in Ville Morte and she knew this one would be no different. "And it's not breaking in if the window is unlocked."

"I don't think that the police will see it that way," Frank protested.

"Well, they'll have to catch us first. And nobody is around. The entire town, including all the police, are at the *fais do-do*." She pulled herself up and sat on the ledge of the window.

"Betty! This is ridiculous. Get out of there."

"Aren't you the least bit curious as to what's in that file?"

"Of course I am, but we can't do this."

185

"You don't have to do anything, just stay where you are and keep a lookout." She swung her legs over and disappeared into the dark office.

"Goddamnit, Betty," Frank hissed as he stepped into the shadow of the building.

With only the light from the streetlamp outside, Betty began to riffle through the scattered papers on the desktop. She knew what the file looked like, she had seen it on the day she interviewed Luke, but none of these were it. She tried the top drawer.

Locked.

She reached in her hair to pull out her lucky bobby pin. The one that had been specially made for her. When she pulled it out, her hand brushed against the peony Luke had tucked behind her ear and knocked both the flower and the pin to the floor. Betty heard it clink on the wooden floorboards.

"Shit," she whispered and dropped to her knees to find it.

Meanwhile, Frank was still outside, crouched down next to the building. His heart was pounding as he waited. He couldn't believe he had let Betty talk him into this. There was no way they were going to get away with it.

A strange sensation came over him. The hairs on the back of his neck stood up and despite the warm night, he had goosebumps on his skin. Frank had the distinct feeling of being watched. Something rustled in the bushes behind him. He whipped around to see what the noise was, only to find Le Bleu happily trotting up to him with a wagging tail.

"Hey girl," he said with relief. She sat down next to him, and Frank scratched her head while they waited for Betty together.

Betty crawled on the floor, trying to feel around in the dark for her hair pin. She knew she didn't have much time. The only way this plan worked was to be lickety-split about it.

"Damnit." She pushed the desk chair aside and reached her hand under the desk. Her fingers groped around in the dust bunnies. Time was wasting, but she didn't want to give up just yet. Finally, her fingertips found the missing pin.

Frank aggressively petted Le Bleu in a vain attempt to calm his anxiety when suddenly, she stood up on full alert. Her body was stiff as she turned to face down Main Street. She tilted her head from side to side to hear better and took a few steps forward, her nose sniffing at the air.

Frank stepped farther into the shadows. "What is it, girl?" he asked and listened carefully. Le Bleu ran off around the corner toward the sound.

"Eey, it's Le Bleu." Frank heard a drunk man greeting the little dog and then Le Bleu returned the greeting with a friendly yap. Frank recognized the voice; it was Romero. He was being escorted to the station in handcuffs by Luke.

"Fuck," Frank whispered to himself, and he pressed his back against the wall. He was certain that they were about to be found out. His mind raced as he tried to think of a reasonable excuse as to why he would be outside the police station.

The two men came around the corner. Romero stumbled along as Luke pulled him by the arm up the street.

"Is dis really necessary?" Romero slurred.

"*Mais*, I'd say so. You cain't just go around punchin' da priest and startin' fights, Romero."

Le Bleu walked alongside the men and circled around them, keeping them confined to the sidewalk. She was herding them up the street away from Frank.

He heard their voices fade away as they walked into the

station.

Frank stuck his head in the window and saw Betty on her knees struggling to pick the lock. "Hurry!" he said in a hushed whisper. "Luke just brought Romero in."

A light from the hallway glowed under the door.

"Damn. Damn. Damn," Betty said. She had been working on the lock, but it was old and tricky.

"Betty, just leave it, we have to get out of here," Frank pleaded with her.

"No. I almost have it." She couldn't give up now, she was too close. The sound of footsteps and muffled voices were getting closer.

She felt the lock click and the drawer opened. There it was, sitting right at the top. Betty snatched the folder and raced to the window

"Got it." She waved the file and handed it to Frank as she climbed out the window.

"Let's get the hell out of here." Frank took her by the hand and led her around the back of the police station to avoid Main Street.

They rounded the other side of the building and were about to make a run for it.

"Wait." Frank pulled Betty back by the hand into the shadows. A group of lively people were leaving the *fais do-do*. He looped his arm around her waist and pressed her tight against his body so that they were face to face. Adrenaline pumped through their bodies. They were glued together in an intense stare. Frank felt the rush of exhilaration. He felt alive. Their chests heaved together with a fiery lust in their bellies. Betty could feel his breath on her lips, and she yearned to be closer.

Then the noise of the crowd faded away and they were alone again. But it didn't feel like they were alone. A cold shiver ran down Betty's spine. She sensed a darkness around them. She knew someone was watching.

Betty swallowed hard. "Come on, let's get out of here before we get caught."

* * *

"Their faces, my God," Betty exclaimed as she spread out the crime scene photos across her bed. "I've never seen anything so brutal in all my life."

She was fascinated and couldn't look away. Frank, on the other hand, couldn't stand the sight of them. Those photos made his stomach turn. He decided to read the written report instead, but that was worse.

As he read the description of exactly what had been done to those teenagers, he couldn't help but think of Avril. What if something like this happened to her one day?

Suddenly, he felt sick. Frank tossed the report aside and began to pace the room nervously.

"You okay, Frank?"

"No. I'm not okay." He felt like he couldn't breathe.

Betty rushed to him. "Here, sit down." She took him by the hand and sat him down on the bed.

"They were just kids. What he did to them..." Frank couldn't finish the sentence; he could hardly catch his breath.

"Just put your head between your knees and take slow deep breaths. I'll fix you a whiskey."

He rested his forearms on his thighs, held his head in his

hands, and tried to erase the images of the four dead teens from his memory.

Betty sat down next to him. "I know it's hard." She rubbed his back. "It's hard not to see the faces of the people we love in the victims. I see my family in them, too." She took a sip of the whiskey and gave herself a beat to remember her dead. Frank sat up and she handed him the drink. He gulped it down in one swallow.

She rested her hand on his knee. "This man is a monster, but we can't afford to look away. We're going to help catch him."

He looked her deep in the eyes. Her kindness touched him because it was genuine and rare. Everyone knew Betty was strong and ambitious, but few people knew that it was fueled by her deep sense of compassion. Frank felt privileged to know the softer side of Betty Boudreaux. Not many people did.

He wanted to lean in and kiss her, but he held back. Instead, he grabbed her hand and laced his fingers through hers. He felt a rush when he touched her. Betty felt it, too. It scared her how much she cared about him. She turned her gaze away from him and to the empty glass in his hand. "Another?" she asked.

Frank closed his eyes and squeezed her hand while he imagined what it would be like to stay with her. "No." He let go. "I think I'm going to call it a night. I can't look at any more of this." He stood up and walked to the door.

"Knock if you change your mind about that drink," Betty said as she fixed herself a glass.

Frank looked down at his feet. He didn't want to leave. His eyes met hers and he gave her a sad smile. "See you in the morning, Betty."

"See you in the morning, Frank." She raised her glass to him as he left her room.

Chapter 18

Frank sat in the creaky old wicker chair in his cabin, drumming his finger on the arm. He was restless and couldn't sleep. His thin white undershirt clung to his broad muscular chest in the sticky Louisiana summer. He told himself he couldn't sleep because the air was too thick, but he knew that was a lie. He knew exactly why he couldn't sleep. It was because of her. He just couldn't stop thinking about Betty.

Frank decided that a walk would be the best thing to clear his head. He aimlessly strolled around the grounds of the boarding house, past the garden, and down to the dock on the bayou. He stood there for a while, looking out at the water, and thinking about how different his life could have been. With his hands in his pockets and his head hung low, he walked back toward the cabins.

Before he realized it, he was standing in front of Betty's cabin, as if he had been pulled there by some unseen force. Against his will, he raised his hand and knocked on her door.

He held his breath, almost hoping that she wouldn't answer. A moment later, the door cracked open. Betty peeked outside, clutching her dressing gown. Her face relaxed and softened when she realized it was Frank. She opened the door wide to let him in. He walked inside and closed the door behind him as she poured a couple of whiskeys.

He stood behind her and very gently placed his hands on her hips. She closed her eyes and let herself sink into him. She put her hands on his and pulled his arms around her tiny waist. He buried his face in her neck. Like the streets of New Orleans, she smelled of wild jasmine. His warm breath on her nape made her entire body tingle.

He whispered in her ear so softly that she almost couldn't hear him, "I love you, Betty."

She turned to face him, looking up into his sad blue eyes she saw the torment written all over his face. She wanted to comfort him, but instead, she ran her fingers through his thick brown hair and let her hands slide down his neck and over his chest. He pulled her close to him, their bodies pressed tight against each other. They both knew it was wrong, but they couldn't stop their faces from drifting closer and closer, until their lips just barely brushed together.

"I can't," Frank whispered with a sigh.

"I'm not asking you to," replied Betty.

Reluctantly, they began to release each other from their embrace. He grazed her delicate cheek with the back of his hand before turning away. He walked out of the room without looking back. He knew if he did, he would never be able to leave her.

* * *

Moonlight shone through a broken window of the shack. It deepened the shadows while casting an unsettling glow about the bedroom. No Face lay on his dirty mattress and stared at a hole in the ceiling.

He felt giddy, like a schoolboy with a new crush. He couldn't get the image of that exquisite face out of his mind. The face of a real man. He had to have it; it suited his taste better. He couldn't have found it at a better time. His face itched. The maggots were getting worse.

This time would be tricky. The couple was older than the others; he might have to forget about the girl. Too bad, she seemed plucky.

But if he played his cards right, he might be able to grab them both. She could be his first blonde.

He closed his eyes and conjured up images of all the nasty ways he could play with them. He could feel the snap of their bones. Dreamed up what their screams might sound like.

He stirred below the waist.

He envisioned a cold steel blade slicing through their skin. His mouth began to salivate. He could almost taste the tangy copper of their blood.

The pressure against his pants grew tighter.

He could stick his filthy prick in their unnatural places. Violent and vicious. Bring them into his darkness and eviscerate them.

The more he thought about their pain, the more aroused he became. He slipped his hand down his pants, let his hand hover over his full erection. But he stopped himself, resisted the urge. The release was more satisfying after a hunt. The final act of defilement.

Instead, he moved across the room, floorboards creaking under his weight. He sat down in a rickety chair by the window, picked up his old accordion, and began to play. It hadn't been tuned in twenty years, but his ear had become accustomed to its dissonant notes.

A physical form of his malicious will, the eerie music echoed from the house and drifted down the bayou. Seeking to destroy.

Chapter 19

After Frank left her room the night before, Betty stayed up drinking her feelings until she passed out. A thunderstorm and heavy rain beating down on the tin roof woke her around noon. She pulled the covers over her head and went back to sleep for a few more hours.

Once the rain stopped, she felt restless and decided to go searching for Beaux Guilbeau's grave alone. But as she tried to pull away from her cabin, her car got stuck in the mud. Frank heard the commotion and came out to help her. By the time they got the car unstuck, the sun was just beginning to set, and there was only a couple of hours of daylight left. Frank insisted on coming along. He couldn't bear the thought of Betty being stranded alone at night if the car got stuck again.

She let Frank drive her car, she was too hungover, and the mood between them was quiet and awkward. Betty flipped through the radio stations to fill the silence. Frank couldn't even look at her.

There was nothing but sugarcane fields for miles. It was tall and green from all the summer rain. Up ahead on one side of the road, the sugarcane disappeared.

The sun had just begun to set and in the distance, they could see the church. It was set back a little way from the road, surrounded on three sides by an untamed forest. The steeple was still standing, but the back of the church was lost to a fire several years back. A new church was built in the center of town, and this one was left to rot.

Frank turned the car down an unpaved road that led to their destination. He stopped a few feet in and shut the car off. "We better walk the rest of the way. Looks too muddy to drive."

Betty got out of the car without speaking and started in the direction of the graveyard. She regretted not wearing more sensible shoes, but in her current state of mind, she was more concerned with getting Frank's attention rather than her own sensibility. Frank followed behind her, making sure to keep his eyes to himself.

The overgrown graveyard sat in the shade of the church. It was small and didn't take long for them to find what they were looking for. In the far corner of the graveyard, farthest from the church, was a tombstone that read: *Beaux Guilbeau 1903-1922.*

"He was young when he died," Frank observed.

"The same age as Edgar." Betty stepped closer and rested her hand on the tombstone. She thought being here would somehow give her a certain insight, but when she touched it, she felt nothing. "I'm not sure what I was expecting to find." She looked over at Frank; he was staring at his shoes. "Are we okay?"

Keeping his head down, he answered, "Listen, Betty, I've been thinking. Tomorrow I'm going back to New Orleans. I'm going to resign from the paper."

"What?! That's ridiculous. Why on earth would you do that?"

"Betty," he said softly and looked at her with his sad blue eyes.

"You're a real son of a bitch, Frank." Betty stormed off in the direction of the church.

Frank followed her and stepped in front of her. "Please don't be like this."

"Oh, shut up Frank," Betty snapped at him. "How could you be so selfish?"

Frank was shocked, "Selfish? I'm trying to do right by my family. How is that selfish?"

"We promised these people that we would do whatever it takes to bring their children's killer to justice, and now you're about to break that promise. If you walk into the office tomorrow and quit, Alan will kill this story."

"You're already here. What is Alan going to do? Come down here and throw you over his shoulder to take you back?"

"Have you met Alan? That's exactly what he's going to do."

"Is that all you care about, getting a story? This is my family we're talking about."

"Look around, Frank, there's no one here. One sheriff and a couple of deputies are not going to solve this on their own. Do you really have so little self-control that you can't set aside your personal feelings?"

"I don't trust myself around you!" Frank yelled. He hung his head. "This thing between us is too strong. Don't pretend like you don't feel it, too." He didn't know what to do. There was no way to get out of this while being a good guy. No matter what he did, someone would end up hating him.

He lifted his head and looked up at Betty, but she was looking past him, her eyes wide with fear. Her whole body had gone stiff and rigid. Frank turned to follow her gaze. In the shadow of the church stood a huge figure, watching them with an unnatural stillness. He took a menacing step forward and blocked their path back to the car.

Frank stood in front of Betty to protect her.

The ghoul raised his arm straight up in the air and fired a single shot from his gun, signaling the start of the hunt. The sound made Frank and Betty jump.

"Run!" Frank screamed. He grabbed Betty by the hand, and they ran full-speed in the direction of the forest. There was no time to focus on fear, only survival. They might be able to lose him in the dense woods then circle back to the car.

The humid summer air made it hard to take a deep breath. Their lungs were on fire, their hearts ready to explode, but they kept running. There was no other choice.

Thick mud sloshed under their weight. Mud flung up from beneath their feet as they entered the forest. The ground was soggy and smelled of dank earth. Low hanging branches slashed Frank across his face. He tightened his grip on Betty's hand as they dodged fallen tree limbs and zigzagged their way through the trees.

No Face charged behind them with determination in every step. When Betty turned her head to look back, her foot landed in viscous mud. She lost her balance and fell face-first to the ground.

Frank felt her hand leave his, but his feet were faster than his brain and he ran several feet ahead before he slowed down. He whipped around to go back for her. For a split second he froze and watched as No Face grabbed her by the ankle and pulled her toward him.

"Frank!" Betty screamed as she reached out for him. She felt utterly helpless.

No Face yanked Betty up by the back of her hair to face him.

She looked at his terrifying face and she couldn't breathe, she couldn't scream, she could only stare. His face was crawling with maggots eating away at a layer of rotten gray flesh. Soft pus leaked from open sores around the edges of his face. Betty could smell infection coming off of him. Underneath the first layer of dead flesh, there appeared to be a second face. In the gleam of sweat, it looked as though the face were melting.

"Don't you touch her!" Frank yelled as he charged at No Face with a large branch that had been lying nearby. Frank swung it and hit him in the ribs, causing him to drop his gun. He tossed Betty to the ground and focused his attention on Frank. After all, he was the real prize.

"Come on, you bastard," Frank taunted him as he swung the branch. There was no way in hell he was going to let that filthy beast put his paws on Betty again.

No Face stood just out of Frank's reach and when he swung the branch once more, No Face grabbed it and pushed it into Frank's gut. It knocked the wind out of him and Frank fell to his knees, gasping for air. No Face stood over him and grabbed Frank by the throat. He stared at Frank's beautiful face and licked his lips. His tongue flicked away a stray maggot. He squeezed his massive hand around Frank's throat.

The borders of Frank's vision started to go black. He fought to stay conscious. All he could think about was what had been in the police file. He knew what their fate would be if he lost.

Suddenly, there was a loud bang and No Face screamed out. He let go of his grip on Frank and turned around. Betty stood there with the gun raised. She had shot him in the shoulder. He started to move toward her, and she fired again, shooting him in the thigh. He screamed once more but did not fall, only stopped.

Frank coughed and gasped for air. Breathing was painful, but he had to fight back. He grabbed the branch and rushed at No Face. This was his only chance to stop him, so he put every ounce of energy he had into one powerful swing and hit him in the temple, finally causing him to fall unconscious.

Frank and Betty stared at each other in shock and horror. He held out his hand to her. "Hurry, we don't have much time before he wakes up."

She ran to his side. Frank grabbed her by the hand. Together, they ran out of the forest and into a meadow. Betty hobbled along, trying to keep up, but she was missing a shoe. Her uneven gait caused her to stumble.

Frank bent down and helped her up. "We've got to hurry, Betty," he pleaded.

"It's my shoe," she cried.

"Take it off. It's okay, I've got you."

Betty slipped the shoe off her foot and they fled back to the car. Frank put her in the passenger's seat. He ran around the front of the car and climbed into the driver's seat. Slamming on the gas, he whipped the car around and sped away, toward the boarding house.

Slowly, No Face started to come to. He had been right; they were more challenging than the teenagers. But despite his loss tonight, he smiled. He saw how committed they were to each other. He *could* have them both, all he had to do was bide his time. If he snatched one, the other would surely come calling.

* * *

Betty and Frank burst through the door of her cabin and quickly shut it behind them. Betty sat on the edge of the bed. Her whole body shook. Frank reached for the lock on the door but then remembered that none of the doors in this town had any locks. He dragged a chair across the room and tucked it under the doorknob. He went to the window and peered out from behind the curtains.

"Did he follow us?" Betty asked frantically. "Is he out there?"

"No. I don't think so," Frank said, still looking out the window.

"Why don't you give me that gun, Betty?"

"What?"

Frank turned to her. "The gun. The gun you used to shoot him with. Where is it?"

"I don't...I don't know. I must have dropped it." Frank let out a disappointed sigh.

"Oh god, do you think he has it?"

"Probably."

Betty stood up and paced the room, leaving a trail of bloody footprints behind her. "What if he comes back? I don't have my shoes."

"What?"

"My shoes, Frank, my shoes." She raised her voice. "I lost them. What the hell am I going to do without my damn shoes?" She was short of breath and her voice cracked with panic.

Frank could see she was in shock, so he wrapped his arms around her in a tight hug. "Hey, hey," he spoke in a soothing voice. "He won't find us. And we'll get you some new shoes."

She buried her face in his shoulder and sobbed. "I was so scared. I thought we were going to die."

Frank stroked her hair. "I'm here. I won't leave you. I'm

right here. I promise I won't let anything happen to you." He felt the tension leave her body and she melted into him.

Betty lifted her head, and they were cheek to cheek. For a long time, they stood that way, letting their feelings pass between them in silence.

Neither of them could fight the pull any longer. They turned toward each other until their lips touched. The kiss was soft and tender at first, and then uncertainty gave way to sureness. They pressed their bodies together. Frank slid his hands down the curve of her waist, and gripping her hips, pulled her closer. There was no space left between them. Betty ran her hands up his broad muscular back. An intense rush, like fire exploding in the pit of their bellies, burst through them as they gave into desire. Everything became electrified. They pulled back from each other, breathless and lightheaded.

Betty looked up at him and brushed her fingertips along a cut across his cheekbone. "You're bleeding."

"So are you." His eyes shifted to the bloody footprints on the floor.

"Oh," she said, surprised. She hadn't even noticed the cuts to her knees and feet.

"Here, let's get you cleaned up." Frank sat her down on the edge of the bed and knelt down to examine her injuries. Her legs were covered in mud and blood. It was hard for him to see the extent of the cuts.

"We need to clean this."

She watched him fill a bowl with warm water from the bathroom. He came back into the room, grabbed the bottle of whiskey, and knelt down in front of her. Dipping a rag in the water, he began cleaning the wounds on her knees and feet.

"The cuts don't look too deep, but I am going to have to

disinfect them." He reached for the bottle of whiskey. "This might sting." He rubbed the alcohol on her knee, and she sucked in her breath. Frank gently gripped the back of her knee and lifted it closer to his mouth. He blew on her cuts to soothe the sting of whiskey.

She couldn't take her eyes off him. He had been so brave tonight, and now he was being so attentive. Frank truly was a good man. In that moment, she realized that she loved him. Her body ached for him.

Betty reached over and ran her fingers through his hair. He closed his eyes and rested his cheek on her smooth thigh. Her hand stroked his face, and her finger grazed his lips. He wanted her so badly, to taste her at least once. Frank looked up at her, she had the same yearning in her eyes. Betty leaned back on her palms, then she opened her legs for him. That was all the invitation he needed.

* * *

Frank woke in the middle of the night to find himself still naked in Betty's bed. He lay on his stomach and looked over at her.

She was awake, smoking a cigarette with her back resting against the headboard and a sheet tucked under her arms to cover her bare breasts. She stared blankly into the darkness of the room, letting her cigarette burn between her fingers.

Frank rubbed his hand over the top of her thigh. "Hey, you okay?"

She looked down at him with a smile and ran her fingers through his hair. "I can't sleep." She put her cigarette out in the ashtray on her bedside table. "Every time I close my eyes, I see his face, that awful face."

Frank sat up. "We just need to get your mind on something else." He cupped her cheek in his hand and pulled her face in close. Tracing her jawline with his finger, he kissed her tenderly on the lips.

He ran his hand down her back. She let the sheet fall and pressed her breasts into his chest. He kissed her again, this time hard and passionate. Betty ran her hands down the length of his body and stopped at his backside. She felt something embedded in his skin and plucked it off of him.

"What is that?" Frank asked.

"My button." She giggled and bit her bottom lip, remembering the way he had torn open her dress last night.

Frank blushed a little. He looked around and noticed their clothes all about the room. The smell of their sex still lingered in the air.

"You know," Betty started, "you still owe me that story of your troubles in '42."

Frank sighed. That story was the last thing he wanted to get into right now. He stretched his arm around her, and she tucked herself into the crook of his shoulder, nestling her head against his chest. He kissed the top of her head and breathed her in: New Orleans jasmine.

He loved her, truly loved her, and in that moment, he could deny her nothing.

Frank tilted his head back, stared up at the ceiling, and let his mind take him back to the past.

IV

France Winter 1942

Chapter 20

I t all happened in a blur, but I can remember every detail of that moment, the memory of it seared into my brain. They say your life flashes before your eyes, but mine didn't. Even though I knew I was going to die, as my plane hurled itself toward the ground, all I could think of was my training.

I had been stationed in Rougham, England for nearly a year serving as a pilot. It was early January '42, just a few days after the turn of the new year, when they sent us on a mission over occupied France. On our way back, we got ambushed by German pilots. Even though my Spitfire was faster, we were outnumbered by three to one. The Nazi scum all started firing on me at once and the bastards shot me down. There was no time for emotions, especially not fear. I had to think fast because I was going down hard.

A grove of trees emerged into my visual. If I could steer the plane onto that grove, it might give me enough leeway to avoid a direct crash and slow the plane down before it hit the ground. To say that the treetops softened the blow would be a gross exaggeration, but I was right: it gave me enough cushion to slow the plane down.

The plane nosedived through the dense trees, causing my body to slam around the cockpit. My ears began to ring as the piercing sound of branches scraping against metal filled the space around me. The trees tore through my plane. It sent metal flying everywhere and ripped a gash through the side. I thought my heart would explode, it was pounding so hard against my chest.

The cabin began to fill with thick dark smoke that burned my eyes and lungs. I held my breath while the plane shook violently and headed toward the ground. With a white-knuckle grip, I pulled up on the wheel and lifted the nose right before it slammed into the terrain. The plane landed on its belly and skidded past the grove into an empty, snow-covered field.

When it finally came to a stop, I couldn't see anything through the smoke. Gasoline was leaking somewhere; I could smell it. My ears were still ringing, but I heard the crackling of fire. I knew I only had a minute, maybe two, if I was lucky.

I tried to unbuckle my safety harness, but it was jammed. Then suddenly, all the emotions I had been keeping at bay broke through and flooded me. Fear seized my mind, and I began to panic. I had survived the crash but now I was going to die, burned alive.

I continued struggling with the harness, but it wouldn't budge. All I could do was scream out in dismay. Then the pain came. I looked down at my leg and saw bone. There was also a sharp piece of shrapnel lodged into the side of my broken leg. I grabbed ahold of it and pulled, cutting up my hand in the process. Blood began to pour out of me. I worked quickly and used the shrapnel to cut away my safety harness.

I began to grow weak as I continued struggling to free

myself. I couldn't breathe through the thick smoke and felt light-headed from blood loss. My vision became blurry. I knew I was about to lose consciousness.

Out of nowhere, the hatch opened, and a hazy face appeared in the smoke. I thought I must be dead, and an angel had come to take my soul. That was the last thing I remember before everything went black.

* * *

The next few days were spent in a fever dream. When I woke, I found myself in a small room. It was bare except for the bed I lay on, a bedside chair, and a picture of the Virgin Mary hanging on the wall.

I couldn't remember if the plane crash was real or something that I dreamed. But my leg was definitely in pain, a constant throbbing. I pulled the covers back and found my leg secured in a crude splint. Whoever pulled me out of that plane went to great lengths to save me.

I heard footsteps out in the hallway. The door opened and an old man walked into the room. He was short with white hair and wire-rimmed glasses that sat on the edge of his large hook nose.

"Bonjour, monsieur." He sat down in the chair and lit a pipe. "You are an American G.I., non?" His French accent was thick, but his English was perfect.

"Yes, sir."

"Do you know what has happened to you?"

"I crashed my plane and broke my leg?" I didn't have the confidence to answer in the affirmative.

He chuckled. "Yes, that is correct. I know you must be confused. We had to sedate you to perform the surgery. You broke your femur. It was not too bad. I was able to clean the wound and set the bone."

"How long have I been here?"

"About a week or so."

"Thank you," I said. "Thank you for saving me."

"Well," he puffed on his pipe, "I cannot take all the credit. It was Ava here who pulled you from the plane." He pointed to a young woman standing in the corner of the room. I didn't know how long she had been standing there. I didn't even notice that she was in the room, she sort of just blended in with the wallpaper. When I looked at her, she turned her face away from me and stared down at her feet.

"Thank you, Ava," I said. All she gave me was a timid nod of her head. I turned back to the man. "I'm sorry, I didn't get your name, sir."

"I'm afraid I cannot give you my real name, but you can call me Doc. The anonymity of our members is paramount. You are now under the care of the French Resistance. I have been able to get you false papers." He reached into his coat pocket, pulled out a set of documents, and handed them to me. "We were also able to get you civilian clothes, which was no easy task. You Americans are built differently." He chuckled and took a puff of his pipe. Then he grew very serious. "You need to leave France as soon as possible, and here is where our problem begins. You cannot walk on that leg. It will take a long time to heal. Three, maybe four months."

"Months?" I exclaimed.

"Yes, months. It is true that it is a risk for you to stay in one place for so long, but there is no other option. Our most common way of getting evaders out of France is over the Pyrenees Mountains and into Spain. In order to make that journey, your leg must heal properly. Listen to me carefully: under no circumstances are you to walk on that leg without my approval. Now, my work requires me to travel, so Ava will be taking care of you. I will return as soon as I can to check up on you. Do you understand?"

"Yes sir, I understand."

He stood up and his smile returned. Doc patted me on the shoulder. "This is why I love American GIs, they know how to take orders."

* * *

I didn't know how I was going to survive the next few months if the past couple of weeks were any indication of how my time here would be spent. There weren't any books to read or radio to listen to, there wasn't even anything interesting on the walls to look at; surely, I would die of boredom, or madness.

Ava was there, of course, but she never spoke to me and rarely made eye contact. She brought me my meals and tended my wounds, but I could tell I made her nervous. Who could blame her? I was a stranger in her home, so I tried not to be too much trouble.

One morning, I spent hours watching the sunlight crawl up the wall. I never felt so helpless in all my life. My body needed rest but my mind needed stimulation. Being trapped in that bed made me feel like I was coming out of my own skin.

Then I heard Ava's footsteps coming down the hall. She

came into my room with a tray of food, her eyes turned down to the floor the whole time. Without a word, she set the tray in my lap and turned to leave. I could feel my desperation bubble up inside of my throat.

"It's Ava, right?"

She froze like a scared animal and nodded her head.

"Do you speak English?"

She stared at her hands and picked at her cuticles, then slowly lifted her eyes to look at me. "I speak small English," she answered, unsure of herself.

"We were never introduced. I'm Frank." I could see she was nervous, so I tried to speak softly. "Will you please join me for breakfast?"

Still not speaking, she moved to the chair next to the bed and sat down. Her eyes shifted around the room, unsure where to look, and she started chewing on her fingernails.

"So, you live here with Doc? Is he family?"

"No." She shook her head. "No family."

"You don't have any family? What about your parents?" She shrugged her shoulders. "The nuns raised me."

"You're an orphan?"

"*Oui*." She nodded. "*Orpheline*."

"*Orpheline*," I repeated. "Sounds prettier in French."

"I teach you French. You teach me English."

"That sounds like a swell idea. I need something useful to do around here. I'm going stir-crazy." I smiled at her.

She blushed and looked down at her hands again. "Tell me your *famille*," she said.

"*Famille*," I repeated. "I don't have much to speak of. I left home as soon as I could. They don't even know I enlisted."

"You are the orphan, too."

214

I scoffed to myself. "Yeah, sort of."

Over the next month, Ava and I became good friends. I grew very fond of her over that period of time. She laughed easily and blushed often. I found myself feeling protective of her; something about Ava seemed innocent and fragile.

She told me how she was dropped off on the steps of a remote convent when she was just a few days old. The nuns took her in, even though it wasn't an orphanage. They raised her but were never warm to her. Ava learned from an early age to speak only when spoken to, to be seen and not heard, although being seen wasn't very well received, either, and that breaking the rules wasn't worth the punishment she received.

There were no other children there. She grew up isolated and with no friends. Her loneliness was constant.

When Ava was around six, a couple came to adopt her. They took her home with them after meeting her only once. Ava recalled being excited to leave the convent and have a family. So she did her very best to be a good child like the nuns taught her. It took less than a week for them to bring her back. The couple said Ava was too melancholy and they wanted a child with more spirit. No one showed interest in her after that.

On her seventeenth birthday, the nuns told her she could either join the convent or leave. Ava waited her whole life to escape that place, so she left. That's when she met Doc, who was in fact a doctor. His wife had been in ill health and needed help around the house. He was the only doctor in the region and spent a lot of time traveling.

Eventually his wife died, and Doc couldn't stand to be in the house for more than a night or two.

Ava and Doc didn't really share affection for one another. It wasn't love or loyalty that bonded them together, but pity. He knew Ava had nowhere else to go and didn't have the heart to send her away. She knew he couldn't sell the house because it reminded him of his wife, but he couldn't stay for the same reason. It worked out for both of them; Doc could stay gone for as long as he needed and Ava had a safe place to stay.

Once the Nazis invaded France, Doc made connections within the Resistance and through his travels was able to provide information on German defenses. With Ava's help, they used the farmhouse as a safehouse for those hoping to escape France.

Usually, evaders only stayed a night or two until their false papers came through and they could be moved to Paris. I was the longest house guest they had so far.

Ava's story resonated with me. My childhood had been just as glum.

My father was a violent man and a mean drunk. He used to slap us around but my mother got the worst of it. Sam, my older brother, did his best to protect me. He hid me under the bed or in the closet when my father started up his yelling. But I heard everything, and I saw the evidence of his cruelty on my mother's face.

The summer I turned ten, she split. Everything got worse for us after that. I couldn't stand to be in that house, so Sam and I worked the fields from sunup to sundown to avoid my father's abuse. Sam was fifteen and quit school to work full-time so we didn't lose the farm. He said it was too late for him but insisted that I finish school and find my way out of the hell we called home.

Slowly, I watched Sam turn into my father. That frightened me more than anything, to see a good person turn into a monster. I began to question if I could be capable of such horrible things and worried that this poison would leak into me.

I tried to limit my time at home to only sleeping and buried myself in school. I hid away at the library to study and signed up for every sport I could so that any spare time I had would be occupied. My hard work paid off and I got accepted into college.

One day, a military recruiter gave a talk at my university. He spoke about how the military teaches honor and how it can turn an ordinary man into an honorable one. I was sold. I would do anything to keep myself from turning into my father and brother. I wanted nothing more than to be a good man, but if I could be an honorable one, all the better. So I enlisted in the Army Air Corps and became a pilot.

I was ashamed of where I came from, and I think Ava was, too. That shame bonded us together. We understood each other in ways that happy people didn't.

The only thing keeping me from going insane was Ava's constant companionship. She had become my best friend.

Doc popped in about every three weeks to check my progress. He never stayed more than one night and spent most of his time locked in his office. I had been on bed rest for nine weeks when he came for another check-up.

He walked into my room as usual and gave me a puzzled look. "Still in bed?" he asked.

"Yes sir, doctor's orders," I replied.

He turned to Ava. She stood in the corner of the room chewing on her nails. Doc lifted my bed covers to see my leg still in a splint.

He furrowed his brow at Ava and shook his head before covering me back up.

"Ava, a word."

She followed him out into the hallway, and I could hear him raise his voice to her.

"Why is his leg still in that splint? I told you three weeks ago to remove it and start exercising his leg. Now his muscles have atrophied. Because of you, his progress has been set back by weeks. Ignorant girl, what were you thinking?"

"He was not ready," she answered in a meek voice.

"He was not ready, or *you* were not ready? You have become too attached, Ava. He cannot stay here forever. If you care for this man, you will help him get out of France as quickly as possible. Now go, remove his splint, and explain yourself to him. Stupid girl."

I heard Doc march down the hall to his office and slam the door.

I didn't like the way he spoke to her. She must have misunderstood his instruction. We cared for one another, and I knew she would never do anything to intentionally hurt me.

A few minutes passed, and Ava came into my room carrying a cane. She set it against the nightstand and took a seat in the chair next to my bed. I could see that she had been crying. She kept her head down and didn't speak as she began to remove the splint.

"Don't listen to him, Ava," I said. "I know you didn't mean anything by it. You're doing a real good job of taking care of me and I'm grateful for you."

Ava wiped her eyes. *"Merci, François."* She still wouldn't look at me.

I could tell she felt awful about her mistake. I reached out and squeezed her hand. "I'm serious, Ava, I wouldn't be here if it weren't for you. I owe you everything."

She looked up at me. There was something dark behind her eyes and it bothered me.

* * *

Several more weeks passed, and we spent our time much the same way as we had before. We talked and joked and enjoyed each other's company. She continued to teach me French, and I helped her improve her English. In the evenings, I started assisting her with the cooking; standing at the counter chopping vegetables built up stamina in my leg.

It felt great to finally be up and about, but my muscles were weak from lying in that bed for so long. Thank God for Ava, she was by my side everyday encouraging me and letting me lean on her. She stretched my leg out and exercised it. Soon I was able to walk with the aid of a cane, thanks to her.

A storm rolled in one night and it made my leg ache all over. Even with my cane, I had a hard time getting around. I tried to help Ava with dinner, but she insisted that I rest.

She brought a tray of food up to my room and sat with me. She watched me eat with an anxious look in her eyes.

I took my first bite. There was a bitter aftertaste to it, but I didn't want to be rude.

"This is delicious," I said. "What is it?"

"Coq au vin," she answered. "Or cock in wine."

I nearly choked on my food when she said it. "Rooster," I chuckled. "In America, we say rooster."

"Rooster," she repeated with a smile.

Even though the food tasted bad, I ate it all. I didn't want to disappoint her. She had spent all day working on this meal.

I immediately regretted it. My stomach cramped up and within thirty minutes, I was vomiting uncontrollably.

Ava never left my side. She rubbed my back as I leaned over the side of the bed and threw up into a bucket. She didn't complain when she had to empty it several times throughout the night. She wiped my brow and cleaned my face. I couldn't even keep water down and my sides hurt from all the retching.

The storm raged on all night. Lightning flashed violently outside, and every crack of thunder shook the little farmhouse.

I was drenched in sweat and weak. Ava crawled into bed with me. She pressed a cold washcloth against my face and wrapped her arms around me. She kissed my forehead and stroked my hair. I rested my head on her chest and felt a comfort I hadn't known since my mother left.

The bout of food poisoning knocked me out for days and I wasn't able to exercise my leg. I began to wonder if I would ever escape this room. At first, my sickness brought Ava and I closer together, but the more I regained my strength, the more she smothered me with her constant hovering.

Then one night, everything changed. We were going to bed, and she lingered in my doorway. I could tell she had something on her mind by the way she picked at her fingernails. Before I realized what was happening, she leaned in and kissed me. It was quick, like she had to work up the nerve to do it. I didn't have time to react before she scampered down the hall to her room.

I lay in bed all night thinking about that kiss and a knot formed in my stomach. I knew she had a crush on me, it was impossible not to see. All the blushing, and the way she laughed at my stupid jokes. The dreamy far-off look in her eyes when I helped her with her English or the cooking. She thought I didn't notice, but oftentimes I could feel her staring at me when I wasn't looking.

I did not reciprocate her feelings. I only saw her as my friend. It all seemed innocent enough, but things were different now that she had kissed me. The thought of telling her that I didn't feel the same way made me sick. She had so little confidence, this would crush her.

But the idea of playing along felt wrong to me. I didn't want to lead her on. I went back and forth in my mind trying to figure out the right thing to do. I decided it was best to just ignore it. My leg was healing quickly and with any luck, I'd be gone soon.

Over the next couple of weeks, things seemed normal. Except the staring became more frequent. She stopped being so shy about being physically close to me. Touching my back, holding my hand, rubbing my leg. On several occasions, I woke in the morning to find the ashtray next to my bed full of cigarette butts. Clearly, Ava had been in my room during the night while I slept. Being around her made me uncomfortable now.

One night, as I drifted in and out of sleep, there was a knock at my bedroom door. I got out of bed to answer it and was surprised to see Doc standing there.

"Come, Frank. We must talk."

I followed him to the sitting room where Ava was waiting. Her eyes were puffy and red from crying.

"The time has come for you to go," he said. "There is a route out of France that doesn't require you to go over the mountains. We cannot waste this chance, the window of opportunity is small, and we are lucky to have found it."

I nodded. "I'm ready."

Ava sat beside me, quietly wiping away her tears.

"Now you will need help navigating your way around," Doc continued. "So Ava will accompany you on your journey to Paris and pose as your wife until you make contact with your host."

I looked over at Ava and she gave me a weak smile. I had a feeling that playing the part of my wife had been her idea.

Doc went on to explain what to expect on our journey. He said that all passengers were subject to random searches and document checks from Gestapo agents. If approached, the best thing I could do was pretend to be deaf and that Ava should answer all my questions for me. Even though I had been working on my French for the last several months, it wasn't good enough to pass as a Frenchman.

He instructed us that, once the train arrived in Paris, we should wait by the first kiosk inside the main hall and look for a man with a red feather tucked in the band of a dark green hat. We were not to make direct contact with him but follow at a distance, and he would lead us to our next destination.

Doc gave each of us fake wedding bands and our train tickets. He told us to get some rest; we were leaving for Paris first thing in the morning.

Chapter 21

I t surprised me how crowded the train station was so early in the morning. We were among hundreds of people on their way to Paris. The station was littered with Gestapo agents and Nazi soldiers. It was nerve-racking.

Ava could see how anxious I was, and she took my hand. I turned to her and smiled. It helped having her by my side and I was glad that she was with me. I decided to put Ava's clingy behavior behind me. She was my best friend, and this was our goodbye.

We boarded the train and crammed into our third-class seats. I felt the tension in my body ease once we were settled. This part should be easy; just a short two-hour train ride to Paris. All I had to do was keep my head down and my mouth shut.

Everything was going smooth until about halfway through the trip. At the front of the train car, I spotted a Gestapo agent checking papers. I looked at Ava to see her reaction, but she didn't notice him. She was too busy gazing down at the fake wedding ring on her finger. She had that far-off dreamy look on her face again. Something about it unsettled me.

The agent was coming down the aisle. I nudged Ava with my

foot to get her attention. When she looked up, she accidentally made eye contact with him. I could feel her body tense up and there was a flash of panic in her eyes. The agent noticed and came straight for us.

"Papers," he demanded as he eyed me and my cane.

Ava reached into her pocket and produced both our documents.

"How did you hurt your leg?" he asked me.

I had to pretend that I couldn't hear. I wasn't sure where to look or what to do with my hands. Every movement felt like it could be interpreted as suspicious. I thought for sure we were going to be caught. Adrenaline pumped through my body, it made my skin itch, and I started to sweat.

"He's deaf," Ava answered for me.

"Lame and deaf." He looked at me with disgust as he took the papers from her. "Born deaf?"

"No," Ava responded. "He hurt his leg in a farming accident. There was an infection, his fever was too high, and he lost his hearing."

He scanned over our documents. I could see that he was bored talking to Ava already, but I was impressed with her fast thinking. He handed our papers back and moved on to someone else. Ava had saved me yet again.

We had no more trouble after that, but the trip took longer than expected. There were delays due to Allied raids and the train had to be diverted. What should have been only a couple of hours took us six. Finally, we arrived in Paris around three in the afternoon.

Hand in hand, Ava and I disembarked from the train. We found the kiosk and waited for the man wearing a dark green hat with a red feather.

We stood there for what seemed like hours but was really only a few minutes. My anxiety started up again. The station was crowded that day and overrun with German soldiers. I began to worry that something went wrong, and we had been abandoned. But then Ava squeezed my hand. She'd spotted him.

He made eye contact with us and slightly bowed his head. He turned and walked out of the station, leading us out onto the streets of Paris.

Both Ava and I were overwhelmed by the sights and smells of the bustling city. Well-dressed people rode bicycles and walked hurriedly to get on with their day. But there was an undercurrent of something unnerving in the air. As we walked through the crowded streets, I could see why. Giant swastika banners hung from old buildings. The streets were packed with German soldiers and many hotels and office buildings had armed Nazi guards keeping post outside.

Ava looped her arm in mine and did her best to help me along. My leg was killing me, but we had no choice but to keep up. If we got lost in the crowds, I would have no way out of France. I pushed through the shooting pain and relied on Ava and my cane to keep walking.

After a brisk twenty-minute walk, we turned the corner to a quiet residential street. The man in the hat turned down an alleyway and walked into the side entrance of a three-story apartment building.

My heart sank when I saw him walk up a flight of stairs. I didn't know if my leg could take it. Again, Ava came to my rescue, and I had to lean on her for help. By the time we reached the third floor, I was drenched in sweat and out of breath. It took everything I had to get to the top floor.

225

We followed him to the end of the hall. He gave a series of short rhythmic knocks on the door. It opened and there stood a woman dressed all in black, with dark hair and piercing blue eyes. She ushered us in quickly and exchanged a few short words in French to the man in the hat before he left.

She shut the door and turned to us. "Please have a seat." Her French accent was completely gone.

"You're American?" I asked.

"Originally from New Orleans, yes. But I've been in Paris for nearly thirty years now."

"You came over when you were a child?"

She let out a boisterous laugh. "I might just have to keep you around. I'm much older than I look, darlin'."

With Ava glued to my side, we sat down on the sofa.

"Have the two of you eaten? I have some wine and cheese if you're hungry."

"That would be great. I'm starving." I watched her glide into the kitchen. She was tall and slender with a rich exotic air about her.

It was then that I noticed Ava still clutching my hand. I didn't know how to handle it. I wanted my hand free of her, but I didn't want to hurt her feelings. So I left it there. When the lady of the house returned and handed me a wine glass, I used it as an opportunity to let go.

The lady sat down and draped herself across her chair. "I see why Doc insisted on this route for you. There's no way you could make it over the Pyrenees on that leg."

"I could barely make it up three flights of stairs with it."

She smiled but didn't laugh at my joke. "So I spoke with my contact, and everything is set for tomorrow night."

"Tomorrow?" Ava asked. There was panic in her voice.

"Yes," the lady said sternly. "It has to be tomorrow night. We have a man who works out of England. He manages air drops of supplies for the Resistance. Occasionally, he takes evaders out of France and back to England on his plane. We told him of your situation, and he's agreed to take you on board. But these special missions take months to plan, so this is your only chance." She looked at Ava and then back at me. "I advise you to take it. They only do these drops at night, so someone will be here to collect you just before sundown. Sleep during the day and say your goodbyes tonight."

Ava said nothing and just stared into her glass of wine as if the answer to her troubles would magically appear.

The three of us spent the rest of the evening drinking wine and chatting. Our hostess enchanted us with tales of New Orleans. I was fascinated and knew then that when I returned to America, New Orleans would be the place I settled.

In the wee hours of the morning, we decided to call it a night. The guest room was small and only had one bed.

"I'll sleep on the floor; you take the bed," I said to Ava.

"There's room for two," she said as she sat on the edge of the bed.

I was too tired to protest and to be honest, the thought of sleeping on the floor sounded awful. I sat on the bed next to her and knew that it was time to say goodbye.

Holding her hand, I started, "I'm going to miss you, Ava. I can't ever thank you enough for what you've done for me. I think you're the first real friend I ever had. I'll never forget you."

Tears streamed down her face. "I love you," she blurted out in between sobs. She leaned in and kissed me. I let her, but I pulled away when she started to unbutton my shirt.

"No, Ava."

Her breath caught in her throat and her lip quivered. "Just this once."

"No. I can't." I held her as she buried her face in my shoulder and cried.

Ava lifted her head and pressed her cheek to mine. In thick French, she whispered in my ear, "*S'il vous plaît, François.*" Her hand moved up my thigh, across the scar. A subtle reminder that I owed her.

Ava clung to me, dug her nails into my skin, and wouldn't let go. She pressed her body against mine and kissed my neck. Then she slipped her hand down my pants and rubbed me.

"Ava, stop." I pushed her off of me. She tumbled to the floor and began to weep. I didn't mean to shove her so hard. "I'm sorry. Are you okay?" I reached down to help her up.

She grabbed my left arm with both hands and pulled me down. My leg was weak from the journey, and I lost my balance. I fell to the floor and landed on my bad leg. A jolt of pain left me breathless.

Ava put her hands on my shoulder to lift me, I thought she was helping but instead, she pinned my back against the bed frame. She climbed on top of me and put all her weight on my left leg. The pain was so intense that I couldn't see straight.

She clung to me once again and straddled me. "Please, please." The kissing and rubbing started over. "You want it. I can tell." She grabbed me between the legs.

I didn't want to sleep with her, but it had been a long time since I had been with a woman, and my body reacted to her touch.

"Ava, stop. Please don't do this." But I knew she wouldn't stop until I gave her what she wanted. My head was swimming with wine, and I was exhausted and in pain. I didn't have the strength to fight her. So I let her put me inside of her. All I could do was close my eyes and think of Veronica Lake.

Afterwards, Ava slept next to me while I lay awake in bed and tried to reconcile my feelings. Violation. Shame. Guilt. How could I let her do that to me? Why didn't I fight harder to stop her? Was she right, did I secretly want this? Was this my fault? Did I lead her on? I didn't think I had. Those feelings of friendship were real for me and my gratitude genuine. I owed this woman my life. But in the end, Ava betrayed me. She used my weakness against me to take what she wanted. Maybe this made us even?

I didn't want to think about it anymore. It didn't matter now, anyway. I was leaving France for good. I'd never have to see Ava again. I could chalk it up to a bad one-night stand and move on.

Ava was still asleep when I woke up the next day. I didn't wake her to say goodbye. I couldn't bear to go through all of that again. All I wanted was to get away from her.

I left the apartment quietly and just as before, I followed my escort at a distance to the train station. It was the last train of the day and less crowded than yesterday. Not many Germans were leaving Paris, so there was little trouble on the train.

It was a short trip to a small village southwest of Paris. Once we arrived, I again followed my escort. The sun was starting to set as we walked nearly ten miles to an out-of-the-way farmhouse. My leg was throbbing by the time we got there.

Still following him at a distance, we rounded the corner of an old barn. There, a truck waited for us. We climbed in the back with four other men and started down a dirt road into the fading light.

We drove without headlights in the darkness of night to an empty field. Everyone got out of the truck, each with a flashlight, and hid in strategic spots in the tall grass. I didn't have to wait long until I heard the rumbling of a plane overhead. They all turned on their flashlights to signal the landing area.

The plane touched down and the men quickly began unloading their supplies. It took less than five minutes. I boarded the plane and by midnight, I was headed back to England. I had done it. I escaped.

* * *

Once I returned to England, they awarded me the Purple Heart for my injuries sustained in the line of duty. Policy dictated that evaders were prohibited from participating in combat missions, so they took me off flight status and put me to work in an administrative position.

It didn't bother me; in fact, it gave me time to brush up on my journalistic skills. Active duty didn't allow me to publish my work, but I did it for myself. It helped kill time while I waited on my disability discharge to go through. Then I was heading straight for New Orleans to start a new life.

I had been in England for about a year. It was April of '43 when I received a letter on my desk. It was from Ava. She had left France and was in London. She wanted to see me.

I wasn't sure what I felt reading that letter. I wanted to put the past behind me. I thought about just ignoring it, but I knew she'd show up there looking for me if I did.

On the other hand, it might be nice to see my friend again.

Maybe if I saw her one last time, it would erase some of the memory of that painful goodbye. We deserved something better. So I wrote her back and told her I would visit in a couple of weeks when I was on leave.

I walked into the tea room of her hotel on a Saturday afternoon.

It wasn't very crowded—not many people were visiting London those days. The host informed me that Ava had called down and changed the table reservation to room service. She would be serving afternoon tea in her room, suite 425.

I made my way to the elevators and watched the doors open and close, open and close. I didn't want to be alone with her; she might get the wrong idea again. But she was expecting me, and it went against my nature to stand up a lady. All I wanted was a meaningful goodbye, something pleasant we could look back on over the years.

However, she did have a way of manipulating me that went over my head. But I was wise to it now, and I would be forceful with her if need be. So I got on the elevator, went up to the fourth floor, and knocked on her door.

She opened the door to her suite and threw her arms around my neck in a tight hug. "I'm so happy to see you, Frank."

"It's good to see you, too, Ava." I pulled her arms off me and took a step back. "You look well. How have you been?" She wore makeup and a new dress.

"Come, have tea." She grabbed my hand and led me to a small table set with afternoon tea. Something about her was different but I couldn't put my finger on it.

"So, are you just visiting or have you left France for good?" I asked as we sat down.

"There is nothing left for me in France."

231

"That's war, I suppose." I gave her a halfhearted smile and sipped my tea. I didn't know what else to say to her. Maybe coming here was a mistake, after all.

Nothing much had changed between us. She still had her crush, I still didn't. After about thirty minutes of awkward conversation, I was ready to leave.

"I should probably head out," I stood up.

"Wait." She grabbed my hand and stopped me from leaving. "I have something for you." She left me in the sitting room before I had a chance to protest. When she came back, my heart stopped. Ava held a sleeping baby in her arms.

Ava came over to me and showed me the child. "Her name is Avril. She is yours." She tried to hand her to me, but I backed away.

"No," I said, dumbfounded. "That could be anyone's child. She's not mine."

"François, she is yours. Hold her, you'll see." Ava held the baby out to me.

"No!" I yelled. The baby woke up and started to cry. I had to get out of there.

"François, please."

"That's not my child," I said and stormed out of the suite. I needed a drink, and I made my way to the pub around the corner.

I sat on my barstool and ordered a whiskey. This couldn't be happening. It wasn't my fault; she forced me to sleep with her. Even though I knew it was possible, I couldn't accept that I might be the father of Ava's child.

I didn't know what to do. I could leave London and never look back. My discharge papers would be finalized soon; I could deny that any of this happened and disappear into

America. She'd never find me. But that would make me a coward, like my own father. I couldn't run from this. I never saw myself as the kind of guy who would get a girl in trouble, much less leave her that way. I was a good man, an honorable man.

What if Ava was telling the truth? What if the baby was mine? How could I abandon my child, and in the middle of a war, no less? I convinced myself that the only way to know for sure was to hold her, so I went back.

As soon as Ava put her in my arms, I fell in love. Avril looked up at me and smiled. She had my eyes. She had my nose. There was no use lying to myself, this was my daughter. I'd never felt that kind of love before. I became a father in that moment, and I knew she needed me.

I stared at Avril, mesmerized by my child. There was no other choice, I had to do right by them. Within a week, Ava and I were married.

I thought that in time, I would learn to love Ava, but the truth is the more I try, the more I resent her, and the more I resent her, the guiltier I feel. I care for Ava, I truly do, but I don't love her the way a man should love his wife. I wish I did love her; life would be easier that way, but I just don't. I never did. And I can't forget what she did to me.

But I love my daughter. She's the only good thing that ever happened to me. If I left Ava, she would take Avril away from me. I can't live without my daughter, and I can't have my daughter without Ava. I'm trapped.

Chapter 22

Ava checked her watch before bringing her finger to her mouth.

She moved on to chewing the skin around her nail beds; there was nothing left of her fingernails.

Over an hour passed since the last bus dropped her off in Berwick, a little town on the edge of Morgan City. This would be her third bus change. She left Avril with Bridget, the neighbor, and boarded a bus from New Orleans in the middle of the night. She had no choice but to go down to Ville Morte and find her husband.

How did it come to this? Why must he always make her chase him? After all this time, how could he still not see her? She saved his life. She nursed him back to health, gave him a beautiful child, and moved to a strange country for him.

Hadn't she at least earned the right to be seen, to be respected? She was his wife, goddamnit, and he had disregarded her for the last time. She would make him see her.

Ava had nothing but time to think. She thought about what she would say to Frank once they were face to face, insults ready to fire in Betty's direction. She hated her so much she could strangle her with her bare hands.

Her rational mind gave way under the pressure of insecurity.

She felt herself being sucked down in a spiral of her own making and there was nothing to grip onto to pull herself out. Anger ripped right through her.

Finally, a neglected bus pulled up to her stop. She waited as people trickled from the open bus doors. She clutched her bag to her chest and stepped inside. Instantly she was assaulted by the mingling of stale air and twelve hours' worth of varying body odors.

Scanning the bus, she saw a seat next to an open window. Across the aisle sat a scoundrel, and his eyes watched her walk the length of the bus. Being watched was an unfamiliar feeling for her, and he made her feel especially uneasy.

Ava sat down and slipped her hand inside her bag. Her sore fingertips searched until they brushed against warm metal. Her hand rested there. She would have to remember to thank Bridget for shoving the gun in her bag.

* * *

Betty gave her full attention to the notepad propped up on her thighs. The pencil flew across the page with wide strokes. She never made it out of bed. Her hair was a tousled mess. She didn't have any makeup on and wore only a bedsheet around her naked body.

Frank looked at her from across the room, a cup of coffee in each hand. He found her natural beauty stunning. His chest tightened. Once they were back in the city, it would all be over. This version of himself, gone. The lightness, the freedom would disappear, and he would go back to being melancholy old Frank.

He walked across the room and pushed those thoughts aside; he didn't want to ruin this moment by thinking of the future.

"What are you up to?" He handed her a mug of coffee before climbing back into bed.

"It's a sketch of that man." She took a sip of coffee and set it down on her nightstand. "I can't get his face out of my head."

Frank moved closer and kissed her on the shoulder, then rested his chin there to get a better look at the sketch.

"Jesus Christ." The words came out slowly as he examined the drawing. "Is that what he looks like? I didn't get a good look at him, it was too dark last night. I see why they call him No Face."

"Jacqueline Quibodeaux was right, No Face is a *tataille*." She stared down at her sketch. Something clicked in her brain.

Frank felt it in her body. "What is it?"

"Hand me the police file."

He grabbed it off his nightstand and handed it to her. Betty flipped through it and pulled out the photographs of the boys. Her eyes darted between the sketch and the photos.

"My god." Betty turned to Frank. "He's wearing them. He's skinning their faces off and wearing them."

Frank examined the evidence; the brutality of it all stunned him. "He's wearing them until they rot off. That's why he went after the second couple. He needed a new face."

"He'll do it again," Betty said.

"And soon."

"When he tries," Betty's eyes lit up, "we'll catch him."

"We'll catch him," Frank confirmed.

Betty leaned in and kissed him hard. Frank grabbed her waist and pulled her close so that they were pressed heart to heart.

A knock at the door made them both jump. "Betty, it's *Tante* Mad, *cher*."

"Just a second," Betty called out and motioned for Frank to keep quiet. She wrapped herself in a sheet and opened the door just wide enough for her face. Sunlight poured through the crack in the door.

Madeline raised her eyebrows when she saw Betty wearing nothing but a bedsheet. "I'm sorry ta disturb you." She tried to peek past Betty into the room.

"Oh, that's okay. What can I do for you?"

Madeline's eyes fell on Betty's face and the corners of her mouth turned up in a knowing grin. "I don't know if you seen Frank today, I jus' tried knockin' on his door, but he don't answer. So if you see him, tell him dat Viv is expecting him today for his second treatment on his leg."

Betty blushed. She knew that Madeline knew Frank was in her room. "Ok *Tante* Mad. When I see him, I'll let him know."

"Thank you, *cher*." She turned and walked off the porch. "Y'all have a nice day," she called out.

Betty closed the door and made her way back to bed. "I think we're caught." She giggled and sat on Frank's lap, facing him.

Frank ran his finger through her messy hair. His hand rested on the back of her neck, he pulled her face to his, and gently kissed her lips. "Let's not get caught twice."

"What do you mean?" She smiled.

"The file. I think we got what we need. We should return it."

Betty sighed and rolled off him. "You're a real buzzkill," she teased.

"You know I'm right. The longer we hold on to it, the more

likely it is that we'll get caught with it." He raised his eyebrows at her.

"You're right. Just let me make a few more notes. I'll stay here while you go to *Tante* Viv's. By the time you get back, I'll be done."

"Any ideas on how to return it without getting caught?"

Betty gave him a playful smile and a quick kiss. "No, but I promise to have a plan by the time you get back."

Chapter 23

Frank pressed his foot against the accelerator and sped down the road. He'd finished his session with Vivian and was on his way back to the boarding house, but he passed up the turn. An uncontrollable urge took over, and he had to go back to the graveyard. While Betty couldn't stop thinking about that face, he couldn't stop thinking about that gun.

He slowed down and turned the car onto the road that led to the graveyard. Gravel crunched under the tires. He parked in the exact spot he had the night before, believing that if he could retrace their steps then perhaps he might find the gun.

A cloud drifted across the sky and revealed the sun. Its light shone down on the tall grass and bathed the yellow flowers of the meadow in sunlight. He remembered running through them last night and how the sharp stickers scratched his ankles.

Walking closer, he saw where the shoulder-high grass had been disturbed. It must've been the path they took last night to escape. He knew finding the gun would be a long shot, but he had to try, so farther into the meadow he went.

Something caught his eye. It wasn't the gun, but one of

Betty's shoes. He bent down and picked it up. She had been so upset about losing them. If he went into the forest, maybe he would find the other one for her. He thought of how happy she would be if he brought her shoes back. The idea that he could make her smile made up his mind for him and he continued on the path until he came to the edge of the forest. Even in the daylight, there was something eerie about the place.

He thought about going back; instead, he kept walking. But the farther he went in, the stronger the urge to turn back became.

Suddenly, everything went quiet. The birds stopped chirping, the bugs stopped humming. There was only the sound of a weak breeze tickling the trees. The forest became still, as if a predator lurked nearby.

* * *

Vivian took a deep breath and continued to stare at the telephone. She had seen the cuts and bruises on Frank when he came for his healing session. He told her the whole story of how they'd been attacked last night, and it disturbed her in more ways than one.

Ever since the murders began, she had a strange suspicion and now, after hearing his story, it didn't seem quite so strange. There was only one thing to be done, so she picked up the phone and dialed Madeline.

It rang twice before Madeline answered.

"Hey *cher*, it's Vivian. Can you come by the shop?"

"*Mais*, yeah."

"Swing by and pick up Suzette. I think it's time to pass a broom."

* * *

Betty sat on the edge of the bed trying to bandage her feet with a cotton cloth she found in the bathroom. She regretted not going with Frank to see Vivian, she would have done a better job at doctoring up her feet.

It was hard to focus; she kept reliving last night with Frank. His hands gripping her hips. His lips on her breast. She could still feel him deep inside of her. Frank awakened her body in a way that no man before him ever had. Every time she thought about it, the same rush she felt from that first kiss pulsed through her.

The sound of a car coming up the driveway snapped Betty back into reality. Thinking it must be Frank, she rushed to the window to peek outside.

It was Luke. He parked his patrol car in front of the main house. Betty's heart raced as she watched him walk onto the front porch and inside the house.

She glanced over at the file on the nightstand. This might be the opportunity she was looking for. She could sneak over and just slip the file into his car. It would be risky, but if she was quick enough, she knew she could pull it off.

Without thinking it over, Betty snatched the file off the nightstand and slipped outside. She crouched down and scurried across the lawn barefoot. About halfway there, she started to second-guess herself. A chill ran down her spine; there were eyes on her, she could feel it. Something told her to turn back and hide in her cabin, but she didn't listen. This was her best shot at getting rid of the file.

She darted toward the car and gently tugged on the handle of the passenger door. All she had to do now was to slip it under the seat and she would be in the clear.

Her heart nearly leapt out of her chest as a heavy hand gripped her shoulder.

"Well, well, well, if it isn't just who I was looking for, Miss Betty Boudreaux. What are you doing in my car?" Luke asked. He guided her away from the car with the hand he had on her shoulder. "I hope you're not trying to steal from me again." He closed the door and leaned against the car.

"I don't know what you're talking about," Betty lied.

"That file you got in your hand has been missing since Saturday night after the dance. And I found this in my office that night." From his pocket, Luke pulled out the peony he had given her to wear in her hair that night.

Betty's heart dropped. She knew she had been caught; there was no talking herself out of this one.

"You got anything to say for yourself, Betty?"

She knew what came next, so she took a deep breath and looked him square in the eyes. "I'd like to call my lawyer."

Chapter 24

"What's all this?" Matthew walked into the bedroom and found Robert neatly packing clothes into a suitcase.

"Betty called," Robert answered.

"Betty? Is everything okay?"

"She's been arrested. Again. And as her lawyer, I need to be there. So it looks like I'm going to Ville Morte."

"I can't say I'm surprised." Matthew sat down on the bed and watched Robert bustle around the room, grabbing things and organizing them into his suitcase. "Betty sure knows how to make a mess of things."

"You're telling me." Robert folded a shirt and tucked it in his suitcase. "I had to call her Aunt Vivian and tell her that Betty has been arrested. And then I had to tell her to keep an eye on some fella, Frank."

"I think that's her assistant."

"Oh, the cute one?"

"The cute one."

"Hmm. I guess I'll find out if he's really that good-looking, because apparently, he's involved in all this, and the police are looking for him. But Vivian told me that Frank left hours ago and there's no way to get him a message without the police finding out. So it's only a matter of time before he gets picked up, too."

"Looks like you have your work cut out for you." Matthew reached for Robert's hand. "How about I come along?"

"Really?" Robert sighed with relief.

"Sure, I have a few days off and Betty needs our help. This will be a great way to start mending fences." He stood up and placed his hands on Robert's hips. They swayed together. "Besides, you're blind as a bat at night. You'll make me a widow if you drive all that way alone."

Robert laughed and threw his arms around Matthew's neck. He leaned in and gave him a soft kiss.

"Who knows," Matthew said, "maybe it will turn into a quiet romantic getaway."

"Well then, let's get you packed."

Chapter 25

B etty stared up at the ceiling of her jail cell. Her cot was so uncomfortable that she considered lying on the dirty floor but then thought better of it. Just because she had made a mess of things didn't mean she had to look like it. And she sure made one hell of a mess.

She tried to tell Luke about No Face, but he wouldn't listen. He didn't believe her, just assumed that she lied to get out of trouble. She didn't blame him; it was a fair assumption. So, Betty kept her mouth shut and waited for Robert.

Before today, she hadn't spoken to him or Matthew since leaving New Orleans. Even though she knew he would be professional about things and do his best to help, the uncertainty of where they stood in their friendship weighed heavy on her and she braced herself for an icy reception.

Then, of course, there was Frank. She never saw herself as a homewrecker, but that's exactly what she became. It was wrong, she knew that, and she tried to resist, but this thing between them was bigger than her. She had never experienced a love like this before. He saw her for who she was and not what she could give him. Not only did he understand her, but he encouraged her in a way that made her better. Frank made her feel safe enough to be vulnerable. With him, she had nothing to prove.

But Frank would choose his family; good men always did. They would finish this assignment, he would resign from the paper, and she would never see him again.

But on second thought, maybe he wouldn't need to resign. When Alan found out that she'd been arrested, again, he very well might fire her. There was only so much he would put up with from her.

No job. No friends. No Frank. As soon as she returned to New Orleans, her life would be in shambles.

The sound of jingling keys echoed through the empty hall and intruded on Betty's thoughts. With a slow and heavy step, Luke made his way to the holding cells. Disappointment weighed him down. All those years spent pining away for Betty, and this was how things turned out. What a complete waste.

The whole ordeal made him feel like such an idiot. She had lived in his head for so long, but the person he longed for had been nothing more than an unfulfilled teenage dream. He could see now that he didn't know her at all; she had just been using him.

"You're free to go," Luke said. He turned the key in the lock and swung the cell door open.

Betty stood up and walked through the open door. "That's it?"

"I'm releasing you into the custody of your lawyer. I've agreed to drop the charges as long as you leave town immediately." He spoke coldly to her.

Betty hung her head and stared at the floor. Here was yet another person she hurt in the wake of her recklessness.

"Luke…"

"The exit is that way." He pointed down the hall.

There was nothing left to say, so she turned around and walked away from him.

Luke felt a sense of relief as he watched her leave. At last, he was free of the ghost of Betty Boudreaux.

She came to the end of the hall and rounded the corner to find Robert pacing the lobby. Her nerves threatened to get the better of her. She didn't know what to expect from him. "Robert," she called to him softly.

"Oh, thank god," Robert said and pulled her in for a tight hug. "I was worried he would change his mind."

Instantly her nerves were eased. "Fat chance of that, he really wants me gone," she joked.

"Our little troublemaker." He put his arm around her shoulder and escorted her out of the station.

As soon as she stepped outside, her eyes fell on Matthew. He leaned against the car smoking a cigarette. "Up to your old tricks again, I see." He smiled and held his arms open for a hug.

Betty walked into his embrace, squeezed him back, and rested her head on his chest. It was exactly what she needed but more than she deserved. A rush of emotions flooded her; she hadn't realized how much she'd missed her best friend.

Matthew whispered in her ear, "I'm sorry for what I said. I didn't mean it."

"No, you were right. I've been a horrible friend to you. I'm so, so sorry."

Matthew pulled back and gave her a puzzled smile.

"What?" Betty asked.

"In all the years I've known you, this is the first time I've ever heard you apologize."

"Well, that can't be true, can it?" She turned to Robert.

Robert waved his hands dismissively in the air. "That's neither here nor there." He placed a hand on each of their shoulders. "Let's all just agree to be better friends to one another."

"Agreed," Betty and Matthew said in unison.

"Wonderful. Now let's get going," Robert replied.

"Where to?" Betty slid into the back seat.

"Your Aunt Vivian's shop. When I talked to her on the phone, she insisted we go there as soon as we picked you up."

"Is Frank with her?"

"Um," Robert started, "I'm not sure. He wasn't there when I called." He saw a flash of panic in Betty's eyes. "But I'm sure he's with her by now. In the meantime, why don't you fill us in on what's been going on, especially with Frank." He winked at her.

Betty blushed and told them everything that had happened since she arrived in Ville Morte.

When they pulled up to the boutique, Betty saw her car parked out front next to Madeline's car. She should have been glad for it; it meant Frank was there waiting for her. But something in the back of her mind told her otherwise. She had a bad feeling.

The trio walked into the store. No one was in front, and all of the lights were off.

"You sure she's here?" Robert asked.

"She should be. *Tante* Viv," Betty called out.

The door to the back parlor swung open and Vivian walked into the room. "Oh Betty, I was worried sick." She gave her a quick hug. "Y'all hungry? I got some food in the back."

248

"Starving actually," Robert said.

"You must be Robert." Vivian shook his hand. "We spoke on the phone earlier."

"Yes. And this is Matthew."

"It's nice to meet you." Vivian shook his hand as well. "Y'all come on in the back. Make yourselves at home."

"Where's Frank?" Betty asked Vivian.

She pulled Betty aside into the hallway that led to the healing room. "He's not here."

"What do you mean, he's not here? My car is out front."

Vivian took a deep breath before she started. "Madeline and Suzette found it abandoned in the old cemetery. They spotted it from the road and didn't want to leave it there. Suzette drove it back."

Betty looked at Vivian in confusion and she started to understand her bad feeling.

"Vivian, where is he?" She could feel herself start to panic.

"We don't know yet, but I think the man from last night took him."

"Oh my god. Oh my god." Betty began to pace the hallway.

Vivian rested a hand on Betty's shoulder. "We have a way to find him. Come with me."

Betty followed Vivian into the healing room. There were white pillar candles lit all around the room. Madeline and Suzette stood at the table in the center of the room. A black iron pot filled with water sat in the middle of the table. Next to the pot was a blank piece of parchment paper.

"What's going on?" Betty asked.

"We gonna scry for him," Suzette answered.

"Scrying? I don't have time for this nonsense. I have to go find Frank." Betty turned to leave the room, but Vivian caught her by the arm.

"This is the only way to find him in time. You have to trust us."

Betty looked Vivian in the eyes, and her gut told her Vivian was right. "Okay," she relented.

Vivian led her to the table. "Hold out your hand."

Betty obliged and held her hand over the table. Vivian turned Betty's palm up and pulled a knife from her garter.

"What are you doing?" Betty asked.

"A little blood of a loved one helps," Madeline replied.

Vivian pricked the tip of Betty's finger and let the blood drip into the pot of water. "Come with me, Betty. We'll let them work their magic." She led Betty out of the room and turned to look back at her friends. "Y'all sure y'all don't need me?"

"We sure," Madeline said. "You tend ta da girl. We'll tend ta dis."

Vivian and Betty returned to the parlor.

"Now what?" Betty sighed.

"Now we wait," Vivian replied. "But in the meantime, why don't you have a seat? You deserve to hear the whole story."

Betty sat down on the couch next to Matthew and Robert.

Vivian took a deep breath. It was the first time she'd ever told a soul about what had happened. "It was 1922. Your father, Amos, had just been accepted into law school at LSU. Everyone was so proud of him, especially your mama. They had been married for a couple of years by then but decided that it was for the best if he went to Baton Rouge alone for the time being. He would send for you and Marie as soon as things were more settled. So you and your mama, Marie, moved in with me."

"I don't remember any of that," Betty said.

"Oh no, well, you wouldn't. You were just a baby then, barely a year old. Anyway, I was happy to have the two of you. Marie had always been special to me. I had seen the gift in her from a young age. I started teaching her to use it when she turned thirteen. Madeline and Suzette eventually joined us when they opened themselves up to their own gifts. We formed a bit of a circle—*passin' a broom,* we called it.

"Marie was still young then, only seventeen. But she was very happily settled down, unlike our cousin Babette. Babette, she was the same age as your mama, and I always thought she was a little jealous of Marie. I had a hard time trusting Babette, but she was family, so when she came knocking at my door, I let her in."

V

Ville Morte, LA 1922

Chapter 26

"Oww." Babette winced and jerked her head back as Vivian examined her split lip.

Vivian tightened her grip on Babette's jaw to keep her still. She dipped a cloth in some homemade salve and dabbed at the cut.

"How did this happen?" Vivian asked.

"It was Beaux, wasn't it?" Marie walked the floor of Vivian's kitchen with her baby girl in her arms.

Babette sat silent.

"You have to stop seeing him," Marie insisted.

Babette looked up at her with dark eyes. "I love him. Like the way you love Amos."

"Don't you dare compare Beaux and Amos. They are not the same," Marie hissed. "Amos would never strike me."

"She's right, you know," Vivian chimed in. "He won't change."

Babette slapped Vivian's hand away and leaned back in her chair. "It seems you'll both get your wish. He's leaving town with his band." She wiped away her tears, but it did no good because the tears kept falling. "He told me last night that he was leaving. I begged him not to go. But he wouldn't listen, so I threw a drink in his face. That's when he hit me."

"Oh, Babette." Marie handed her baby to Vivian and sat down next to Babette. She wiped the tears from her cousin's face and embraced her. "It's for the best. You can be free of all this now."

"I don't want to be free of it." Babette pulled away from Marie.

"Don't you want to marry a good man?"

"No." Babette raised her voice, "I want to marry Beaux."

The baby started to cry.

"Beaux will never marry you, Babette," Vivian said as she rocked Betty to quiet her down. "And let's pray that he doesn't come back. For your sake."

"And what would a spinster like you know of love, Vivian?" Babette snapped.

"Better a spinster than a corpse." Vivian stood up from the table, angry, and took Betty into the sitting room. She'd had enough of the Beaux and Babette saga.

It had been the same story for the past two years. Things between them would be sweet and romantic for a while and then gradually it would build up to a dramatic and often violent end. They would swear each other off, then spend the next couple of weeks trying to woo each other back through jealousy and manipulation. And thus, the cycle would start again.

Vivian sat in a rocking chair by the window and rocked the baby. She could hear Babette crying as she left the house. Marie came into the sitting room and sat down next to Vivian.

"I was thinking, maybe we could invite Babette to pass a broom with us."

"No," Vivian said. "I know the two of you are close and

you can't see it, but there's a darkness in her. I've seen it in another before, and I can't imagine what would have come of that situation had Maw Maw taught her the gift."

"I do see it, Vivian, but maybe it would do her some good to be around the light. Perhaps we could teach her to channel that dark energy into something good."

"I've been trying to steer that girl toward the light for as long as I've known her. There is a dark streak that runs through our family and it's strong in Babette."

"Please, Vivian. She's our cousin, and like a sister to me. Babette needs our help."

Vivian huffed through her nose. "I'll think about it. But I need to talk to Suzette and Madeline before anything is decided."

* * *

After Babette left Vivian's, she walked home down a lonely dirt road. The gray sky overhead threatened rain and she was glad for it. It matched her mood. She couldn't imagine a bright sunny day when her soul sat so heavy in her body. A gust of wind rustled the sugarcane that grew on either side of the road. It was late spring, and the cane was still young, only three feet tall.

Babette reached the crossroads where the main highway cut across the dirt road. To the west led out of town. She stopped for a moment and watched the sugarcane sway. The weight of first love's heartbreak made her pensive and she thought the cane looked as though it was waving goodbye. A sob caught in her throat and she knew she needed to move

257

on, so she turned east, back toward town.

At the edge of the crossroads was a steel bridge that connected the east and west banks. The winding road of the east bank led through the forest and back into town.

Babette walked along, lost in her own pain, when a quick sharp whistle reached her ears and she perked her head up. She knew it was Beaux before she even saw him. That had always been his way of getting her attention.

He stood at the end of the bridge, leaning against the railing, his long legs stretched out in front of him. Beaux wasn't like most Cajun boys; he had a certain *je ne sais quoi*.[45] He was tall, almost six-foot-four. His body was broad and lean, with blonde hair and cold blue eyes. His facial features were sharp and angular. He took after his grandmother whose family line immigrated to Louisiana's German Coast. She had been a Trosclair before she married a Guilbeau and her people came from a long line of accomplished accordion players.

"Beaux, you're still here?" Babette walked to him. For a moment, she thought he changed his mind about leaving town, but then she saw the worn duffel bag and his grandfather's accordion case at his feet.

"Waitin' on my ride." He flicked his cigarette over the side of the bridge. "I was hoping I'd see you before I left." He lifted her chin and turned her face to the side so he could get a better look at her busted lip. "I gotcha pretty good there, huh?"

Babette didn't say anything, she just looked down at the ground.

"Geez, I'm sorry, Babs. I just got so angry I couldn't control it." He bent down and nuzzled her neck. "You know you make

---

[45] Je ne sais quoi: a quality that cannot be described or named easily.

me crazy, baby," he whispered in her ear. He wrapped his arm around her waist and pressed her against his hips. "Please forgive me."

Babette couldn't resist him when he was being sweet to her. She brushed his hair away from his face. "I forgive you, Beaux."

"That's my girl." He kissed her on the temple.

She rested her hands on his chest and looked up at him with her big doe eyes. "Take me with you."

"Can't. No wives allowed on the road. Band rules." He twirled her dark hair in his fingers; he knew she couldn't be mad at him when he did that.

"I'm not your wife," she said playfully.

"Not yet." He smiled down at her.

"Well, when then?"

"Maybe when I get back."

"How long will that be?"

"That's what I was trying to tell you last night, but then you went and threw that drink in my face."

"Sorry," Babette mumbled.

Beaux tugged at her hair gently. "I know you are, baby."

"Answer my question," she whined. "When you coming back?"

"End of summer. Should be back before fall starts."

"And then you'll marry me?"

"If you wait for me."

She looked up into his cold eyes. "You know I will."

He leaned in and kissed her hard. It hurt, but she liked it. She liked the way his tongue pressed against her cut and opened it up, the copper tastes of her own blood.

He pulled back and looked at her with hunger in his eyes

259

while he licked her blood from his bottom lip. He wiped the blood from Babette's mouth then brought his thumb to his lips and sucked it off.

A wagon full of rowdy musicians pulled up next to them on the bridge, but Beaux kept his eyes on her.

"*Allons-y,*[46] Beaux," the driver called to him.

"Ride's here." He tugged at her hair one last time.

"You'll write me, won't you?"

Beaux tossed his duffel into the wagon without answering her, carefully loaded up his accordion, and jumped in the back. The driver snapped the reins and the wagon jerked forward.

"Give 'em hell, Babs," Beaux yelled out to her with a wink and a laugh.

She stood on the bridge at the crossroads and watched him disappear into the west. He left her with a dangerous amount of hope.

* * *

The next afternoon, Vivian had Madeline and Suzette over for coffee.

The three women sat at Vivian's kitchen table, catching up on the latest goings on around town.

"*Mais*, let me ask y'all sumthin'." Suzette sipped her coffee. "Eva since ma mother-in-law, Madame Trahan, passed," she crossed herself, "God bless her mean ol' soul, I been thinkin' 'bout updating the dress shop."

"Well, it's yours now," Madeline said, "she left it ta you. You

---

[46] Allons-y: Let's go

can do whateva ya want wit it."

"You should definitely cleanse it, make sure she's not still hangin' around," Vivian joked.

"You right about dat." Suzette laughed. "Listen Viv, I was wonderin' if you'd like ta come work wit me. I always loved your designs. And we got a space in da back dat used ta be storage; we could turn dat into ya healing room. Dat way, ya wouldn't have ta work out ya house no more."

"I don't know how ya do it, Viv. People knockin' on ya door all hours of da night for dis an' dat," Madeline added.

"Oh Suzette, I would love that. I don't know what to say." Madeline gave Vivian a little pat on the arm. "*Mais*, say yes."

Vivian smiled at her friends. "Of course. Yes." She took a sip of her coffee before she changed the subject. "Now that that's settled, I need to talk to y'all about the circle."

Both Madeline and Suzette sat up straight and leaned in closer. Vivian had their full attention.

"Babette came over yesterday."

"Oh Lord." Suzette rolled her eyes.

"What happened now?" Madeline asked.

"Beaux busted her lip. Again."

"I know he's ma brotha and dats why I love him, but he's *pas bon*,"[47] Suzette said. "Always has been."

"As I'm sure you already know, he's leaving town. And Marie thinks it would be a good idea to bring Babette into the circle, to help her see things a little more clearly."

"I think Marie is right," Madeline said. "Babette could mos' certainly use some guidance."

"I don't know," Vivian disagreed. "Remember what hap-

---

[47] pas bon: no good

pened with Clothilde?"

Madeline clicked her tongue. "Viv, you have ta stop blamin' yaself for Clothilde. What's done is done. Babette is still young, dis could be a turnin' point for her. She needs healing after everythin' Beaux put her through."

"Not ta take sides here," Suzette piped up. "But it wasn't all Beaux's fault. Babette did some ugly things ta him, too."

"Well, dats true," Madeline agreed. "But I think if we can help, we should help."

"I'm wit Madeline an' Marie on dis one."

"Well, looks like I'm outvoted." Vivian sighed. "I'll invite her to pass a broom for the full moon circle."

* * *

Later that week, the five women gathered at Vivian's home for the full moon. The house was nestled on the edge of a dense forest. Once everyone arrived, they gathered their supplies and headed out into the woods.

Vivian walked alongside Babette while the others went ahead. "Tonight, we're gathering together to honor the gifts that The Great Mother has bestowed upon us," Vivian explained to Babette.

"What do you mean by gifts?" Babette asked.

"Your inner senses. The ability to sense things beyond the other side of the veil. There are four gifts. Clairvoyance is to see. Clairaudience is to hear. Claircognizance is to know. And clairsentience is to feel."

"Which are you?"

"I'm a clairsentient."

"Which am I?"

"We're about to find out." Vivian turned to Babette and smiled.

They reached a small clearing in the woods. The others were already there and stood around a small bonfire in a circle.

"Everyone, ground and center," Vivian announced. Then she turned to Babette. "Let me show you how." She stood behind Babette and spoke softly in her ear. "Close your eyes and take long steady breaths through your nose. Try to make your inhales and exhales of equal length. Feel the rhythm of your body." Vivian placed her hand on the top of Babette's head. "Now, imagine a bright white light flowing from the crown of your head, up to the heavens, and connect it to the full moon overhead. See the beam of light pulse with the energy of the moon and let it flow back into you through that beam of light and into the crown of your head. Now connect the energy beam from your crown to your third eye." Vivian moved her hand to Babette's forehead. "Now your throat." Again, she moved her hand to where she wanted Babette to direct her energy. "Your heart. Your center. Your root. Once you've connected all your points, let the light spill out into the rest of your body until you are filled with it."

Babette's entire body began to vibrate and in her mind's eye, she was bathed in a brilliant white light. "I can feel it," she said, surprised.

Vivian left the circle and returned with a small wooden box in her hand. She stood in front of Madeline and presented the box to her. "Sister, what do you hear?"

Madeline took the box in her hands and closed her eyes to focus. "Laughter. Lots of laughter from many different voices." Madeline handed the box back to Vivian, who moved

263

to stand in front of Suzette.

"Sister, what do you see?" Vivian asked Suzette.

Suzette did as Madeline had done and focused her energy on the box. "Green. Everything bathed in green light."

Vivian took the box from Suzette and stood in front of Babette. "Sister, what do you sense?"

Babette took the box from Vivian, and her fingertips began to tingle. Then she was overcome with emotions that were not her own. She knew that they were attached to whatever was in the box. "I feel joy and freedom."

"Ah," Vivian said with a smile, "another clairsentient." She moved on to Marie and asked, "Sister, what do you know?"

Marie had done just as the others before her had done. She looked up and smiled. "I know it's an absinthe glass."

Vivian opened the box and held up a small crystal absinthe glass for them to see. "All the way from Paris. Together, my sisters, there is nothing we cannot do."

* * *

That summer, the seeds of renewal were planted, and they were all blessed with abundance and good health.

Babette had thrown herself into learning all she could about the craft to distract herself from the fact that Beaux didn't write a single letter to her all summer. But she still clung to the hope that he would marry her when he returned. She didn't tell the others; she kept that secret longing to herself.

Madeline enjoyed being a grandmother for the first time. Her eldest son had just had a son of his own, little Luke Landry.

Marie stayed busy taking care of Betty. It had been hard for her to be away from Amos for so long, but she had the help of her family and friends. Together, she and Amos decided that after Christmas they would find a place in Baton Rouge where they could settle down as family.

As summer waned and the sugarcane grew taller, Vivian and Suzette finished the renovations to the dress shop and transformed it into a beautiful boutique. By the end of the summer, they were ready to reopen.

They decided to throw a grand opening party to celebrate the renaming of the store, *La Corde a Linge*.

The building had a fresh coat of white paint with French country blue trim. Inside, the walls were lined with racks of clothes, all Vivian's original designs. There were tables with hats and gloves and hair ribbons.

Babette and Marie arrived at the boutique around midday, and it was crowded with townsfolk. People browsed around and congratulated Vivian and Suzette on their new venture.

A pair of white leather gloves caught Babette's eye.

"Those are precious," Marie said as she handed Betty off to Madame Boudreaux, her mother-in-law. "You should get them."

"I don't know if I have an occasion to wear them," Babette questioned herself.

"If you don't get them, an occasion will come up for sure, and then you'll be sorry you didn't buy them."

Babette thought on it for a moment. "You're right. I'm gonna get 'em." She smiled the whole way to the counter.

"Good choice, Babette," Vivian said as she boxed up the gloves at the register. "I had you in mind when I designed them."

She was about to thank Vivian when she heard a laugh

coming from the crowd behind her. Her heart beat double-time. She knew that laugh.

When she turned around, she saw Beaux standing in the middle of the room talking to a group of people. Babette had no idea that he had come back into town. It was just like him to show up out of the blue.

She stood frozen, her mind racing with questions. But none of them mattered. He was back now, and he had come back for her. She had prayed for this. Waited for this. Cried for this, and now it was finally happening. Things would be different this time because she was different. She had become a better version of herself.

She wanted to rush to him, but her legs felt unsteady. Slowly, she made her way through the crowd. "Beaux?"

He turned around and looked her up and down with that hungry look in his eyes. "Babette. I wondered if I'd see you here."

The sound of his voice sent tingles through her body. Her heart beat so fast it was hard to catch her breath. "You're back."

"Babs…" He started but stopped when a young woman appeared at his side. She had blonde hair, soft brown eyes, and a pretty smile.

"Hello," the young woman said. Her Mississippi twang instantly grated on Babette's nerves. "Or should I say *bonjour*." She mispronounced the word with a hard R.

"Um, Elizabeth, this is Babette." Beaux rubbed the back of his neck. "Babette, this is Elizabeth. My wife."

The words echoed in Babette's mind and her world came crashing down around her. Everything she'd worked for that summer came uprooted. In an instant, her light was snuffed out. Hatred poured out of Babette's eyes as she looked back and forth between Beaux and his wife.

Suddenly she felt very hot, and the room seemed smaller. She had to get out of there. "Excuse me." She ran out of the building and down the street.

"Babette!"

She heard Marie calling after her. Babette turned around to see her four friends coming toward her.

"What happened?" Marie asked.

Babette turned to Suzette with tears streaming down her face. "You knew about this, didn't you?"

"No. I jus' found out ta'day."

"Liar!" Babette screamed. She was determined that some- one would pay for her pain. "Why didn't you tell me?"

"*Mais*, I can't tell ya what I don't know."

"What is she talking about?" Marie asked.

"Tell them, Suzette. Go on, tell them."

Suzette took a deep breath and turned to the others. "Dat girl Beaux came in wit, well, dats his wife. Apparently dey met on da road."

"See, you did know. And if Suzette knew, then so did all of you. All your talk of sisterhood and you betrayed me. I hate all of you!" Babette turned away from them and ran down the street toward the crossroads.

Marie moved to follow her, but Vivian stopped her. "No. Let her go. She needs time."

* * *

Babette hadn't been at the bridge for very long when she heard that sharp quick whistle. She looked up, and saw Beaux walk onto the bridge. She ran at him.

"How could you?" She shoved him.

"Oh, come on, Babs."

"You promised me! You promised me!" She shoved him again.

Beaux grabbed her arms, his fingers dug into her flesh, and she knew she would have bruises.

"It's not that serious, Babette."

She broke free from his grasp. "Not that serious? You married another woman. Why?"

He shrugged his shoulders and scoffed. "Her family's got money." Babette stared at him in disbelief.

"Look, I got money, you got money." He took a step closer to her. "You're still my girl, Babs." He stroked her face.

"You son of a bitch, I hate you." She slapped him across the face with everything she had inside her.

He snapped. Beaux grabbed her by the throat, slammed her against the railing of the bridge, and pinned her there with his body. Her head tilted up to look at him.

He put his face inches from hers. "You hate me?" His voice was low and intense. Fueled with aggression, he breathed heavily in her face and then he kissed her.

She could feel his rage, his lust. It mirrored hers and made her weak in the knees. The danger of it all gave her a thrill and she kissed him back.

He squeezed her throat just enough to leave her breathless and pulled away. "I don't think you do." He let go of her and backed up. Babette took a step toward him and when he saw that she wanted more, he laughed and walked away.

Chapter 27

That fall, Beaux took a position playing with the house band at Thibodeaux's Tavern. Accordion playing was what his family had been known for, and Beaux was the best anyone had seen in generations. He came alive on stage. His magnetism brought in a crowd and people came from all over Acadiana to see Beaux Guilbeau play.

The way he made his accordion sing was masterful. His great-great-grandfather made that accordion by hand and it had been passed down through the family. Beaux confessed to Babette once that he thought it was magical and superstitiously believed that the accordion was what gave him his talent. He worshipped it above all else.

The next few weeks were hell for Babette. Beaux and Elizabeth seemed to be everywhere. She couldn't escape them. He paraded Elizabeth around town in front of her and when Beaux caught Babette staring, he'd smirk and make a show of kissing Elizabeth. Seeing them together made Babette feel like her insides were being ripped out.

She was aware that he was toying with her and convinced herself that it was only a matter of time before he came back to her. She tried to talk to him a couple of times when he was alone, but he always ignored her. It played on her desperation, and he knew it. It wasn't until Babette noticed the bruises on Elizabeth's neck that she thought Beaux might actually love her. She turned to whiskey to quiet her emotions, but it only clouded her judgment.

* * *

Marie stepped out of the dressing room of the boutique and admired herself in the mirror. "What do we think about this one?" she asked the *tantes*. The boutique was closed for the night, but they all stayed late to help Marie pick out a new dress.

"Black is always a good choice," Vivian said. "It's elegant. It's mysterious. And it's sexy," she teased.

"Whatcha think about ya Mama in dat dress?" Suzette asked Betty as she bounced her on her knee.

"I hope Amos likes it." Marie turned from side to side, looking at the dress in the mirror.

"Ya could be wearin' a potato sack an' Amos would like it." Madeline laughed. "Dat boy is so in love wit you, cher."

Marie smiled at Madeline's reflection in the mirror and then looked down at her hands.

"What is it?" Vivian placed a comforting hand on Marie's back.

"I can't help but think about Babette and what she's going through. I know you said to give her time, but it's been almost three weeks, and I haven't seen her."

"She's been hangin' around Thibodeaux's Tavern," Suzette said. "Gettin' stinkin' drunk almos' every night." She sat Betty down on the floor to play by herself. "Dats what I heard, anyway."

"I just wish she'd let us help her," Marie sighed.

"I don't think you'll have ta wait too long ta get ya wish. Here she comes now." Madeline nodded her head toward the front door.

It was clear that Babette had been drinking when she walked inside the boutique.

Marie went to her and embraced her in a tight hug. "I'm so glad to see you."

Babette didn't return the hug and left her arms limp at her side. "Aren't you all dolled up?" she said with resentment.

"I'm picking out a new dress for when Amos comes to visit in a couple of weeks for his fall break."

"How fun for you." Babette pulled a flask out of her pocket and took a sip.

"Don't start, Babette," Vivian scolded.

"Looks like Vivian doesn't want me here." Her dark eyes stared Vivian down. "She doesn't trust me. I can feel it."

"Can you blame me?" Vivian stood her ground.

"Don't fight," Marie pleaded. "Can I have a moment alone with Babette?"

Madeline and Suzette got up from their chairs and followed Vivian to the backroom parlor. Vivian turned in the doorway. "Should we take the baby?"

"No, she'll be fine with us. Thank you, Vivian," Marie said.

Once they were alone, Marie and Babette sat down in the chairs previously occupied by Madeline and Suzette.

"How've you been, Babette? I haven't seen you in a while."

"How do you think I've been, Marie? I'm miserable."

"Well, we're doing a blessing for Betty on the next full moon. She's almost a year old now. It might give you something nice to look forward to. I hope you'll come."

"What kind of blessing?"

"We're each going to bestow her with something life has blessed us with."

Babette scoffed. "I don't think my life has any blessings to give."

"That's not true. You can bless her with your fierceness." Marie placed a hand on top of Babette's. "I've always admired that about you. If you can learn to not bring it to a dark place, you could have so much more out of life."

Babette squeezed Marie's hand. "I'll be there." She teared up a little in the warm glow of Marie's good intentions. "You're right, it has been a while. I've missed you."

"I missed you, too."

Babette relaxed and leaned back in her chair. "So, what's everyone else giving her?"

"Well, Vivian is blessing her with independence. Madeline with grace and beauty. And Suzette is giving kindness."

"What about you, Mama? What are you blessing her with?" Marie looked at Babette sheepishly. "True love."

"I really am happy for you and Amos. If anyone deserves true love, it's you."

"You'll find it too one day. I know you will."

Babette took another sip from her flask. "You know Beaux won't even talk to me."

"I'm sorry you're going through this."

"Well, he's the one who's about to be sorry." She smiled to herself.

Marie knew that smile and grew concerned. "What did you do, Babette?"

She rolled her eyes at Marie. "It's not that bad."

"Babette, tell me what you did."

"I may have stolen his grandfather's accordion."

"*Oh, mon dieu*. This is what I'm talking about. Why do you always have to take it to such a dark place? Why can't you just leave him be?"

"Of course you're on his side. You're all on his side," Babette snapped.

Marie leaned over and stroked Babette's arm. "No one's on his side. We just want to help you."

Babette yanked her arm away and glanced out the window. She sucked in her breath and turned back to Marie. "Good. Because I'm about to need it."

Beaux came storming up the steps of the boutique and barged in through the door. "Where is it, Babette?" He charged at her.

"I don't know what you're talking about," she lied but the smirk on her face gave her away.

Beaux yanked her out of the chair by the back of her hair and forced her to her knees. "Where is that accordion, Babette?" he growled through clenched teeth.

Marie let out a shriek and jumped out of her chair but stood there, frozen.

He tightened his grip on Babette's hair. "That accordion means everything to me. It's my livelihood. Now where is it, you stupid bitch!" he yelled.

Babette knew exactly which nerve to pluck. "Looks like you'll have to go work at the sugarcane mill." A wicked grin spread across her lip. "Just like your daddy."

He lost it and brought his enormous fist down on her nose. Her head snapped back, and blood sprayed through the air. Her head spun as Beaux yanked it upright. Blood gushed from

273

her nose, covering her lips and dripping down her chin. She looked up at him with bedroom eyes and taunted him without a word.

Marie screamed and the *tantes* came running out from the back parlor. Beaux lifted his fist again and brought it down on her face with the unmistakable sound of her cheekbone cracking.

"Grab the baby!" Vivian yelled. Marie scooped up little Betty and Vivian rushed them to the healing room in the back of the boutique.

He slammed his fist into Babette's face again.

Suzette rushed at him and beat him with her fists as hard as she could.

"Stay out of this, Suzette." He shoved her into a rack of clothes, and she hit the wall.

Madeline grabbed a broom and flew at him. She hit him over and over with the handle. Still holding onto Babette by the hair, he used his free hand to snatch the broom away from Madeline. Beaux swung and struck her in the ribs. She fell to the floor, gasping for air. He had knocked the wind out of her.

He raised his fist to hit Babette again but stopped short when he felt a sharp pain in his side. Vivian stood next to him. She had pulled a knife from her garter and stuck him in his flank. The prick of the knife was just deep enough for him to know that Vivian had him. She grabbed his hair and pulled his head back so she could whisper in his ear.

With a steady voice she said, "Lord knows I have a tender heart for the devil's creatures, but I will put you down, Beaux Guilbeau, if you don't leave here right now."

He knew Vivian wouldn't hesitate to plunge it to the hilt

if he didn't obey. He lifted his bloody hands in the air as a gesture of surrender and Babette fell to the floor.

"Just calm down, Vivian," he condescended to her.

She slid the knife in just a little deeper. "Why don't I walk you to the door, Beaux." With the knife still in his side and her hands gripping his hair, she ushered him outside and released him.

He turned around to face her. "I still want my accordion. This isn't over yet."

Vivian glared at him. "It better be." She slammed the door in his face and rushed to Babette's side. "Help me get her to the back," Vivian said to the others.

Ignoring their own injuries, Suzette and Madeline helped Vivian carry Babette to a couch in the back parlor. Vivian examined Babette. She was covered in blood, her nose had been broken, and her face was starting to swell.

"We need to clean her up," Vivian said. "Suzette, get me some soap and water, a clean cloth, and a jar of rose salve. Madeline, I need something for her bite down on. Her nose is broken, and I have to set the bone."

Madeline and Suzette ran to the healing room to grab the supplies for Vivian. Babette lay on the couch, barely conscious.

"Oh Babette," Vivian said with pity in her eyes as she held her hand and stroked her hair.

It was well into the night by the time Vivian finished attending to everyone's injuries. She insisted on staying the night with Babette at the boutique. No one wanted to see Marie go home alone with the baby, so Madeline invited her to stay the night at her house and extended the invitation to Suzette. She knew that Suzette, like herself, was too wired to sleep. If they were both going to have a sleepless night, they might as well spend it together prattling in her kitchen over coffee.

"How ya doin', Suz?" Madeline handed her a cup of coffee and sat down at the kitchen table with her.

"I'm alright. Dis ain't da first time Beaux's thrown me into a wall."

"He got his grandma's temper, dats for sure." Madeline sipped her coffee.

"Pph, talk about."

"All dat ova an accordion." Madeline shook her head.

"Well, it's more dan jus' an' accordion. It's been in our family for generations, an' he's had his eye on dat thing since he was a little boy. Na dat don't excuse what he did. But in his mind, it's sacred."

They both let out a deep sigh and sipped their coffee.

"Ooo child, an' when Vivian pulled out dat knife."

"Oh, I know," Suzette said. "Vivian's not one to be trifled wit, cher."

"Well, I guess not. She done been halfway aroun' da world, her."

"I'll say dis much," Suzette leaned back in her chair. "I'm glad she's wit us."

* * *

Vivian couldn't sleep either, and paced the floor of her healing room. She fiddled with a skeleton key in her hand as she replayed what Beaux had done in her mind. His threat that it wasn't over rang in her ears and she knew that something had to be done.

Her eyes fell on the locked armoire in the corner. She was still unsure, but it called out to her. If ever there was a time to use its dark magic, it was now. She stood in front of it and said a silent prayer that she was doing the right thing. Her hand slipped the key in the lock. She opened the door and a *frisson*[48] ran down her spine.

In the morning, Vivian woke Babette with a fresh cup of coffee. "How ya feelin'?"

Pain seared through her sore body, but Babette managed to sit up. "Like hell."

She caught a glimpse of herself in the mirror, and she didn't recognize herself. He had broken her face. It was swollen and purple. Her nose twisted in an unnatural curve, slashes freckled her skin, and she couldn't open her left eye. Babette's lip began to quiver and the memories of last night came flooding back.

"Try not to cry." Vivian sat down next to her on the couch. "It's not good for your nose."

"I'm so sorry, Vivian."

She grabbed Babette's hand. "You have nothing to be sorry for. No matter what you did, you did not deserve this."

She couldn't look Vivian in the eye.

"I know you think that I don't understand how you feel, but Babette, I know everything that you feel." She let go of her hand and reached into her pocket. "Use this if he ever tries to attack you again." Vivian placed a glass vial of thick black liquid on the coffee table. "Careful not to get any on yourself. It melts the skin."

---

[48] frisson : a chill

* * *

Too ashamed to show her face around town, Babette hid out at Vivian's house until she healed. A week went by without incident until one night, Marie showed up at the boutique in a panic.

"What's wrong?" Madeline asked.

"It's Babette," Marie answered

"What happened now?" Suzette asked.

"I went to drop Betty off with Amos' parents for the night. When I got back to the house, Babette was gone, and I found this note." She handed it to Vivian. "She went to meet Beaux."

"Oh, dat little fool," Madeline scoffed.

"The note said she's going so she can give him the accordion," Marie continued. "But I know she has no intention of giving it back." She shook her head. "I have a really bad feeling. I think he's gonna kill her."

"We gotta do sumthin'," Suzette said. "Did da note say where dey goin'?"

"No," Marie answered.

Vivian took a deep breath. "Alright, let's get the scrying bowl. We can ground and center. Maybe we can find them before things get out of hand."

* * *

Hidden behind the tree line on the east bank of the bridge, Babette sat on the accordion case and waited for Beaux. She had every intention of giving it back. Tonight, she would be done with him for good.

Out of the darkness from the west bank, Beaux appeared on the bridge. His quick sharp whistle filled her with fear.

"Babette," he called out. His tone didn't give his mood away and she stayed in her hiding spot.

"Babs," he called her again.

She felt a little easier; he only called that when he was in a soft mood.

"I'm here." Babette came out from behind the trees but remained in the shadows.

"Babs." He started toward her.

"Stop!" she yelled. "Don't come near me."

Beaux hung his head and ran his fingers through his hair. "Look, I'm sorry, okay. Just let me make it right."

"You wanna make it right?" Her heart was filled with sorrow.

"Yes. I'll do anything you want. Anything you want, baby."

"I want you to get down on your knees and beg for my forgiveness." He cocked his jaw and huffed, "It's always a game with you, isn't it, Babs."

"Do you want your accordion or not? Because I can always throw it into the bayou." She kicked the case toward a slope on the bank.

"Alright. Alright," he said and reluctantly knelt to the ground.

When he got down on his knees, she stepped into the light of the moon and walked across the bridge to him. His face fell when he saw her. He didn't realize the damage he had caused. He hated himself. If another man had done this to her, he would have killed him.

"I'm sorry. I'm so fucking sorry." His voice cracked and all he could do was weep at her feet. He grabbed the waist of her dress and looked up at the woman he destroyed with his love.

Babette slipped a gloved hand into her pocket and wrapped her fingers around the vial Vivian had given her.

"Please, please forgive me," he begged.

"No," she said and smashed the vial in his face.

* * *

Vivian, Madeline, Suzette, and Marie gathered around the table in the healing room. A black iron pot sat in the middle of the table. Candles lit the room. They all held hands and gazed into the black water.

Vivian let out a gasp. They all knew what she felt and looked around the table at each other, wide-eyed with dread.

"Madeline, what did you hear?"

Madeline took in a deep unsteady breath. "Screamin'. Da mos' awful screamin'."

They turned to Suzette. "I saw a body." She fought back tears. "A body lyin' in da crossroads." She covered her mouth and let out a sob.

"Viv, whatcha felt?" Madeline asked.

She looked around the table, shook her head and closed her eyes. "I felt death."

They turned to Marie; her lip quivered. "Someone's dead. I know it." She covered her face with her hands. "I just don't know who," she cried.

Suzette rubbed Marie's back to try to comfort her.

"Well, we're not gonna find out sittin' around here," Vivian said and moved toward the door.

"I got ma buggy outside." Madeline followed Vivian's lead.

Marie and Suzette dried their tears and the four women rushed into the night.

As they approached the crossroads, they could see a dark mound lying in the middle of the road. Madeline stopped the buggy; they climbed out and ran to the body.

Suzette fell to her knees and sobbed when she saw her baby brother face-down, sprawled out in the middle of the street. Madeline rested a comforting hand on her shoulder. Vivian and Marie breathed a sigh of relief that it was Beaux and not Babette. Suzette collected herself and turned the body over.

Marie screamed. She ran to the ditch and vomited on the side of the road.

All of them were horrified by what they saw. Chunks of his face were gone. Some skin had dissolved down to the bone. Streaks of deep, black, charred flesh ran down his cheeks. Beaux had no face.

Suzette couldn't stand to look at it any longer. She turned the body over the way she'd originally found it. She made the sign of the cross and began to recite The Prayer for the Departed.

Vivian turned to Madeline. "Stay with them. I'll look for Babette." She hurried to the bridge and found Babette crouched down on the side of the road with her knees pulled up to her chest.

"I didn't mean it. I didn't mean it," she mumbled under her breath as she rocked back and forth. She didn't even notice Vivian standing there until she knelt down beside her and gripped her shoulders.

"I didn't mean it. I didn't mean it, Vivian." She couldn't catch her breath and started to hyperventilate.

Vivian wrapped her arms around Babette and held her tight.

"It's okay. You're okay. Just breathe. Breathe with me."

"I didn't mean to kill him. I didn't think it would be that bad. I just wanted to hurt him, but not like this."

"Tell me what happened." Vivian smoothed Babette's hair.

"I hit him with the vial. He started screaming like a wild animal. I saw his face melt away." She let out several heavy sobs. "Then he got up and stumbled into the crossroads. The screaming stopped and he collapsed." She covered her face with her hands and wept. "Is he really dead?" she asked in between sniffles.

"Yes," Vivian answered. "He's gone."

"No!" Babette wailed. "What did I do? What did I do?"

"Is she alright?" Marie called out and came running with Madeline and Suzette right behind her.

Vivian stood up and pulled Babette to her feet. "She's not hurt," Vivian answered. She held Babette's face in her hands. "You're gonna be ok."

She started to calm down and her breathing returned to normal.

Babette looked at Suzette. "I'm sorry, I'm so, so sorry," and the tears started again.

Suzette stared her down for a moment. She grabbed Babette, pulled her close, and wrapped her in a hug. "Ya did whatcha had ta do," she whispered in Babette's ear. They held each and mourned the loss of Beaux.

"What am I going to do? They'll give me the chair for sure."

"No," Vivian said. "Not if we can help it. No one has to know what happened here. We can throw him into the bayou. It wouldn't be a stretch to believe he got drunk and fell in. The gators will make quick work of him and by the time he washes ashore, you, Babette, will be long gone. No one's seen you in the last week; we can say you left before he disappeared."

"Where am I supposed to go?"

"Shreveport," Marie said. "We have cousins in Shreveport."

"I can getcha on da train tonight," Madeline added.

Vivian noticed Suzette's silence and asked, "Suzette, are okay with this?"

Suzette wiped a stray tear from her eye. "He was ma blood an' I loved him. But y'all, y'all are ma sisters. You done suffered enough by his hand, Babette. I won't let him you hurt no more. We gonna getcha outta dis, cher."

They dragged his body back to the bridge and lifted him up, then hurled his body over the side of the bridge. Babette picked up the accordion and tossed it in after him.

The five women stood on the edge of the bridge, arms linked together, and watched his body float down the murky waters of the bayou.

Chapter 28

"It was the last time all of us were together. Babette made it to Shreveport and started a new life. We never heard from her again. Marie moved to Baton Rouge with Amos that Christmas like they planned. We waited for Beaux's body to pop up, but it never resurfaced. After a year, he was officially declared dead, and his wife moved back to Mississippi after the funeral."

"*Tante* Viv, why did you wait to tell me this?"

"We swore we'd never speak of it again, and we didn't. We put it behind us and moved on. When these murders started, it never crossed my mind that it could be Beaux. Not until Frank came in today and described the man who attacked you last night. As impossible as it is to believe, I know it can't be anyone else."

The door to the healing room cracked open, and Suzette and Madeline came into the parlor. Betty held her breath and waited for them to speak.

"Frank's alive," Suzette said.

"Oh, thank god," Betty breathed out.

"But he's in alotta pain," Madeline added. "I don't think ya have much time."

Betty grabbed hold of Robert's hand and squeezed hard.

"Do you know where he is? How do we find him?" Matthew asked.

"I saw it clear as day," Suzette answered him. "He's at da ol' Guidry camp. It's been abandoned for nearly fifty years. Nobody goes out dat way too much no more." She handed him a piece of parchment paper with a crude drawing of a map on it. "If you follow dis map, you'll find him."

Matthew took it from her and looked it over.

"Da only way ta get there is by boat," Madeline said.

"By boat?!" Betty exclaimed.

"Don't worry, cher, dere's a *pirogue*[49] on da dock at da boarding house. But y'all need ta hurry."

Betty jumped up out of her seat. "Thank you," she said to the *tantes* and gave them each a quick hug. "Come on, boys, let's go."

The three of them rushed out of the boutique.

Vivian stood up from her chair. "Y'all up for a protection circle?"

"*Mais*, yeah," Madeline said.

"Pooyie," Suzette sighed. "It's gonna be a long night."

* * *

Matthew parked his car as close to the boarding house boat dock as he could without getting stuck in the mud. The sense of urgency was palpable among the trio as they jumped out of the car and rushed to the dock. The *pirogue* sat in the water just as Madeline said it would.

---

[49] pirogue: small flat-bottom boat

"It's too small," Betty remarked. "There's no way the three of us plus Frank will fit."

"I'll go." Robert stepped up.

"Betty," Matthew said firmly, "you need to stay here."

"Like hell I do. One of you can stay. I'm going." She tried to walk past him toward the boat, but Matthew sidestepped in front of her and blocked her way.

"Listen to me, Betty, Robert is stronger than you are, and we don't know what we're facing. The longer we stand here arguing about who's going and who's staying, the more likely the chance we'll be too late."

Images of the dead boys flashed across Betty's mind. The mutilated bodies. The missing faces. She couldn't stand the thought that the same fate was about to befall Frank. Betty knew Matthew was right, there was no time to argue.

"Go, go. I'll wait here for you." Her heart raced as she watched them get into the *pirogue* and paddle away into the darkness.

* * *

Frank slowly opened his eyes. His senses were foggy and dull. His whole body hurt; the only part of him left untouched was his face. After the last horrendous beating he took from No Face, he must have passed out.

In the back room of the shack, he lay hogtied and naked on the bloodstained floor. He wasn't sure where he was but by the smell of decay, he knew he was in the kill room.

He couldn't remember how he got here. The last kick in the head seemed to scramble his memories. Every time he tried to recall what happened, it came back patchy, hazy. Like trying to hold onto a dream. The last thing he remembered clearly was bending down to pick up Betty's shoe.

He was worried about her. Certain words and images from the police file kept crashing down on him. If he was here and that maniac followed his M.O., then that meant Betty was already dead. The thought of her violent death threatened to crush him.

The sound of heavy footsteps made his heart beat faster. He could feel the rotten floorboards shake as they got closer and closer, until that evil presence stood right behind him. Without a word, No Face reared his foot back and kicked him dead center in the back of the head. Frank saw stars. The room began to spin, and he braced himself for another brutal beating.

* * *

The muggy night air wrapped itself around Matthew and Robert as they made their way upriver. Robert sat at the front of the *pirogue* and held up their only source of light, the hurricane lamp that had been left in the boat. Matthew sat in the back and steered using a single paddle.

The bayou was dark but alive with creatures of the night. Locked in an eternal loop of crescendos, the cicadas performed their hymns. Fireflies twinkled over the murky water and floated toward the shore, where glowing eyes watched them paddle along. Swarms of mosquitoes bit and sucked at them. They tried to slap them away, but every time they squashed a bug, another was there to take its place.

Robert lifted the lantern; he spotted something in the water up ahead. "Move a little to the left, there's a log." He watched as the log sank below the surface of the water and disappeared. "Shit. It's a gator." He tried to keep his voice from cracking with fear.

As they drifted along, they heard the shrieks of the gators' supper cry out into the night. Then heavy thrashing at the water's edge, and finally, the silence of death.

They continued on their journey upriver. Neither of them spoke, except to give direction. They were too focused on the task at hand to maintain any sort of conversation.

"I think this is it. This is the bend," Robert said, holding the lantern up high for Matthew to see.

Matthew steered the *pirogue* toward the inner corner into the cypress trees, where the water became shallow. He paddled until the water gave way to soggy ground. A few more good rains, and this area would be under water. They pulled the *pirogue* onto the shore and tied it to a cypress knee for good measure.

Robert examined the crude map drawn by the *tantes*. "This way," he said, and they walked deeper into the trees.

Matthew held out his hand to Robert.

"I'm not a child, Matthew. I don't need you to hold my hand to keep me from being frightened."

"No, but maybe I need your hand to keep *me* from being frightened."

"Sorry." Robert gave Matthew a soft smile. "I get snippy when I'm scared."

"I know."

Robert took Matthew's hand and together they walked toward an unknown fate.

Chapter 29

Frank floated in and out of consciousness. His body lay limp on the floor. There was no fight left in him, not even when he felt No Face readjusting his restraints so that his hands were tied over his head.

No Face grabbed him by the legs and dragged him through the shack. Frank could feel the splinters digging into his back as he was pulled across the grimy floor.

A whiff of fresh air hit his nostrils. He was outside. Frank hit his head on the back porch steps as No Face yanked him into the yard. He hauled Frank over to a large tree and looped a rope around his hand restraints. No Face tugged on the rope and lifted Frank off the ground. Then he secured the rope around the tree trunk and left Frank to dangle naked in the wind.

No Face walked back to the porch. The yard around it was littered with an array of junk, scrap metal, old tools, and rotten wood planks. All things he had scavenged and stolen over the years.

He dug through his treasure trove of trash, tossed a rusty shovel to the ground, then continued rummaging until he found what he was looking for.

Moonlight bounced off an eight-inch filet knife he gripped

in his hand as he marched back toward Frank.

Matthew and Robert ran toward the sound of Frank's screams. They crouched behind the tall marshland grass and watched in horror as No Face sliced away a long strip of flesh from Frank's flank.

His screams pierced their ears, and they tightened their grasp on each other's hands.

"I hope you have a plan," Robert whispered.

Matthew turned to him. "Not a good one."

No Face watched with delight as a stream of blood ran down Frank's leg and dripped from his toes onto the ground. The sound of Frank's screams made him hard. What was left of the rotten flesh from the Babin boy's face hung loose around No Face's jaw and flapped about as he licked Frank's blood from the chunk of skin he just removed.

Frank nearly passed out from the pain, but his mind clung to thoughts of Betty. The red dress she wore on his first day at the paper. The powdered sugar on her nose that morning at breakfast. Dancing at the *fais do-do*. The way she challenged him. The way she awoke his passion. Their time together was too short, he wanted more. Frank knew he was going to die here tonight, and he wanted to die thinking of her.

No Face moved to Frank's other side. He lifted the knife, ready to tear away another strip of flesh.

"Beaux Guilbeau!" a voice yelled.

No Face whipped around at the sound of his old name. He saw Robert standing next to the steps of the porch.

"Where did you hear that name?" he growled and started walking toward Robert.

"Let that man go," Robert demanded.

Anger rose up inside of No Face like a storm surge and he

charged at Robert.

Robert turned to run up onto the porch but when his foot landed on the third step, it crashed through the rotten board, and he tumbled to the ground. No Face was on him in an instant. He grabbed Robert by the neck and lifted him off his feet.

The massive hand tightened around Robert's throat and with his last bit of breath, he managed to squeak out one word: "Babette."

Fury burst through No Face's eyes. "You dare say that name to me!" he screamed, his hot breath hitting Robert in the face. He slammed him into the porch rail.

Robert struggled for air but managed to get out a few more words. "She's in Shreveport."

"Lies," he hissed and tightened his grip. Robert couldn't breathe, and the edges of the world began to fade.

Suddenly, No Face's head whipped to the side as Matthew swung a shovel against his head. No Face dropped Robert and stumbled sideways. He lifted his eyes and saw Matthew standing just out of arm's reach, the shovel raised and ready to strike again.

Free from the monster's grasp, Robert ran to Frank and started to get him down from the tree.

"Come on you son of a bitch," Matthew mumbled under his breath.

No Face sized him up and as he made his move toward Matthew, he picked up a hammer lying in his junk pile. Matthew backed away quickly, but he was too fast and tripped over some of the trash lying in the yard. No Face saw he had the upper hand and lunged at Matthew with the hammer raised high above his head, ready to strike.

Out of the tall grass, like a flash of lightning, Le Bleu came running.

She jumped up and sank her teeth into the back of No Face's thigh. He howled in pain and tried to reach behind him to grab the dog, but he couldn't reach her. Le Bleu locked her jaw tight. She pushed her paws against his leg and in quick, jerky movements, pulled at his thigh. Then she whipped her head back and forth, tearing the muscles in his leg. He switched his focus from Matthew to LeBleu and while No Face was trying to get the dog off of him, Matthew saw his opportunity and took it.

Matthew grabbed the shovel, jumped to his feet, and charged forward. He rammed the shovel through No Face's groin, the blade puncturing the soft area of his body. Matthew pulled the shovel back, yanking it out of him. No Face let out a screeching roar as he fell to his knees. Blood spurted from his crotch. Matthew lifted the shovel like a baseball bat and swung it across his skull with a loud crack. No Face tumbled over and lay lifeless on the ground.

Matthew ran to help Robert with Frank.

Frank's eyelids were heavy but lifted long enough to look Robert in the eyes.

"Betty sent us," Robert said in a comforting voice.

"Betty?" Frank was so weak he could barely speak. "Is she…"

"She's safe," Matthew answered. He took his shirt off and put it on Frank. "But we need to leave, now."

"Can you walk?" Robert asked Frank.

"I'll have to," Frank said. "Just get me the hell out of here."

Matthew and Robert each took one of Frank's arms and put it over their shoulders. They held him up by his waist, careful to avoid the gash along his ribs, and the three men ran back through the swamp.

* * *

Betty paced the length of the dock. She felt powerless and anxious. Doing nothing went against her nature. She needed to feel useful. All she could think to do was pray, so she prayed to every god she had ever heard of to bring her boys back safe.

Time seemed to stretch on forever. She wasn't sure how long she had been out there, but the more time that passed, the more worried she became.

She stared out into darkness. In the distance, a faint light drifted closer. Her heart began to speed up. Was it them? Had her prayers been answered?

"Betty!"

She heard her name and ran to the end of the dock. "Robert!" she returned the call.

"Start the car! Hurry!"

She raced across the dock and up the sloped bank. A thousand questions ran through her mind, mainly: was Frank alive? The car was where they left it facing the river. She hopped in the driver's seat and turned the key in the ignition. The headlights illuminated the bank. She held her breath and waited. Then finally, the three men came up the slope. Betty let out a gasp when she saw Frank's condition.

He was so weak that he could barely hold his head up. Matthew and Robert propped him up between them. Even though Frank tried his best to walk, they practically had to drag him. He was naked from the waist down and covered in blood. It dripped from his legs and soaked through his shirt.

Betty froze. She didn't know how to feel. She was elated that he was alive but heartbroken by what he must have endured.

Matthew and Robert fumbled to get him in the back seat. Robert stayed in the back with Frank while Matthew got in the front seat with Betty.

"Go. Go to the nearest phone." Matthew looked over his shoulder in the back seat. "He needs a doctor, Betty."

"There's one at the main house." Betty put the car in gear, whipped it around and sped off in the direction of the boarding house. "What happened out there?"

"I think I killed him," Matthew said.

"No Face?" Betty asked.

"Yeah. But I'm not sure. I didn't check. I just wanted to get out of that hell hole."

"It doesn't matter." Betty pulled up to the main house and parked the car. "The only thing that matters is that you're all alive."

"Betty," Frank groaned from the back seat.

"Hold tight Frank, we're going to take care of you. Let's get him inside, boys."

They worked together to get him out of the car and onto the porch.

"Here," Frank said and sat down in a wicker porch chair. "I'll be fine here."

Betty knelt down in front of him and held his face in her hands. She turned to her friends and said, "Robert, find us some first aid. Matthew, call Vivian and the police."

"How about some water, Frank?" Robert asked.

"That would be nice. And maybe something to cover up with."

"You got it," Matthew said. He and Robert went inside the

house and left the lovers alone on the porch.

"Oh god, Frank." Tears fell from her eyes.

"I'm okay, Betty." He kissed the palm of her hand.

"Here, let me see this." She went to unbutton his shirt, but he stopped her.

"I'm okay." He lifted her chin and looked her in the eyes. "I'm alive. And I'm here with you. I'm okay."

"I was so worried." She started to cry softly. "I was afraid I would never see you again. All I could think about were those boys and what he had done to them."

"I know. I know." He grabbed her hands and held them tight. "I thought he got to you first. I thought you were dead. I thought I was as good as dead. All I could think about was you, us. And the only thing I wanted was more time with you. More time to love you, to fight with you." He placed his hand on the back of her neck. "To kiss you." He pulled her face to his and kissed her hard.

Betty felt that kiss throughout her entire body. She wanted more, too, she didn't want things to end between them.

The kiss ended abruptly when they heard the sound of a gun cock.

Chapter 30

A bright light struck Ava in the eye and stirred her
awake. It took a moment for her to remember where
she was, but it all came back rather quickly. She
arrived in Ville Morte late that afternoon. The sound of her
native tongue being spoken in the street and written on signs
delighted her; she would have loved Ville Morte if it weren't
for the circumstance that brought her here.

She made her way into Romero's grocery just as he was
closing up for the day. They had a pleasant conversation in
French, something she hadn't indulged in for ages, and he
offered to give her a ride to the boarding house on his way
home.

When she got there, she knocked on the door, but no one
answered. There didn't seem to be anyone on the grounds at
all. No one answered when she knocked on the cabin doors,
either. She wondered if maybe Romero didn't understand her
French and brought her to the wrong place. All the doors were
unlocked but she didn't feel right about waiting alone inside a
stranger's house, so she walked along the wrap-around porch
until she found a bench on the side porch. It had been a long
journey, and she was tired, so she lay down on the bench and
fell fast asleep.

The headlights from Matthew's car was what woke her. She heard panicked voices and a whole lot of commotion coming up the front steps. It made Ava nervous. Fearing that she may have found herself in a precarious situation, she slipped her hand into her bag and pulled out the gun she borrowed from Bridget. Slowly, Ava got up from the bench and crept around the side of the house to investigate, careful to stay hidden in the shadows.

What she saw shattered her. There was Frank with his dick hanging out and that harlot Betty on her knees in front of him. Were they going to fuck outside like animals? Their hands were all over each other. Ava heard his declaration of love for Betty and then she watched her husband kiss another woman with a fierce passion that he never gave to her.

It was the last straw. She had been right all along, and now her anger was vindicated. All her fury bubbled up inside her and she couldn't contain it. Her whole body shook with the rage of betrayal.

Ava stepped out of the shadows and with a shaky hand, raised the gun, then cocked the hammer. "Get away from him," she demanded.

Frank didn't know what to do, he was still reeling from his injuries.

Betty froze. All she could do was clutch Frank's hand.

Ava pointed the gun directly at Betty and took a step forward. "Get away from him," she repeated.

Betty turned to Frank, he gave a silent nod and said, "Do what she says." There was only so much he could do to protect her in his state, but he was going to do his best to keep her safe. Betty let go of his hand, stood up slowly, and backed away from him.

Ava walked across the porch and stood in front of Frank. He hung his head; he couldn't look her in the eyes. "I'm sorry, Ava," he said.

"How could you? After everything I have done for you."

"Ava, please put the gun down." Frank tried to remain calm.

"I could have let you die. I saved your life!" Ava yelled.

"No, Ava, you ruined my life," Frank raised his voice.

She glared down at him in disbelief. Then she raised her hand and slapped him across the face so hard her hand stung.

"Stop!" Betty cried. "Can't you see that he's hurt?"

Ava whipped her head around and snarled at Betty like a wild animal.

"Ava, please," Frank pleaded with her.

Ava turned her attention back to Frank. "GET UP!" She let out a scream so deep that it burned her throat.

"I can't walk."

Ava pressed the barrel of the gun to his forehead. "Get up," she said through gritted teeth.

"Okay. Okay." Frank held his hands up in surrender and cautiously stood up.

Ava grabbed him by the arm and pulled him down the steps. He could barely walk and stumbled to the ground on his knees.

Betty couldn't stand to watch him leave. She had just gotten him back. Before she even knew what she was doing, she ran off the porch and rushed at Ava. Betty pushed her and Ava slammed into Matthew's car. The last bit of sanity Ava had left was gone, and she saw red.

"HE'S MINE!!" Ava screamed. She lifted the gun, pointed it at Betty, and pulled the trigger.

Betty clutched at her stomach where the bullet hit her and fell backward, gasping for air.

"No!" Frank yelled as he crawled to her body. "Betty. Betty." He held her face in his hands, and he couldn't stop the tears from coming.

Ava watched her husband cry over his mistress. The love she had for him drove her to madness and she didn't recognize herself anymore. How did it come to this? Shooting a woman in the streets. Surely, she would go to prison for this. But Ava already found herself in the prison of her own mind, condemned to live in the shadow of Betty. Frank was never going to see her. There was only one way to get out from underneath this, only one way to sever the tie. If it's the last thing she did, she was going to make him pay for her pain.

"François," she called out to him.

Frank turned his head and watched her raise the gun. "Ava, no."

She stared him in the eye as she pressed the barrel to her temple and pulled the trigger. In her last moment, Ava knew Frank would blame himself. He never saw her in life, but she made damn sure he would see her in death. The thought of him torturing himself for the rest of his life gave her a deranged pleasure.

The sound of the gun firing made Frank jump, and he watched her body slump against the car, brain matter on the ground.

"No, no, no." He crawled to her body. The guilt of what he had done to his wife came crashing down on him like a dark wave. He cradled her lifeless body in his arms. "I'm sorry, Ava. I'm so very sorry." He wept. Frank did love her, just not the way she wanted him to. This was all his fault.

Every choice he made regarding her had been a misstep. He had done wrong by her, destroyed his wife and the mother

299

of his child. In that moment, he wished he had died in that plane crash.

"Frank!" From somewhere behind him, he heard his name being called and it brought him back to the present.

"Frank!" Matthew called out again. "We need your help over here." He and Robert were huddled over Betty, who was struggling to breathe.

Frank gently laid Ava's body on the ground and closed her eyes for her. "I'm sorry," he whispered one last time before rushing to Betty's side.

Matthew put pressure on the wound while Robert propped her head up in his lap.

"Talk to her," Robert instructed Frank. "Hold her hand. Help is coming."

Frank gripped her hand tight and stroked her face. "Stay with me Betty. Stay with me."

"Frank?" Betty's eyes searched for him.

"I'm right here. I won't leave you. Stay with me."

"I…" She gasped for air. "I can't breathe."

VI

New Orleans, LA Sunday March 31st, 1946

Chapter 31

Frank sat on a bench in the cemetery, looking up at the sky. A warm breeze caressed his face. The sky was bright blue and cloudless, a beautiful spring day by all accounts.

Every Sunday, he came here to reflect. He couldn't bear to carry his guilt around every day; it would paralyze him. But he couldn't bear to put it down, either.

He picked up the bouquet of white roses next to him and walked over to the grave. There Avril sat in front of her mother's tombstone, chatting away. She looked up at Frank and smiled.

"Hi Daddy."

"Hi Sunshine. You ready to go?"

She nodded, then stood up and kissed the tombstone. "I miss you, Mommy."

Frank's heart was consumed with guilt as he laid the rose on Ava's grave. By his account, his indifference had killed her. He needed to make it up to her in some sort of way. So he came here for a weekly penance and made sure to tell Avril what a wonderful person her mother had been. He hoped it would be enough.

Avril put her tiny hand in his, and together they walked solemnly through the cemetery. Frank noticed that she was unusually quiet.

"You okay, Sunshine?"

She shrugged her shoulders.

"Are you feeling sad?"

"I miss Mommy."

"She loved you very much, you know."

"I know. And she's wiff me in my heart." Avril repeated the words that all the grownups had been telling her.

"I think we need some cheering up," Frank said. "I don't know about you, but ice cream always cheers me up."

"Ice cream!" Avril's face lit up.

As they walked through the gates and onto the street, Frank felt his heart lighten. It took some time, but he had learned how to leave his grief at the gates, until next Sunday when he would pick it up again and allow himself to feel every ounce of sorrow.

They rode the streetcar to the Walgreens on Canal, and each had an ice cream sundae. Frank paid and bought one copy of each newspaper they sold. They took the St. Charles streetcar back uptown, and Avril fell asleep on his lap. He carried his sleeping daughter the rest of the way home, to their new house on Octavia Street.

He brought her to her room and laid her down in bed to finish the rest of her nap. He was grateful that she fell asleep on the streetcar and was spared the tantrum of her fighting against naptime. Frank closed the door softly and made his way down the hall to his own bedroom.

The door creaked when he opened it, and he peeked inside. "Oh good, you're awake."

"Of course I'm awake, it's nearly two in the afternoon," Betty replied.

"Yet you're still in bed," Frank teased as he began to strip off his clothes.

"Well, the cat's asleep so I can't get up." She smiled and gestured to Miss Edgar, who was curled up next to her.

Frank crawled under the covers with Betty and kissed her tenderly. "Well, we can't disturb the cat."

The mattress shifted under his weight and woke Miss Edgar up. She shot Frank a disdainful look and then hopped off the bed to find a new place to nap.

"I think she hates me." He laughed.

"Don't feel bad, it took me getting shot in the gut for her to stop hating me."

"I'm not too worried about it." He went in for another kiss but Betty stopped him.

"Did you get my papers?" she asked.

"I did. They're on the coffee table."

"My hero," she said and gave him a quick kiss before scampering off to the living room.

When she came back into the bedroom, her eyes were wide as saucers. She stood in the doorway holding the paper up. "Did you see this?"

"Shh, Avril's asleep," Frank warned her.

Betty closed the door and climbed back into bed. She read the headline to him. "Texarkana Phantom Strikes Again: Teenage Couple Slain. It's him, Frank, I know it."

"It certainly seems that way."

"I had my suspicions after the first attack, but this confirms it. It all fits. The .32 caliber gun, teenagers murdered on Lover's Lane, a masked man. I always thought that when

305

he disappeared, he must have gone looking for Babette in Shreveport. And Shreveport is only a couple of hours from Texarkana. Our No Face is their Phantom Killer. We have to get up there and cover this story."

Frank touched the scar down his flank where No Face carved through him. "There's no talking you out of this, is there."

"No," she said with a smile.

Frank took a deep breath and looked her in the eye. "Let's get the bastard."

Betty threw her arms around his neck and gave him a big kiss. "I love you."

He rested his forehead against hers. "I love you too, Betty."

"What about Avril?" she asked. "She can't be there, it's too dangerous."

"You're right. If only you had a hoard of aunts who could watch her for us." He ran his hand across her thigh.

Betty smiled. "I'll call *Tante* Viv."

About the Author

Theresa Natalie grew up on the Cajun prairies of the Louisiana countryside. As the daughter of an English professor, she had been writing since early childhood and was taught the fundamentals of storytelling from a young age. She attended The Arts Academy of Acadiana to study the art of storytelling through acting and later attended The University of New Orleans to study film making. She currently resides in Breaux Bridge, LA where she is working on her sophomore novel.

You can connect with me on:

- https://www.facebook.com/TheresaNatalieBooks
- https://www.instagram.com/theresa_natalie_books
- https://www.tiktok.com/@theresanatalieboo